ACROSS THE GREAT BARRIER

PATRICIA C. WREDE

ACROSS THE GREAT BARRIER

SCHOLASTIC PRESS · NEW YORK

Library of Congress Cataloging-in-Publication Data available

ISBN 978-0-545-03343-5

10 9 8 7 6 5 4 3 2 1   11 12 13 14 15 16/0

Printed in the U.S.A.   23
First edition, August 2011

The text type was set in Griffo.
Book design by Christopher Stengel

This one's for my dad,
with love.

CHAPTER
· 1 ·

Being a heroine is nowhere near the fun folks make it out to be. Oh, it's nice enough at first, when everybody is offering congratulations and making a fuss, but that doesn't last long. And when the thing they're congratulating you for is getting rid of a bunch of bugs, which you didn't do all by your own self anyway, it feels pretty silly. Not to mention that it annoys the other people who ought to have come in for some of the credit.

The one it mainly annoyed was my twin brother, Lan. He's the seventh son of a seventh son, which makes him a pretty strong magician. It was his spells that held the mirror bugs off of the Little Fog settlement long enough for Wash and William and me to get there. I thought that was a lot harder than what I'd done, but the only people interested in talking to Lan much were the magicians at Northern Plains Riverbank College, and even they were more interested in me than in my brother. What Lan had done was something they understood, but what I'd done was a mix of the Avrupan magic I'd learned in school and the Aphrikan magic I'd studied outside regular hours. The professors all said it was a new thing and got very excited. Even Papa.

Everyone from the North Plains Territory Homestead Claims and Settlement Office to the Mill City Garden Club was only interested in me, Eff Rothmer.

I wasn't used to it. The only folks who'd paid me much mind before were the ones who thought I was evil and unlucky because I was thirteenth-born. I didn't believe they were right, not anymore, but I still didn't like all the attention. I didn't like strangers asking me questions or staring at me when I walked down the street. I didn't like people asking me to make speeches and getting cross with me when I said no. I didn't like folks expecting me to do absurd things for them, like the lady who showed up one day with a train ticket to Long Lake City, saying she wanted me to put a spell on her prize roses to get rid of the aphids. She wouldn't take no for an answer, and Papa had to come out and be stern at her. And it wasn't even a round-trip ticket.

I thought the fuss would die down after a few days, but it kept up all that summer long. William Graham, who'd been friends with Lan and me ever since we moved to Mill City, said it was because the newspaper reporters liked writing about a pretty young girl. I told him I was eighteen and nothing like as pretty as Susan Parker.

William turned beet red, because everybody knew he'd been sweet on Susan before he went East to school, but he stuck to his guns. Then Lan said that the newspapers would call any eighteen-year-old heroine pretty, even if she was sway-backed and had buckteeth. I whacked him with the flyswatter.

By that time, Lan had mostly gotten over his mad, which was a big relief. Or at least it was until the week before Lan went off to study at Simon Magus College in Philadelphia, when he cornered me in the kitchen garden and started asking me all kinds of questions.

"You're going to graduate from the upper school this year," he told me. "Where are you going after that?"

I looked at him. The last few years at boarding school, Lan had sprouted up a good bit taller than me, and he'd grown sideburns and started slicking his brown hair back like an Easterner. He hardly looked like the brother I remembered . . . except for the gleam in his brown eyes. I knew that gleam, and it always meant trouble for somebody.

"I'm staying right here with Mama and Papa," I said warily. "Just like Nan and Allie did. And the other girls, before we moved to Mill City."

Lan rolled his eyes. "That's what I thought. You haven't even considered any other possibilities."

"Other possibilities?"

"After what you did to the mirror bugs at the Little Fog settlement, any of the big universities would be glad to have you as a student. You could probably even get a sponsor, so it wouldn't cost Papa and Mama anything."

"Lan! Don't talk nonsense." I went back to my weeding, but Lan didn't leave.

"It isn't nonsense. You have talent and power; you deserve to get the training you need to use them properly."

I sat back on my heels, rested my muddy hands on my green weeding apron, and just looked at him for a minute.

From the time I was thirteen, when I almost blew up my Uncle Earn at my sister's wedding dinner, I'd had more and more trouble doing normal, Avrupan-type magic spells. It had only been a month or two since I'd figured out that the trouble was mostly in my head. I'd been so worried about being an unlucky thirteenth child that I'd nearly talked myself right out of doing any magic at all, ever, on account of being afraid of what might happen if I lost my temper. For the past five years, Aphrikan magic had been the only sort I'd had any luck with. I was still getting accustomed to the notion that it was a safe thing for me to work Avrupan spells at all.

Oh, I'd learned the basic Avrupan magic theories in school, like everyone else, but I had a lot of catching up to do on the practical side. I still had trouble even with simple things like housekeeping spells. And here was Lan, proposing that I go off to college as if it was me who was the double-seven magician.

"And don't go objecting because you're a girl," Lan went on. "There's lots of girls who study advanced magic. And Mama doesn't need you here, really — not when there's only you and Robbie and Allie left at home."

He ran on like that for a while; I just sat and watched. It was plain as day that he didn't expect me to disapprove more than a token, for form's sake. He ran down a whole long list of answers to objections I hadn't made and worries I hadn't mentioned. It was some time before he noticed that I wasn't saying anything at all.

When he finally did notice, he stopped in the middle of a sentence. We looked at each other for a minute, and then he said, "Eff?"

"I'll think on it," I told him.

"Good," he said, a little uncertainly. Then he grinned, and I could see his confidence coming right back. "While you're thinking, I'll mention it to Papa, so that —"

"If you say one word to Papa before I've had a good long think, I'll sew the tops of all your socks together before I pack them."

"Eff!" Lan laughed, but he looked a little worried, too. "It's a great opportunity. You have to grab it while you can."

"I'm not grabbing anything until I'm sure whether I'm grabbing a fire nettle or a sprig of mint," I said. "You've been thinking about this for a couple of weeks at least. I can tell. I want time to do some thinking of my own."

Lan tilted his head sideways and narrowed his eyes at me. Then suddenly he nodded. "All right. But don't take too long. And don't go getting all tangled up in worries about what it'd be like. Hardly anybody back East is like Uncle Earn."

He left, and I went back to my work. Weeding is a good job to do when you need to think about things, and I needed to think even more than I'd let on to Lan.

Papa had moved the family — well, the younger half of it, anyway — to Mill City when Lan and I were five, but I still remembered what it had been like before. Most of my aunts and uncles and cousins hadn't liked it one bit that I was an unlucky thirteenth child, and they'd taken it out on me every chance they got. We'd gone back East for my sister Diane's wedding when I was thirteen, and none of them had changed much except for being eight years older and eight years meaner. Uncle Earn had been ready to have me arrested or worse, just because I happened to be thirteenth-born.

Mill City was different. It was right at the edge of the country, just this side of the Great Barrier Spell that kept the steam dragons and mammoths and other dangerous wildlife away from the settled parts. Some days it seemed like half the folks in Mill City were looking to move out past the Mammoth River into the Far West, just as soon as the Homestead Claims and Settlement Office approved their applications, and the other half had relatives and friends and customers out past the barrier, even if they didn't go their own selves.

Being so close to the wild country made people here a lot less interested in making up dangers and a lot more interested in plain, practical magic. From Mill City on west, nobody would care if I had two heads and bat wings, if I could work the spells that kept the wildlife from overrunning the settlements. Of course, right that minute I still couldn't work the wildlife protection spells, on account of the trouble I'd made for myself over learning magic, so even in Mill City there was no reason for folks to overlook my bad points. But back East . . . well, Lan had been going to boarding school there for the past four years, and I believed him when he said that not everyone was like Uncle Earn. But even a few people like my uncle would make more unpleasantness than I wanted to face.

I finished the row and began carting the dead weeds over to the compost pile. Lan was right about a lot of things, I could see that. I might not be able to go to one of the big important schools, like Simon Magus College or the New Bristol Institute of Magic, but between all the attention I'd been getting and being the twin sister of a double-seventh son, some Eastern school would surely take me in. It was an opportunity that wouldn't likely come around again, and it didn't seem right to pass it up only on account of a worry that folks might be unpleasant.

I thought about that, off and on, for the next couple of days, and about Lan. Even though we were twins, he'd always been the one to look out for me. We'd been growing apart, though, ever since I had rheumatic fever and got behind a year at school. And for the past four years, he'd hardly even been home summers. I could see that he wanted what was best for me, but I wasn't sure that he knew what that was. Especially since I wasn't sure myself.

I was still thinking when William came around to say good-bye. He still had a year of preparatory school before he went to college, and he was going back early to meet up with a possible sponsor.

"What's this I hear about you coming East to school next year?" he asked.

I scowled. "That Lan! I told him not to talk to anyone about it until I was done thinking."

"You'll never be done thinking," William said. "And he didn't actually say much. So what is it about?"

I glared at him, but I knew there'd be no point to not answering. William didn't look like he'd be difficult about anything — he was thin and sandy-haired and already wore eyeglasses like his father. Most of the time he didn't say much. But when he was curious about something, he was stubborner than a bear after a honeycomb. He'd pay no heed to glares or hints or scowls or much of anything else until you told him what he wanted to know. Sometimes he'd listen if you told him straight out that you didn't want to talk about it, or that you didn't want to tell him, but I knew as sure as anything that this wasn't one of those times. So I said, "Lan thinks I should go off to college when I'm done with upper school."

"So it was his idea." William didn't sound surprised. "What do you think?"

"I —" I looked down at my boots. "I don't know."

"Why not?"

"I just don't!" I said. Then I sighed. I had no call to go snapping at William just because I didn't know what to make of Lan's notions. "It's a completely new idea. I never once thought about me getting schooling past upper school."

"Why not?" William asked. His eyes had narrowed and I could see he was getting ready to be cross about something.

"I just didn't," I said. "I'm not like Diane or Sharl." Diane and Sharl were two of my big sisters who hadn't come West with us. Diane had been saving up for music school when we left; Sharl had finished college and been married.

William looked suddenly thoughtful. "And your sisters who came here — Allie and Nan both went to work as soon as they finished with upper school. Rennie —" His voice cut off abruptly and he gave me an apologetic look.

My sister Rennie had run off and married a settler, a member of the Society of Progressive Rationalists who thought using magic was a weakness. Mama and Papa had been crushed and disappointed, and it tore up the rest of the family pretty bad, too, at the time. But we'd had five years to get over it, and we all pretty much had, even Mama.

"Yes," I said, so William would know it was all right and that I knew he hadn't meant anything by bringing it up. "And Julie got married practically right out of upper school back in Helvan Shores, too. She just didn't run off to do it."

"That doesn't mean you have to do the same."

"I wasn't planning to!" I looked at my boot tips again. "I wasn't planning much of anything, I guess."

"And neither was anyone else," William said. "Don't look at me like that. It'd take a blind prairie skunk all of ten minutes to see that the plans in your family have always been about Lan."

"William!"

"It's true," he said in that tone he had that meant there was no arguing with him. "I think Lan feels guilty about it, too. Which is probably why he came up with this idea about you going East for school."

"It's not just that," I said, because I knew William was right about my twin feeling guilty. "Lan has a whole pile of good reasons."

"Like what?"

I started rattling them off. "It would be a chance for a kind of learning I've never had before. The best teachers —"

William cut me off. "Those are Lan's reasons," he said. "There are other ways to look at the matter. What do *you* want to do?"

I just stared at him for a long minute. That was what Miss Ochiba, who used to teach us magic at the day school, had said over and over — there are always other ways to look at things. I thought I'd learned that lesson through and through, but it hadn't occurred to me to try looking at this proposal of Lan's from any other direction until right that minute.

"Other ways," I said slowly. Lan saw going East for school as a great chance to learn spells and theory from the best Avrupan teachers in the country. Papa would see it the same way, especially if I found a sponsor so it wouldn't cost the family so much, and he'd be especially pleased to have another child go for schooling past upper school. Mama would see it as a chance for me to get some Eastern polish on my manners, and a good way of keeping me far, far away from the settlement territory on the west bank of the Mammoth River.

And I . . . I didn't know yet how I saw it, but I knew for certain fact that I wasn't going to find out by arguing Lan's reasons over and over in my head. I had some more thinking to do, of a different kind. I looked at William and nodded. "Thank you, Mr. Graham," I said. "I needed reminding."

William looked at me for a minute, then just nodded back. One of the good things about William was that he always knew when to stop pushing on a point. "You're welcome, Miss Rothmer," he said. "Anytime."

We spent the rest of William's visit talking about his plans for the next year. I told him I'd write if he would, which I figured meant maybe three times all year. William wasn't much for letter writing.

After he left, I did some more thinking, only this time I wasn't just chasing my tail trying to counter all Lan's reasons why I should do what he wanted. The first thing I thought was that it was what *Lan* wanted, not what *I* wanted. Lan had always loved school, magic lessons especially, and he just kind of assumed that once I got over my problem with spell casting, I'd feel the same.

I didn't, and so I told him the very next day. He wasn't happy about it, but I got him to agree that it was my decision and he would have to let it be. I could see that he thought I'd come around sooner or later, but as long as he didn't go stirring things up right then, I didn't mind. I figured that by the time he was around to bring it up again, I'd have done a sight more thinking about what I did want and how to get to it. Right then, I just knew that it felt wrong for me to go so far away from everyone I cared about and everything I loved, just to get more schooling that I wasn't sure I had any need for.

Lan left on the train the first week in September, still sure that I'd change my mind before Christmas. I didn't try to convince him he was wrong. I wasn't certain that he was. I only knew that between him and William, I had a lot more thinking to do before I finished upper school.

CHAPTER
· 2 ·

THINKING DIDN'T COME EASY THAT FALL. I'D BEEN SURE THAT ALL the fuss about the mirror bugs and the settlement and me would finally die down when Lan and William went back East, but it didn't. Oh, the newspaper people stopped coming around, and they'd quit doing broadsheets a while back when the big fire at the grain mill gave them something else exciting to write about, but it wasn't like anybody forgot about it.

The ones who especially didn't forget were my teachers and classmates at the upper school. Half of them treated me like a circus lion, wanting me to do tricks for them, and the other half thought I'd made the whole thing up and made no bones about saying so. And some of them were jealous because I'd been out past the Great Barrier Spell and seen part of the Western settlement country for myself, and they didn't believe me one bit when I said the part I'd seen wasn't so different from the land around Mill City.

Magic classes were the worst, because everyone expected me to show off, and thought I was shamming when I still had nearly as much trouble getting my spells to work as I ever had. On the very first day, when we were reviewing the solidifying spell, mine turned half of the wooden table black and gooey, so that it collapsed. The mud we were supposed to be working on spattered all over everything, and I spent the rest of class cleaning up the mess. At least my spells had quit exploding, so I didn't have to worry about someone getting hurt.

I went back to spending most of my free time down at the college menagerie with Professor Jeffries. He was the college wildlife specialist, and I knew him pretty well because he used to let William and me come down and practice our Aphrikan magic on the animals, coaxing them to move around or choose one bit of food over another. That was when I'd first grown to love the menagerie, and by extension the Far West that was the true home for many of the menagerie's animals.

Although I didn't have any official position with the menagerie, Professor Jeffries let me feed the animals, even the young mammoth that was the prize specimen in the collection, and sometimes I assisted in the office. There was a new professor in the department, Miss Aldis Torgeson, and she was at least twice as good at coming up with paperwork as Professor Jeffries ever was, so they needed a lot more assisting.

This was why I was at the menagerie on the October day when Washington Morris came by. Actually, Wash got there before I did. I came straight from school, and found him sitting on the corner of Professor Jeffries's desk, waving his hands to emphasize a point, so that the long leather fringe on his jacket flapped every which way as he talked.

Wash was a circuit-rider, one of the six or seven magicians who rode from settlement to settlement to bring them news, share new spells, and help out when the settlement magicians needed helping. He'd been out in the settlements all summer, spreading the anti-mirror-bug spells that Papa and Professor Jeffries had worked out, and I hadn't looked to see him again until spring. His black hair was a mass of frizz grown nearly to chin length, and his beard looked as if he'd used a crosscut saw to trim it. Circuit magicians always got a mite shaggy when they'd been out in the settlements for months, but Wash usually stopped at the barber in West Landing, on the far side of the river, before he came on into town. I thought he must have been in a powerful hurry to have skipped sprucing up.

As soon as he saw me, he broke off and his dark face split in a wide grin. "Hello, Miss Rothmer!" he said, and I could tell that he was tired because the hint of Southern drawl in his voice was a lot stronger than usual.

"Good afternoon, Mr. Morris," I said.

"Wash," he corrected me.

"Not if you're going to call me Miss Rothmer," I told him. "I thought we got that settled last summer."

"Miss Eff, then," he said, still grinning.

I couldn't keep from rolling my eyes, but I let that stand. It should have felt peculiar, being on a first-name basis with a gentleman a good fifteen or sixteen years older than me, and a black man to boot, but Wash never paid much attention to other people's rules, and he had a way of making everyone else forget about them, too. I always thought that was why he spent most of his time out in the wild country: because there was no one there to make rules for him.

"What are you doing back in Mill City so soon?" I asked.

"Supply run," he said. "I gave most of mine to the settlement magician at Evergreen Farms, and I need to restock."

Knowing Wash, that was true enough, but it wasn't anything like all of the truth. I narrowed my eyes at him. "Then what are you doing in Professor Jeffries's office, first thing? He doesn't have supplies to sell."

"Not of the usual kind," Wash said agreeably.

"You're as bad as William," I complained. "And whatever Professor Jeffries has for you, it still doesn't explain why you came straight here before you even got yourself looking civilized again."

Wash laughed. "You sound just like Miss Maryann," he told me, meaning Miss Ochiba. That was how I'd first met him, three years back when Miss Ochiba had asked him to talk to her classes at the day school about the settlements and the open lands of the Far West.

Professor Jeffries gave both of us a look of mild reproof. "Mr. Morris came to deliver a new specimen for the menagerie," he said.

"A new specimen? What did you catch?" I asked eagerly.

"A pair of golden firefox cubs," Wash said. "I had quite a time getting them through the Barrier Spell. Young 'uns have a harder time with it. The ferryman didn't much like me bringing wildlife over, either. I took myself off as soon as we docked and came straight here."

I stared at him. "Fox cubs? In October?"

Wash shrugged. "Firefoxes don't breed quite the same as their natural cousins."

"Still, a fall litter is unusual even for magical wildlife," Professor Jeffries said. "We're lucky you found them."

"It's not so out of the way for those critters," Wash said. "Truth to tell, I'd had my eye on a den I found two years back, hoping one of the family would circle around to use it again this fall. I wasn't expecting goldens, though, and I wasn't expecting the mama fox to be caught by a Gaulish trapper."

"I see." Professor Jeffries pushed his glasses up on his nose and made a humphing sound. "I do wish you could see your way to staying in Mill City for more than a week at a time, Mr. Morris. Your practical observations would be infinitely useful, if we could persuade you to write them out." He frowned slightly. "Or better yet, dictate them to someone."

I ducked my head to hide a smile. Wash's handwriting was dreadful. I knew on account of he'd been sending notes to Professor Jeffries for a couple-three years, and I'd been the one making a clean copy of them for the professor.

"It's Wash, Professor," Wash said with a smile, but then he shook his head. "I'm pleased enough to help out where I can, but staying too long in the city makes me twitchy."

"I've half a mind to assign you to one of my students as a project while you're here," Professor Jeffries said. He was still frowning with his eyebrows, but you could just see that the corners of his mouth were itching to curl up considerably more than he was letting them. Wash had that effect on people.

"If you like," Wash said. "I doubt it'd be worth the effort this time, though. I'm only here for a few days, to resupply and" — he gave me a quick wink — "get a haircut so I don't frighten the new settlers."

"Hmph." Professor Jeffries shook his head. "No doubt you're right. Next time, I shall be ready for you." His frown deepened suddenly, as if he'd thought of something, but all he said was that Wash should take me out back and show me the fox cubs. "And I trust that you will provide Miss Rothmer with any pertinent information regarding their care," he added. "I would not wish to lose a pair of valuable specimens through ignorance."

So Wash took me out to the pen they'd rigged up in the menagerie. The golden firefoxes were a double handful each of long fluffy fur and bright black eyes and cold black noses, just barely past being weaned. Wash said they'd keep their pale, pale gold color until spring, when they'd get their first summer coats and start coming into control of their magic. When they were full-grown, they'd be a light gold on top, almost the color of dry grass, with a deeper gold underneath. And just like regular firefoxes, they'd be able to warm or cool the air around them, though neither animal could actually start fires as far as anybody knew.

Wash told me how to feed the cubs, and what sort of bedding firefoxes used in their dens, and to be sure the cubs didn't get too warm. Then I showed him around the menagerie. The college's collection had grown in the past three years, though we still didn't have very many magical creatures on account of the difficulty of getting them past the Great Barrier Spell. In addition to the scorch lizard and the daybat we'd started with, we'd added a miniature silverhoof and a pair of jewel minks that the professors were trying to get to breed, but most of the animals were ordinary, natural ones, like the mammoth: a prairie wolf, a couple of bison, the colony of prairie dogs that had grown from the two Dr. McNeil brought back, a porcupine, and so on. We'd had a skunk for a while, but even the magicians couldn't do much about the smell, so we'd gotten rid of it.

After we went through everything once, we went back past the cages and pens that Wash thought could be improved on, and Wash made suggestions for changes. By the time we finished, the afternoon was getting on for evening and it was time for me to head home. Wash said he'd walk along with me, as he had a fair number of thanks from the settlements to pass along to Papa.

"And to yourself as well, Miss Eff," he added. "Seeing that it was you that figured out the spell for getting rid of the mirror bugs."

"Don't you start, too!" I said. "I've had more than enough of that all summer long."

"Do tell," Wash said, and so I did. It took me halfway home to cover it all, from the newspapers to Lan's notions about college to my classmates at school. It turned out that Wash knew some of the boys from back in day school who'd gone west to the settlements instead of on to upper school. We gossiped some about them, and it was a considerable relief after all the talk of me and my doings. I'd almost forgotten how easy Wash was to talk to. He never pushed and he always listened, and when he finally said something to the purpose it was always worth hearing. So I was more than a little surprised when, after a short pause in the conversation, he asked after my magic lessons.

I made a face. "It's not as bad as it was, but I still can't make Avrupan spells work properly most of the time. And I haven't had time to practice Aphrikan magic."

Wash gave me a thoughtful look. "You're still at the point of needing practice, then?" he said mildly.

"I —" I stopped. It hadn't occurred to me that there were other ways of learning magic than sitting down to work at it the way we did at school. I felt pretty foolish; Miss Ochiba had told us often enough that you could find a different way to look at *anything,* if you tried. And the most basic part of Aphrikan magic was all about sensing the way the world was and how it maybe could be different if you nudged it a little. It wasn't a separate thing from just everyday living, and learning how to do it didn't have to be separate, either. "I guess that's what she meant."

"Miss Maryann?"

I nodded. "She said once that when we got good at world-sensing, we'd be able to tell if an apple had a worm in it before we bit into it. I wondered at the time why anyone would go throwing spells around before they ate anything, but that's not what she meant. She meant that when you get really good at it, you just do it all the time. And I haven't even been trying once in a while!"

"You've been raised to Avrupan magic," Wash said. "It's natural that you think in terms of specific spells and purposes. Aphrikan magic isn't like that."

I touched the thumbnail-sized whorl of wood I wore on a leather cord around my neck, under my blouse. Wash had given me the charm early in the summer, to help me control my magic. Or at least, that's what I'd thought at the time. Then I'd discovered that there were a whole lot of spells wrapped around it, some of them Aphrikan or Avrupan and some a kind I didn't recognize. Some were very new, and some were very, very old, and a good chunk of them were there to make sure nobody noticed all the magic except people who already knew about it. I hadn't gotten much further than that in the time I'd had to study on it, which wasn't too surprising. Untangling all that old magic so as to get a proper look at it would have been hard enough all by itself; with all the don't-notice spells added in, it was practically impossible.

I started to ask Wash about it, but then changed my mind. Neither Wash nor Miss Ochiba would tell you something if they thought you ought to be figuring it out on your own.

So instead of asking about how the pendant worked, I said, "Who gave you that wood pendant, Wash?"

Wash's eyes crinkled up at the corners and he looked at me like he thought I'd said something extra clever. All he said was, "A conjureman. He was a friend of my mother's. I've had it since I was, oh, three or four."

"Wash!" I said. "And you gave it to me?"

"It's not a keeping thing," Wash said. "I haven't had need of it in years. It was more than time I passed it along, but I never met quite the right person before."

"But —"

"But, nothing." Wash's voice was unusually stern. "I told you once, that pendant only goes one way. Teacher to student. I'll tell you the whole story some other time, perhaps. But meantime, don't you go leaving it in a drawer somewhere. Some things are meant to be worn, valuable or not."

"I'm wearing it now," I said. "I just . . . it didn't seem like something I wanted to show off. So I don't."

"Ah. That's good."

"It seems very complicated," I said tentatively. "The spells that go with it, I mean."

"It *is* complicated," Wash said. "So's the world. Keep it while you can; use it while you need it; pass it on when you've finished."

"Use it for what?" I said, exasperated. "And how?"

"That's up to you," Wash said with a wide grin that made me want to forget I was a grown-up lady, nearly, and haul off and smack him the way I used to smack Lan and Robbie when we were little.

But I could see that I wouldn't get anything more out of him then, and we'd almost reached the house, so I huffed a little and asked where he was going next, after he left Mill City.

"Out to finish teaching the last few settlement magicians those new spells of yours," he said. "After that, downriver for the winter."

I must have looked surprised, because he shook his shaggy head at me and grinned again. "It seems the Settlement Offices up and down the river got together and decided that somebody should train a few magicians farther south, just in case some of those mirror bugs turn up in the Midlands next spring. We don't know how far they spread before we got a handle on them, after all. And it's been a long time since I visited New Orleans."

"New Orleans is a long, dangerous trip," I said, before I thought to remember who I was talking to. Going down to New Orleans wasn't near as dangerous as riding circuit in the settlements, and the reason they'd asked Wash to ride a circuit in the first place was that he was one of the few men who'd gone off to explore the Far West on his own and come back alive to tell about it.

"Not so far as you think," Wash said. "I'll be there well before Christmas, even stopping at settlements. Might even have time to swing east a bit and see how things are changing there, before I come back in the spring."

We turned in at the gate of the big lumber-baron house the Northern Plains Riverbank College had given Papa when we first moved to Mill City thirteen years before. It was a lot quieter now that Robbie and Allie and I were the only ones left at home, even with Papa's students in and out all the time.

I left Wash in the front parlor and went to find Papa and then to make tea. I had a million questions still to ask, but I didn't think Wash would answer any of them right then, and certainly not when he had Papa to talk to. Besides, I had more thinking to do. Wash was almost as good at giving me things to think about as William.

CHAPTER
· 3 ·

THE FIRST THING I DID, THE MORNING AFTER THAT TALK WITH
Wash, was to work on the Aphrikan world-sensing technique
that Miss Ochiba had taught us. Only instead of just doing it
and stopping, I tried to keep it going all the time.

It was difficult. Paying attention to everything at once,
while being very quiet inside your own head, is hard enough
when you're sitting still. Doing it while you are walking around
and talking to people and doing breakfast dishes and solving
math problems and answering history questions seemed pretty
near impossible at first. I kept getting distracted by the warm
feel of a wooden table or the swirly sense of the soap in the
dishwater. The more I worked at it, though, the easier it got. I
still couldn't keep it up all the time, but the more I tried, the
longer it worked.

Oddly enough, one of the first things that happened was
that my Avrupan spell casting got better as soon as I started
doing the world-sensing in class. It was late November before I
tried, because I wasn't sure it would be a good idea to mix
Avrupan and Aphrikan magic, but after my pencil-mending

spell reduced my broken pencil to a heap of splinters and black powder, I figured that world-sensing couldn't make things any worse than they were already.

Two days before Harvest Feast, I walked into magic class concentrating on world-sensing for all I was worth. I almost dropped my books in surprise. The practice tables where we set up our spells were covered with warm spots and cool spots, like someone had scattered snowballs and lit candles over them and left them to melt. My table was the coldest spot in the room, and it didn't take me long to figure out that the reason was the way my spells always went wrong.

That day, Mr. Nordstrom had us working on a spell for balancing an uneven weight from a distance. It was actually a blend of two spells we'd already learned, and the point was to learn to control them both at the same time. A lot of the advanced spells, like the travel protection spells that folks need west of the Great Barrier Spell, use two or more spells at once, so it's important to know how to work with combinations.

I was actually fairly good at the spell for doing things at a distance, because it was so useful at the menagerie. Cleaning the scorch lizard's pen was downright dangerous if you got too close, but with the distance spell, I could just stand outside and lift the mess into the bucket without getting anywhere near the lizard's teeth or breath. I'd never been able to do the weight-adjusting spell, though, so I expected the class exercise to be a failure, as usual.

I set up my table the way the instructions said, with a little wooden teeter-totter at the far end and a stubby candle, a feather, a linen string, a lead weight, and a paper fan in front of me. Most Avrupan spells need a lot of equipment to get them to work when you're learning; it's only after you've practiced a lot that you can do them without the supplies, and there are some spells that only the most powerful magicians can ever learn to do without gear. Being a combination spell, this one needed supplies from both the spells we were supposed to combine, plus some extra things to make the spells work together properly.

I measured the herbs carefully and set part of them aside so Mr. Nordstrom could see that I'd done it properly and maybe give me partial credit. Then I tied one end of the string to the feather and the other end to the weight, and looped the middle around the base of the fan. I started murmuring the spell as I lit the candle and sprinkled the herbs across the fan and the candle flame.

As I picked up the fan (carefully, so as not to let the loop of string fall off), I felt the magic thicken around me like a warm blanket. It gathered around the flame and the fan, getting stronger and warmer as the spell shaped it. I was fascinated; I'd never watched an Avrupan spell casting through my world-sensing before.

And then my spell started to go wrong. Instead of balancing evenly between the candle and the fan, the feather, and the lead, the magic grew hotter around the fan. It was speeding up, too, and I knew that in another minute my paper fan would catch fire.

So I reached out and *pushed* the magic back toward the candle. I'd done something like that at the Little Fog settlement, using Aphrikan magic to make the mirror bugs' magic do what I wanted instead of what it was supposed to do, but I'd never thought about doing it to my own spells. It worked better than I expected. The spell slowed and the magic evened out, and a minute later I finished the casting.

The teeter-totter on the far end of my table shivered. I held my breath. Slowly, the lower arm rose until the bar of the teeter-totter was dead level, just the way it was supposed to be.

I got full marks in magic class that day for the first time since I'd started upper school. After that, I made sure to keep doing my world-sensing whenever I was casting spells. It let me sort of *feel* where things were going wrong before they fell apart, in time to push them back together again. My grades in magic class went right up and stayed.

Of course, improving my spells also meant that Allie made me take on a bunch of the housekeeping magic that I hadn't been able to do before. I'd have been cross about it, except that she made Robbie take over most of the chores that were just plain hard work and no magic. I didn't much mind trading hauling firewood and hoeing the garden for working the fly-block spells and the fast-dusting charms.

Lan and William didn't come home for Christmas that year, not either one of them, nor did most of my other brothers and sisters, but there were letters from everyone. Even Rennie sent a letter, the first we'd had from her since Papa and I had been out to the Rationalist settlement back in June. It was kind of sketchy for something covering all that while, but we didn't have much time for thinking on it because of Professor Jeffries and William.

Professor Jeffries came by just after we got Rennie's letter, with a fat packet that had gold trim and red wax all over it. I knew because I was the one who answered the door for him. He asked to see Papa, and they spent an hour in Papa's study before they came out to have cider and biscuits with the rest of us. And right about then, Professor Graham showed up and the parlor pretty near exploded.

Professor Graham was William's father. He was an angular, intense sort of man, and he hadn't changed much in all the years we'd been in Mill City, except that his hair was a little thinner and his eyeglasses were a little thicker. He had emphatic notions about a lot of things. One of them was magic, and another was William. When he came busting into our house, he was shouting about both of them, and it was a while before he simmered down enough to make sense. He was so mad he didn't even stop to take off his coat and boots in the hall, and Allie and I had to spend nearly an hour later on drying out the carpet where he'd tracked in all the snow.

Between Papa and Mama and Professor Jeffries, they

finally got him set down with a cup of hot cider and some biscuits, though it was plain that Professor Graham was still plenty fussed about something. After a minute, Papa and Mama exchanged a look over his head, and then Mama said, "What brings you by today, Professor?"

For a minute it looked as if Professor Graham was going to explode all over again, but instead he pulled a letter from an inside pocket and handed it to Papa. "That," he said bitterly.

Papa started to read, then looked up. "This is from your son."

"No son of mine," Professor Graham said even more bitterly than before. "Go on, read it."

From the way he said it, I thought he meant for Papa to read the letter aloud, but Papa only nodded and commenced looking over the letter again. It didn't take him long to finish. "Well," he said. "Seems the boy has a mind to choose his own way."

"Choose!" Professor Graham burst out. "Choose Triskelion University, when everything's arranged for him to attend Simon Magus? He's an idiot, and he's ruining his life."

I very near bit my tongue off to keep it still. Professor Graham had been bragging for months about William attending Simon Magus College, same as Lan, so I could see why he'd be upset at the news that William had decided on a different course. But I couldn't say I was surprised, and neither would he have been, if he'd paid attention. William had already messed up Professor Graham's plans for his life twice: once when he talked the professor into sending him to the day school like Lan and me instead of tutoring him at home, and once when he insisted on having two years at the upper school in Mill City, instead of going East for prep school the way Lan had when he finished day school. And William had taken Miss Ochiba's extra class in Aphrikan magic after school for years, same as me, even though his father had made it plain that in his opinion nothing was worth spending time on except Avrupan magic.

William going off to Triskelion fit the same pattern. Triskelion University wasn't anywhere near as old as Simon Magus. It was founded in 1824, just eight years before the Secession War started, but even though it was practically brand-new, its first four classes of graduates had been as helpful in winning the war for the North as the magicians who'd studied at the older, better-known schools. It was the first university in North Columbia to give equal weight to all three major schools of magic: Avrupan, Hijero-Cathayan, and Aphrikan. And Miss Ochiba, who'd taught Avrupan magic at the day school for twelve years and Aphrikan magic after school for six, had been a professor at Triskelion since right before William left for boarding school. I wondered whether that was what had decided him.

Something of what I was thinking must have shown on my face, because Professor Graham rounded on me and snapped, "Did you know anything about this?"

"No, sir," I said, for once thanking the stars that William was such a bad hand at letter writing. "He didn't say a thing about it last summer, and he hasn't written since."

Professor Graham gave me a suspicious look, but let it go. "Well, he'll not have a penny from me for this folly."

"It may not be folly," Professor Jeffries said in a thoughtful tone. Ignoring Professor Graham's scowl, he went on, "Triskelion has an excellent reputation for such a young school, and after that business with the mirror bugs last summer —"

"Nonsense!" Professor Graham said sharply. "He needs a solid grounding in higher Avrupan theory if he's to get a teaching position with one of the great Eastern universities. Triskelion can't provide that."

"I don't think William wants to be a teacher," I said before I could stop myself.

"What?" Professor Graham looked mad enough to have an apoplexy. "I thought you said you didn't know anything about all this!"

"I-it was something he said a long time ago," I stammered. "Back before he went East for school."

"Boyish nonsense!" Professor Graham said. "He'll come to his senses soon enough."

"Perhaps," Papa said. He glanced at the corner of the mantelpiece, where the little wooden squirrel sat that my brother Jack had carved. Jack had gone for a settlement allotment the minute he turned eighteen, though Papa and Mama were both against it. He'd stuck to it through two years of waiting until the Settlement Office found him a place, and now he was out in Bisonfield, starting on his five years of working to earn his claim.

"Eff," my mother said, "would you bring some more biscuits from the kitchen, please?" She handed me the platter even though there were still three biscuits left on it.

I could see she wanted me away for a while. I took my time in the kitchen, but when I brought the biscuits back, Mama handed me the cider pitcher to fill. I went back out and added two sticks of kindling to the cookstove so I could heat up the cider. I wasn't any too keen to go back to the parlor while Professor Graham was that angry, and I didn't know how long it would take Mama and Papa and Professor Jeffries to talk him out of his mad. Professor Graham had a powerful temper.

When I finally came back out with the pitcher, Professor Graham was gone and Mama and Papa and Professor Jeffries were talking real serious. I poured more cider for everyone and then took Professor Graham's cup and plate to the kitchen without being asked. I washed up the dishes and tidied the kitchen, and when I came out again, Professor Jeffries was gone, too.

Papa and Mama didn't say much about what had happened, but it didn't take long for news to get all over town that Professor Graham had had a gigantic dustup with his son and cut him off without a penny. I was real popular at school for a week, on account of having practically been there when

Professor Graham got the letter. William had been in my class until he'd gone East for school, and most of my classmates remembered him.

I sat down and wrote William a letter right off, to let him know I understood why he hadn't written and to tell him that Mama and Papa didn't seem to think Triskelion University was such a bad choice, though they weren't saying so straight to Professor Graham's face. I thought a long time about what else to write. If William had been there, I'd have told him to his face that going to Triskelion was a fine idea for him and that I wished him well, but every way I tried to write it sounded like I was puffing off my opinion. In the end, I just asked him to remember me to Miss Ochiba if he saw her. I was pretty sure he'd understand.

William didn't write back, but a month after Christmas we got a letter from Lan. He told us all the things Professor Graham hadn't: that William had taken his graduating exams early and found a sponsor to send him to Triskelion before he'd ever written his father about it. Lan sounded a tad miffed that William hadn't told him anything in advance, and a mite disappointed that William wasn't going to be at Simon Magus with him after all, but he mostly sounded cross with Professor Graham. He said that if the professor hadn't gone all obstinate about William attending Simon Magus, William might have changed his mind. I was pretty sure he was wrong about that last bit, but there was no point in writing to tell him so.

I spent the weeks after Christmas thinking real hard about William and his father, and about Lan's and mine. One of the things I thought was that William had been partly right, last summer, when he'd said that all Papa's plans were about Lan, but he'd been partly wrong, too. Papa and Mama expected most of us to make plans for ourselves, once we got past upper school; they only got involved when there was a special reason, like Diane's music or Lan's double-seven magic.

I'd never made much in the way of plans, and I could see it was well past time I did. I'd already decided I wasn't going East like Lan wanted, and I knew I didn't want to work for the railroad like Nan, or get a job with one of the mills. About the only thing I really liked was helping out at the menagerie.

So right about the middle of February, I went to Professor Jeffries and asked him if there was any chance of me being hired on at the menagerie full-time after I finished the upper school exams in the spring.

Professor Jeffries narrowed his eyes at me. "And when would that be, exactly?"

"They start testing in March," I said. "I figured on signing up for an early place, if the settlement folks don't grab them all." The students who came from settlement families all tried to take their exams in March or early April, so as to be home in time to help with planting. Sometimes, if there weren't enough places, they'd just go on home, anyway. Some of them never did get their upper school certificates.

"Hmm. And you think you'd like working here?"

"I know I would." I hesitated. "For a while. A few years, anyway."

"A few years," Professor Jeffries repeated. "And after that?"

"I'm not sure," I said. I knew that I wanted to see more of the wildlands of the Far West, but I didn't want to join a settlement, and the only other job I knew of out on the far side of the Great Barrier Spell was the one Wash did. I didn't think the Settlement Office would hire a girl fresh out of upper school with no experience and no great knack for magic to be a circuit magician, even if I had helped out with the mirror bugs the summer before.

"Aren't you?"

The professor looked honestly interested, and next thing I knew I was telling him about wanting to go West, only not to a settlement. "I don't know how, but I mean to find out," I said. "Maybe somebody will get up another expedition to explore, and I can talk them into taking me along."

"Maybe." Professor Jeffries's eyes crinkled like he was amused about something, but all he said then was, "Well, if and when you pass your exams, I think I can find something for you to do."

I went home that day feeling very pleased with myself. All I had to do was pass my exams. And I wasn't much worried about just passing any of them, except maybe the one in magic, and I'd been doing a lot better with my spells since last fall.

I signed up to take my upper school exams in late March, and as soon as I was sure I'd be doing it, I told Mama and

Papa what I'd arranged with Professor Jeffries. They seemed a little startled, but not unhappy. Mama actually seemed pleased. That is, until I told her that I wanted to see more of the Far West one day.

"Eff!" she said. "You're much too young to make a decision like that!"

Papa gave her a look. I said, "I'm eighteen, Mama. Nineteen in June. And I'm not looking to head out this summer, or even next. I just wanted you to know it was something I was thinking of, so you wouldn't be too surprised when it comes up for real and all."

I don't think Mama heard anything past me saying I was eighteen. That was the age you had to be to claim an allotment from the Settlement Office, the way my brother Jack had done, and though there weren't many women who did, it wasn't unheard of.

"You can't mean to go for one of the settlements!" Mama gasped.

"No, no," I said quickly. "I'm not inclined to farming, and I'm nowhere near good enough to be a settlement magician. Anyway, I don't want to stay in one place. I want to get out where I can see the country and the animals and such."

"I still say you're much too young to be doing something like that!"

"Mama," I said, "I'm only just deciding to work for Professor Jeffries. Far as I know, he hasn't got any expeditions planned. I expect I'll just be doing the same thing I've been doing all along, only I'll have some pay to help with the householding."

"I'm sure Allie could get you a job at her day school. She's always saying that the office could use more help."

"I don't want a job at a day school. I like working for Professor Jeffries, and I already know most of the work. And if something likely does come up in the way of heading West, I'll be in a good place to hear about it."

"Eff!"

"Sara," Papa said, and Mama looked at him and pressed her lips together, and didn't say anything more. Papa turned to me. "It sounds as if you've thought this out very carefully."

"I've been doing just about nothing but think since last summer," I said. I must have sounded a mite cross, because Papa laughed.

"If Professor Jeffries thinks it will do, and you pass your exams, I think it will work out very well," Papa said. "For a short while, at least."

Mama looked crosser than ever. I'd expected her to dislike the notion of me going West; she'd been upset for months when Jack signed up for a settler, and then she got snappish again when he finally got his allotment and left. I hadn't expected her to be this cross, though, not when it was just a notion for somewhere far off in the future. I didn't worry too much. I figured she'd grow accustomed after a while, the way she had when I first started spending time at the menagerie.

That same night, I wrote Lan and William about what I'd decided. They both wrote back right away, for a wonder. Lan's letter wasn't happy; he still thought I should go to magic school, and he warned me that he'd be home in the summer to badger me about it. (He called it "talking it over some more," but I knew what it'd feel like to me.)

William's letter was more of a short note. *Good for you*, it said. *You always have liked animals better than people.* Then it went on to say he'd be heading off to Triskelion as soon as he finished his last term, and gave me his address. It was the first letter I'd had from him all year, and I'd have thought he hadn't gotten any of the other letters I'd sent him, except for the line at the bottom.

P.S., it said, *I'll give Professor Ochiba your message when I see her.*

CHAPTER
· 4 ·

I PASSED MY EXAMS AND STARTED WORKING AT THE MENAGERIE FOR real in April. I was happy and busy, and I didn't pay too much heed to Mama's worrying or to the visits of the new head of the North Plains Territory Homestead Claims and Settlement Office. There were always people from the Settlement Office coming by in the spring, on account of their arrangement with the college. The Settlement Office never had enough magicians, so they'd taken to hiring on some of the magic students during the summer, and of course the college professors always helped out when there was an emergency.

At least, the professors helped out if the emergency was the sort magic could deal with. Magic couldn't do much to replace the oats and Scandian wheat and meadow rice and soybeans the mirror bugs had eaten, and that spring, eighteen settlements failed. A lot more were right on the edge of failing. The only small bit of good news was that the bugs had driven back a lot of the wildlife and had cleared a whole bunch of land that the settlers could plant. If we had a good growing summer, maybe the shaky settlements would get back on a solid footing again.

Meantime, the government in Washington had put a hold on building any new settlements until they'd studied up on the situation. That made a lot of folks in town very cross, including some of the people from the Settlement Office.

"We've solved the mirror bug problem," I heard one of them tell Papa. "And there are acres and acres of land that the bugs wiped clean, just begging to be filled up. But by the time those imbeciles in Washington realize it, the prairie will be back and it'll be twice as hard to expand. Wildlife always comes back stronger after a fire clears an area, and this will be no different."

Papa just hmphed at him, which meant he didn't really agree with the Settlement Office man but didn't want to start an argument right then.

I was busy most of April with the young mammoth at the menagerie. The McNeil expedition had brought him back as a baby, along with a few other samples of wildlife. He wasn't a baby anymore; in fact, it was hard to think of him as only partway grown. He was half again as tall as a tall man, and his tusks were three and a half feet long and as big around as my arm. He could split a rail fence with one blow of those tusks, and he'd done it a time or two, which was why his pen had a high fieldstone wall around it now, outside the rail fence. We still needed the wooden rails, because when he got edgy he'd charge at the wall and do himself an injury if there wasn't something in between for him to take out his mad on.

The mammoth always got restless in spring and fall, when the mammoth herds out on the plains were migrating, and that year was the worst ever. Professor Torgeson had to help out with the calming spells a time or two, and once even Professor Jeffries joined in. "It's because he's growing," Professor Jeffries said.

"That may be true, but it won't make any difference to the college or the people who live around it if he gets loose," Professor Torgeson snapped. She was a tall, rangy, red-haired woman with a marked Vinland accent, and she spoke her mind to anyone, which had already gotten her into difficulties with some of the other professors.

"I think we've been taking the wrong tack," Professor Jeffries said. "He doesn't need calming down; he needs exercise."

"Ride him North and feed him to an ice dragon," Professor Torgeson suggested. She had strong opinions about wildlife, most of them unfavorable.

"An ice dragon would eat the rider first," Professor Jeffries said absently. "They prefer the taste of people to just about anything else."

Professor Torgeson sniffed. "Tell me something I don't know," she said, and her accent was especially strong, like she wanted to remind him that Vinland was a whole lot closer to ice dragon territory than the North Plains Territory of Columbia was.

Her tone didn't put Professor Jeffries out one bit. "Professor O'Leary is planning to teach a class on poetry for magicians next year," he replied. "He thinks our students need more literary background than they've been getting."

Professor Torgeson looked startled, then laughed. "All right," she said. "But you're going to have to put this thing down eventually."

"Possibly," Professor Jeffries said, still staring at the mammoth. "But not just yet. Certainly not until we run out of other options."

"Is he always like this?" Professor Torgeson asked me.

I could see she didn't actually expect an answer, and right then the mammoth whacked the inner rail fence so hard the top rail splintered and we had to step smart to keep it contained.

By the time the mammoth calmed down, we were all hot and damp and thirsty. As we walked toward the offices, we saw Dean Farley standing outside Professor Jeffries's office. "Professor!" he called as soon as he saw us. "We've heard from the Frontier Management Department! We have funding."

Professor Jeffries stopped mopping his forehead and smiled. "Excellent! Professor Torgeson, would you join us? This may concern you."

Professor Torgeson's eyes narrowed, but she nodded. Professor Jeffries turned to me. "Miss Rothmer, I think that will be all for today. Tell your father the good news, if you please, and let him know I would like to stop by tomorrow evening to discuss it, if that would be convenient."

⎯⎯⎯⎯⎯ ◆ ⎯⎯⎯⎯⎯

Professor Jeffries and Professor Torgeson both showed up late the following day. I thought they'd disappear into the study with Papa, but instead Papa had us all sit down together. And then they explained.

For years and years, ever since the McNeil expedition got back in 1850, Papa and Professor Jeffries had been trying to persuade people that we still didn't know enough about the wildlands in the West. The plague of mirror bugs and the failure of eighteen settlements had finally convinced the Assembly in Washington that something needed to be done right away, but they were still arguing about what. Until they decided for sure, they were asking the land-grant colleges in the North, Middle, and South Plains Territories to do wildlife surveys out in the settlements, so they'd have some baseline to compare to.

"Pity they didn't think of this before the mirror bugs showed up," Professor Torgeson said in an acid tone.

"It would have been far more useful, certainly," Professor Jeffries conceded. "On the other hand, this should give us a very clear picture of the way wildlife returns to an area after such devastation. I'm sure you'll do a stellar job, Professor Torgeson."

"The newest person in the department always gets the worst assignments," Professor Torgeson said, but there was no

44

heat in her voice and her eyes had a gleam that said she was looking forward to it.

"We would like to offer you the position of record-keeper and assistant, Miss Rothmer," Professor Jeffries said.

My mouth fell right open. The corners of Papa's mouth tucked in, the way they did when he was trying not to smile, and suddenly I knew why Mama had been so cross when I'd said I wanted to go West one day.

"Papa! You've known about this for months!" I said, and then I remembered that this was supposed to be business and not family. "Excuse me, Professor Jeffries."

"That's quite all right, Miss Rothmer." Professor Jeffries looked like he was enjoying himself. "The stipend is rather less than your current wages, I'm afraid, but the direct costs will be part of the survey's budget. That would be things like food, lodging, feed and stabling for your horse as required, and so on."

"I —" I swallowed hard. "Yes. I accept, Professor Jeffries."

"Excellent," Professor Torgeson said. "We'll be leaving as soon as Mr. Morris returns from Belletriste."

"Wash is in Belletriste?" I said. "I thought he was going to New Orleans for the winter."

"I believe he did," Professor Jeffries said. "But when I tracked him down last month, he was in Belletriste, visiting friends."

"Visiting — oh." Triskelion University was in Belletriste,

which meant that was where Miss Ochiba was now. Also William, but I wasn't sure Wash would think of William as a visiting sort of friend.

"Mr. Morris will be our guide," Professor Torgeson said. She frowned slightly, as if she weren't quite happy about that for some reason. I thought maybe it was because she didn't think she needed a guide, but everyone who traveled across the Mammoth River into the West had a guide, even Papa and Professor Jeffries, who'd been doing it for years.

Wash was one of the best; he'd even gone far enough to catch a glimpse of those Rocky Mountains, all on his own. He hadn't gone far enough to actually start climbing them, of course. Nobody'd ever done that and come back alive, except maybe for three men so stark out of their minds that some folks still said they'd made up their whole story.

"What about his circuit?" I asked. The settlements that were farthest out depended on help from the circuit magicians; I couldn't see Wash leaving them to get along on their own for a whole summer.

Papa cleared his throat. "That shouldn't be a problem," he said. "Wash's circuit is somewhat emptier than it was."

I reddened. The grubs and the mirror bugs had come in from the Far West, right into the middle of the North Plains line of settlements. I'd seen the devastation they caused for myself — acres and acres of dead, empty land that had been forest and fields and prairie. And Wash was circuit magician for the northern half of the North Plains Territory, from midway up the Red River down to the Long Chain Lakes. Most of those eighteen settlements that failed had to have been all along Wash's circuit.

Professor Jeffries coughed and said something about planning our route so that Wash could see to his duties for the Settlement Office as well as taking care of us, and Papa brought out a map. The three of them — Papa and Professor Jeffries and Professor Torgeson — bent over it, pointing and arguing. I moved around to where I could watch, but mostly I just stood there thinking.

First I thought about getting to go West at last. I'd been wanting this since before I started upper school, but except for that one trip last summer that was supposed to be just a visit with my sister Rennie, I'd never been west of the Mammoth River. In fact, that and the horrible trip to Helvan Shores when I was thirteen were the only times I'd been out of Mill City since Papa moved half the family here.

Watching Papa and the other two professors arguing over the map made me realize how little I really knew about the country west of the Mammoth River. Oh, I knew the things everyone did. I could make lists of the two types of wildlife, the natural (mammoths, terror birds, bison, saber cats, prairie wolves, piebald geese) and the magical (steam dragons, spectral bears, swarming weasels, chameleon tortoises, cinderdwellers, sunbugs). I could calculate the yield of a field of soybeans or Scandian wheat or meadow rice, and I could draw a line on the map that showed where the well-charted territory ended

47

and the land began that only a few folks like Wash had ever looked on.

But I also knew that studying up on a thing in school and actually living with it were two different things. Miss Ochiba had made quite a point of that, and even if she hadn't, I'd have figured it out from the letters home that my brother Jack and my sister Rennie had written over the last few years.

More than that, there were a lot of things I still didn't know. There were a lot of things nobody knew about settlement country, let alone the Far West beyond it — that was the whole reason for the survey. Even the circuit-riders got surprised by things sometimes, and they'd had more experience with the wild country than anybody.

By the time the professors left, they'd drawn up a route for us to follow, starting from West Landing and heading west to Lake Le Grande, dipping south and west to the Oak River settlement, and then farther west to zigzag north along the Red River and eventually circle back through the thin spot and down the Mammoth River to Mill City.

The thin spot was the place where the Great Barrier Spell had to cross land. The Great Barrier Spell protected all of the United States of Columbia — and a little bit of Acadia, in the Northeast — from the dire wolves and saber cats and steam dragons and other wildlife of North Columbia. It ran for nearly five thousand miles, all the way up the Mammoth River from the Gulf of Amerigo to the headwaters in Lake Veritasca, and then east through the Great Lakes and down the St. Lawrence

River to the Atlantic Ocean. The rivers and lakes not only made a natural barrier against the wildlife that added to the spell but the flow of water and magic along the rivers also kept the Great Barrier Spell going once it was set up.

But there were 175 miles between Lake Veritasca and the westernmost point of Lake Superior where there was no river and the Great Barrier Spell stretched thinly through the forests. That was why the lumber camps in the North paid so well, and why they were always looking for magicians even though they were inside the Barrier Spell. If any wildlife got through, they wanted to take care of it real fast, before whatever-it-was got to feeling better and started attacking people.

Even the Settlement Office didn't complain about keeping extra magicians up along the thin spot, though usually they grumbled about anything that meant fewer magicians for them to send out to keep the settlements safe. Everyone had heard the horror stories about the dazzlepig that had poisoned three miles of creek, or the short-faced bears that killed four men before the magician got there to stop them. I shivered just thinking about it.

And I was going out on the other side of the barrier, where deadly trouble with the wildlife happened a lot more often than once or twice a year . . . and I still wasn't half as good at working protective magic as most of my classmates. The only person I knew who'd been to the Far West and come back safe without using magic was Brant Wilson, the Rationalist who'd married my sister Rennie. He'd had a whole expedition full of magicians with him, but it was Brant's revolver that had saved them all from swarming weasels.

I'd never shot a revolver, but right after his first trip out to the settlements, Papa had seen to it that everyone in the family older than twelve learned how to handle a rifle, and he'd made sure that each of us younger ones learned as soon as we were old enough. I'd learned, though I didn't enjoy it much. It had been a long while since I'd done any shooting.

The day after Professor Torgeson asked me to go West as her assistant, I got Robbie to take me to the college range for some practice. Robbie was a good teacher, and he made me practice every day no matter how busy I was, until I could hit what I aimed at two times out of three. I'd never make a markswoman, but I was a whole lot better with the rifle than I was with my spells, and at least Wash and Professor Torgeson wouldn't have to spend extra time worrying about protecting me.

The last thing Robbie did before I left was to take me down to Gantz's General Store and buy me a brand-new repeater rifle to take with me. When I objected to the expense, he said that he wasn't spending all his own money; Lan and Jack had both sent a little to help pay for it, and Papa was in on it, too. "Just don't let Mama find out," he told me. "And take it to the range tomorrow for some practice, so you know how it handles before you go."

After considering for a bit, I decided to stick my new rifle and ammunition in with Professor Torgeson's supplies, so that Mama wouldn't notice and ask awkward questions. It was a good thing I thought of it then, because three days later, Wash turned up at last and all the plans and preparations sped up like a dire wolf going after a jackrabbit, and I didn't have time for anything else.

CHAPTER
· 5 ·

WASH WAS IN A POWERFUL BAD MOOD WHEN HE FIRST GOT BACK TO Mill City, but all he would say about it was that Eastern cities didn't much agree with him. I thought that was stretching it some. Belletriste was only about halfway between Mill City and the East Coast, just north of the border of the State of Franklin, and it wasn't all that much bigger than Mill City, especially if you counted in West Landing. Compared to New Amsterdam or Washington, or even St. Louis, it counted more as a largish town than a city.

Wash wouldn't talk about that, either. He didn't have much to say about anything he'd been doing since he left in October. Of course, he didn't have much time to talk to me about anything. Mostly, his time was taken up with Professor Jeffries and Professor Torgeson, getting ready for us to go.

Professor Torgeson was pretty cross, too. She wanted to head West right away, as soon as Professor Jeffries told her about the survey, and she wasn't too pleased to have to wait on Wash or classes or anything.

"We should have been out in the field in early March," she told Professor Jeffries. "We've already missed the entire germination period."

"It's May second and the trees are just now leafing out," Professor Jeffries commented. "If you'd left in March, you'd have been snowed in at least twice, for very little gain."

"We could still get snow," I said. "Sam Gantz says that the year he first came to Mill City, it snowed in June, a good six inches' worth."

"Snow in June, this far south? Not likely," Professor Torgeson said. "Who's Sam Gantz?"

I stared at her, trying to soak up the notion of someone thinking of Mill City as "this far south." I knew Professor Torgeson had grown up on Vinland, and I knew the islands of Vinland were just off the East Coast a fair piece north of Maine. It just never occurred to me to put the two things together before.

"Sam Gantz is the fellow who runs the general store," Professor Jeffries told her. "He's one of Mill City's oldest residents and an invaluable source of information, once you figure out where he's reliable and where he isn't."

I frowned. I wanted to object, because I liked Sam, but I had to admit that he had a fondness for tall tales.

"I would venture to guess that Mr. Gantz was quite accurate about the date of the snow," Professor Jeffries went on. "It's the amount that I question. An inch at most would be my guess, though of course there's no way of finding out now."

Professor Torgeson looked at Professor Jeffries as if she was trying to figure out whether he was joking. Professor Jeffries just smiled and went back to checking over the supplies we'd be taking. There were a lot of notebooks, several pencils, magnifying glasses, and tweezers, as well as some sample boxes enchanted to preserve whatever was in them and a small case full of spell ingredients that might be needed to test and classify things. Professor Torgeson was sure that a careful survey would turn up a lot of new animals and plants, and Professor Jeffries seemed to agree with her.

Picking out what to take was hard, because there wasn't much room. We were only taking one packhorse and what we could each fit into our saddlebags. Allie had near as much of a fit over that as Mama had had when I told her I was going West for the summer for sure and certain.

"Riding horseback isn't proper for a lady," Allie said. "You should ride in a buggy or a wagon."

Papa and I exchanged looks. Last summer, Mr. Harrison had tried to take a buggy West and he hadn't gotten five miles from West Landing before it broke an axle. Wagons were sturdier, but slow, and I'd had my fill of them on that trip. Anyway, Wash had already settled the question.

"A wagon will slow us down too much," he'd told the professors bluntly. "You'll either have to cut your planned route in half or figure on taking two years to cover it, with half that spent holed up somewhere for the winter. Myself, I'd keep the route as is and take a packhorse. Overwintering in the far frontier is chancy."

Nobody wanted to spend the winter in the West — well, Professor Torgeson got excited and muttered a bit about winter fauna and adaptations, but even she was more wistful than really serious about the idea. Once we got Allie to understand that, she stopped fussing about wagons, but she wouldn't let up on clothes. She'd have filled my saddlebags up with petticoats, if I'd let her.

What with all the talk and the fussing, it seemed sometimes as if it'd take months before we were ready to leave, but between Professor Torgeson wanting to get started and Professor Jeffries being real good at arranging things, it actually only took about a week. Early Monday morning, Wash, Professor Torgeson, and I led our horses onto the ferry that linked Mill City with West Landing.

Professor Torgeson seemed a bit absentminded as she tied her horse to the hitching rail. Her eyes kept straying to the faint shimmer in the air about halfway across the river. It dawned on me that she'd never been through the Great Barrier Spell before. Vinland had no need of such a thing, being an island, and what with all the settlement failures, the Settlement Office hadn't called on any of the college magicians for help since she'd arrived.

I didn't have much in the way of time to worry over Professor Torgeson, though, because I had worries of my own.

I'd only been through the Great Barrier Spell twice myself, once in each direction, but I knew that it was a disturbing feeling even when you knew what was happening. Animals couldn't understand and nearly always panicked, especially horses, unless someone cast calming spells on them. Last time, I'd been a passenger, and Wash and Papa and Professor Jeffries had taken care of the calming spells for all our horses. This time, I would be expected to take care of my own.

I'd started practicing the standard Avrupan calming spell as soon as I realized I was going to need it, so I was pretty sure I could do that part. What troubled me was whether I could keep it going when we passed through the Barrier Spell. Being looked over by something that felt as old and large and strange as the magic of the Great Barrier Spell was . . . well, the first time I'd gone through, I'd been convinced it would treat me the same as it did the wildlife, on account of me being thirteenth-born. I didn't think like that anymore, but that Barrier Spell still made me plenty nervous. And if there's one thing that'll mess up a calming spell quicker than anything else, it's if the magician gets distracted.

As soon as Professor Torgeson saw Wash riding down toward the dock, she cast the calming spell on her horse. I hesitated for a second, then started on my own. I was just finishing up when Wash tied his horse next to mine and signaled the ferryman that everyone was ready to go.

He did the spell for his horse as quick and easy as most folks do the candle-lighting spell. Then he turned and inspected my horse and the professor's. He didn't say anything, just gave me a little nod, but I felt better all the same.

Wash and the professor went forward, so that she could watch as we approached the Great Barrier Spell. I stayed with the horses. Despite Wash's approval, I was still nervous about the calming spell, and I wanted to be right there if anything went wrong.

The ferry cast off and made its slow way toward mid-river. The shimmery haze got more and more shimmery as we got closer, then turned into a curtain of tiny rainbows that flickered and moved like the waves on the surface of the water. The horses shifted, as if they could tell they were drawing nearer to the greatest magical working in the New World.

I looked at the horses, wondering what I was going to do if my spell did go wrong. I wasn't good enough yet to cast it again in a big hurry. Then I smiled. All year in school, I'd been doing my Avrupan spells by using the Aphrikan world-sensing to tell when they were going wrong. I ducked under the hitching rail and braced myself against it with both hands. Then I let myself get very quiet inside my head, and felt outward for everything else, especially the spell I'd just cast.

I'd done something similar by accident the first time I went through the Great Barrier Spell, so I thought I knew what the spell would feel like: huge and strong and ancient-seeming, even though Mr. Franklin and Mr. Jefferson and the others had only gotten it going a few years before the Revolutionary War. It felt like Avrupan magic and Hijero-Cathayan magic and Aphrikan magic all mixed together, and then some. Nobody could figure out how they'd done it, and nobody wanted to poke at it too hard trying to find out, on account of maybe making it fall apart and letting the wildlife back in.

That first time I'd crossed the Mammoth River, it had felt like the Barrier Spell itself was looking me over, checking to see if I was a danger that shouldn't be let through. It hadn't been a pleasant feeling, and I'd been careful not to do any Aphrikan magic on the return trip. Now I had a moment of misgiving; I wasn't sure whether being very quiet would be enough to keep the spell from noticing me. But it was too late for second thoughts; the ferry bell was ringing to warn everyone that we were almost at mid-river. A moment later the ferry hit the spell with a little bump.

Little rainbows shivered across the deck toward me. The horses jigged and pulled against the hitching rail, and I could feel mine fighting the spell I'd put on him. I sank deeper into the magic to try to calm him. Without thinking, I fell into the breathing pattern of the Hijero-Cathayan concentration technique that Miss Ochiba had taught me when I was thirteen.

The Great Barrier Spell reached the part of the ferry where I stood with the horses. It didn't seem to pay me any mind, though I didn't have too much time to think on it right then. That horse of mine was fighting the calming spell worse than ever, and I could see it wasn't going to hold.

I reached for the nearest natural magic source. I'd gotten in the habit of doing that whenever my Avrupan spells started to go wrong — twitching and tweaking them from outside to make them work, anyway. But there was no natural source of magic within reach except the power of the river, and the Great Barrier Spell was using all of that.

I bit my lip, clenched my hands around the hitching rail, and poured as much of my own power as I could reach into the spell. Distantly, I felt something warm against my chest. The weak spots in the calming spell tightened up. My horse gave a great sigh, shook his mane, and settled down. And a few seconds later, we were through.

I hung over the hitching rail, panting. As I did, I felt Wash's wooden pendant swing and settle a few inches below my collarbone. It was cool again, but I knew it had been the source of the warmth I'd felt a minute earlier. Right that minute, though, I wasn't thinking much about it. I was just hoping that Wash hadn't noticed what I'd been up to, because I was pretty near certain that he'd guess I'd been tweaking my Avrupan spells and wouldn't think much of me doing it.

"Nice job, Miss Rothmer," said an accented voice above me. I jerked my head back to see Professor Torgeson pushing sweat-damp hair back from her forehead. "Fixing a spell on the fly like that is a useful talent," she went on. "I'm glad you have it."

I straightened, though I still felt shaky and exhausted. "Thank you," I said uncertainly. "But I always thought it was better if your spells didn't need fixing."

The professor laughed. "True enough, as long as you're working with a predictable situation. The wildlands aren't predictable, though."

"Wildlands?"

"The land that men haven't tamed," Professor Torgeson said. "From my home, that's most of the mainland; from yours, it's all of North Columbia that's outside the Great Barrier Spell."

"Oh," I said. Over her shoulder, I saw Wash studying me and my horse. His face was a dark, expressionless mask, and when he saw me watching, he turned away. My heart sank. He'd noticed what I'd done, right enough, and he frowned on it just as much as I'd thought he would.

I wanted to head off somewhere and curl up in a ball, like I used to when I was five and my cousins back in Helvan Shores hectored me, but I couldn't. There was no place on the ferry to go, and as soon as we docked, I had my hands full with my horse and the extra baggage and supplies. As our guide, Wash got to handle necessities like food and fire starters, but Professor Torgeson told me that as her assistant, the equipment and magical supplies for the survey were my responsibility, and we should begin as we meant to go on. I had to see that everything we'd packed up in Mill City was still there and safely unloaded.

The main worry was the extra boxes we were sending on to settlements farther along on our route, so that we could pick them up later. With all the settlement failures, there weren't so many carriers going back and forth, and we had to change our plans some. That meant repacking some of the preserving jars and labels, a couple of blank journals, ink, and about half of the extra spell-casting ingredients, so as to get the right amount to the right places. It took the rest of the day to get it all done and sent off.

Wash didn't say a thing to me all that afternoon that wasn't about the business in hand. At first, I felt lower than a snake's belly, but after a while I started to get a mite peeved. I hadn't done anything except make sure my horse stayed calm, the way I was supposed to.

I went to bed grumpy and woke up grumpier. I'd gotten in the habit of working on my Aphrikan world-sensing first thing every morning, but that day I didn't. I told myself it was because it felt peculiar to be sitting there concentrating while Professor Torgeson bustled about the hired room we shared, but really it was just bad temper.

Neither Professor Torgeson nor Wash noticed my mood, which didn't help matters any. My horse did, though. He was skittish the whole time I was saddling him, and I thought for a while I was going to have to put a calming spell on him again. I didn't know if I could get it to work, though, not without using Aphrikan magic to prop the spell up from outside, and that made me grouchy all over again.

Fortunately, the packhorse was dead calm, and by the time I had her loaded up, I'd gotten over some of my grump. I triple-checked everything — the last thing I wanted was for

Wash or Professor Torgeson to find a loose rope or an unbalanced load on the very first day. I was glad I had, too, because the professor and Wash each checked everything over again before we all mounted.

Once I was in the saddle, my horse settled down. Then Wash took the lead rein for the packhorse and led us out onto the streets of West Landing.

CHAPTER · 6 ·

WEST LANDING WAS THE OLDEST SETTLEMENT ON THE WEST BANK of the Mammoth — at this end of the river, anyway. It was founded right before the Secession War, though back then it was just a couple of big warehouses built of mortared fieldstone, meant to make it easier to catch the free timber that floated downriver from the lumber camps up North. The settlement had hung on through the war, just barely, and then started growing fast when the war was over and all the Homestead Claims and Settlement Offices started working at getting the Western Territories settled before anybody else laid claim to them.

Riding through the town settled me down even more. I liked the feel of West Landing, from the double-wide dirt streets to the people in their long tan dusters and home-sewn calico. A lot of the folks recognized Wash and waved when they saw him. One man yelled to him that it was about time he got out on circuit.

"Take it up with the Settlement Office, Lathrop!" Wash yelled, and the man made a show of rolling his eyes, then grinned back.

A few of the men on horseback turned to come along with us for a little way, so they could ask Wash about what was happening farther out in settlement country or back at the Settlement Office in Mill City. Some just wanted to complain about the way the North Plains Territory Homestead Claims and Settlement Office was handling everything from the mirror bug problem to the freeze on new settlements. One or two had information to pass along.

"There's a pack of prairie wolves causing trouble down by Swan Prairie," one man told us. "Watch your horses, if you're heading that way."

Wash nodded. "Thanks for the tip."

"You're welcome. Safe journey, Wash, ladies." The man touched his hat brim to Professor Torgeson and me and rode off. A large young man on a chestnut horse took his place almost immediately. He asked about our route, and looked put out when Wash said we were swinging south to the Oak River settlement before we headed back west and north.

"Blast it, I was hoping you were heading straight for the Raptor Bay settlement," he said. "Isn't that normally your first stop?"

"Not this year," Wash said. "We're for Oak River first, then west and north until we get to St. Jacques."

"Ah." The rider frowned, then hesitated. "So you won't be passing near Raptor Bay at all?"

"I wouldn't say that," Wash drawled. "I think we'll be

near enough to drop a letter by, though perhaps not as soon as you'd like."

The young man flushed slightly. "Would you? There's supposed to be a supply carrier going out in another week, but you know what they're like — it'd take a message weeks to arrive, if the wagon master even remembers to deliver it. And if I leave without sending word, it could be months before I get another chance."

Wash laughed. "Shipping barges do make stops," he said. "And even if your captain is in a tearing hurry, he'll overnight in St. Louis."

"Well, I know, but —"

"Give me the letters, Charlie, and I'll see that your parents and your girl get them in as reasonable an amount of time as I can manage," Wash said.

"Thanks, Wash!" The young man pulled some folded-over papers out of his pocket and handed them over. Then he bobbed his head at Professor Torgeson and me, and rode off.

"Wash! Mr. Morris!"

A little shiver went down my spine, and I felt a cool spot against my chest. I turned to see a pretty black woman standing on the boardwalk, waving. She was a few years older than me, with warm brown skin the color of the smooth bark on a young maple tree. Like most of the folks in West Landing, she wore a tan duster buttoned up close. Three inches of calico ruffle and a pair of neat high-button boots showed at the bottom. The tall black man next to her made a what-can-you-do-with-her? motion. He had left his duster open, and I could make out a gray work jacket and trousers under it.

Wash's mouth quirked, and he rode over. "Morning, Miss Porter, George."

"This is a nice surprise," the woman said. "You usually come through West Landing in March. Or have you been gone and come back once already this year?"

"No, ma'am," Wash said. "It's an unusual year."

"How long will you be in town?"

"I'm afraid we're leaving this morning." Wash made a little movement with his free hand to indicate the professor and me.

"Then I shouldn't keep you. Safe journey — but next time you're through town, try to make time to visit us."

"Mother would love to see you," the man with her said, nodding. "But not if she finds out Elizabeth has been accosting you on the street like a fancy woman."

"George! I did no such thing," Miss Porter said. "Besides, Mother won't mind if it's Mr. Morris."

George and Wash exchanged a look over her head, then Wash touched his hat and rode back to us.

It kept on like that all the way through West Landing. Some of the folks who came over to chat with Wash asked to be introduced to the professor and me, but most of them just tipped their hats to us before they rode off. It took us nearly an hour to get through the main part of town.

Once we got out of West Landing at last, Wash and Professor Torgeson started up a conversation about how to manage the survey we were supposed to be doing. The professor wanted to stop and take samples right off, but Wash pointed out that most of the things this close to the Mammoth River had already been collected. Also, if we did too much stopping and starting, we wouldn't make it to the first wagonrest by nightfall.

They talked over various ways to go on, with me listening hard with both ears the whole time. I didn't have much to add, but if I was going to help the professor, I had to know what I was supposed to do. Eventually, they settled on using the wagonrests as base camps, at least while we were still close to the Mammoth River. We'd stay for a day or two when the professor wanted to collect samples and make observations, and move on when she finished.

Once we got past the middle settlements, though, there wouldn't be any wagonrests. "That," said Wash, "is when things will get interesting."

Professor Torgeson pursed her lips. "In Vinland, when we use the term *interesting* in connection with the mainland, it usually means something like 'you'll have to watch that a short-faced bear doesn't get your supplies, and maybe you' or 'a pack of dire wolves was hunting a unicorn in that area last week; if they didn't catch it, they're probably hungry enough to go after you and your horses.' Is it the same here?"

Wash laughed. "Pretty much, except it's plains creatures we'll need to keep an eye for."

"Steam dragons and saber cats and so on," the professor said, nodding. "I know them in theory, but I haven't seen many in life, and I certainly haven't met up with any in their natural environment."

"If it's all the same to you, Professor, I'd as soon we didn't meet up with any of those particular critters this trip, either," Wash said.

"If nobody ever gets a look at them, we'll never find out what to do about them," Professor Torgeson said tartly. "Look at what happened to that expedition back in 1850 — they'd all have been eaten by swarming weasels if that one fellow hadn't gotten off a lucky shot and killed the swarm leaders. None of them knew that weasel swarms *had* leaders."

"It wasn't just luck!" I said before I thought. "Brant's mother kept bees; he said the way the weasels moved reminded him of the bees, so he looked for something like a queen bee and shot that."

"Eh?" Professor Torgeson looked at me. "And how do you know that, Miss Rothmer?"

"Brant Wilson married my sister Rennie," I said. "Later on, I mean. He and Dr. McNeil came to our house after the expedition got back. My brothers were mad after stories about what they'd seen, so they told us all about it."

"Pity the whole tale didn't get into the journal accounts," the professor said.

"Maybe Dr. McNeil thought it would mislead people," I said. "Swarming weasels aren't really that much like swarming bees, and the swarm leaders certainly aren't queens."

"Yes, but the similarity in movement may be important. Someone should look into the reason why, but if no one knows about it, no one will think to investigate."

"It's kind of hard to investigate a mob of critters that are trying to eat you," Wash pointed out.

"Which is why the first thing we need to learn is how to keep them from getting interested in eating us," the professor replied. "So that we can watch and learn. The magicians in New Asante have proven it can be done; if we apply their methods —"

"I can't rightly claim to be up-to-date on exactly what the New Asante conjurefolk are doing, but Aphrikan ways of spell working don't generally mix well or easily with Avrupan-style magic," Wash said in a very dry tone.

"I'm sure that if —" Professor Torgeson broke off, looking at Wash as if it had only just occurred to her that he might know a bit more about Aphrikan magic than she did. "It never hurts to consider new methods," she said after a moment.

"Now, that's a true thing," Wash said. "Though west of the Great Barrier, it's best to be cautious about when you stop considering and start practicing. What will turn away one animal may call up a worse one. I speak from experience."

"Oh?"

Wash shook his head ruefully. "During the war, when I was in the army, we had a little spell for keeping the flies off in summer. One of the men in my company said it made some kind of sound, up high where most folks can't hear, that drove the bugs away."

Professor Torgeson gave him a quizzical look. "I've heard of the spell, but . . . during the war? You mean the Secession War?"

"I do indeed, and I'll take that skeptical tone as a compliment, ma'am," Wash said with a grin. "I was a large lad, and like a good many others, I lied about my age to join up. That was the third year of the war, and by then the army wasn't looking too hard at anyone willing to volunteer. I was seventeen when I was mustered out after the Southern states surrendered."

I did some quick math in my head. The third year of the war was 1835. Wash must have joined the army at fourteen or fifteen, in order to have been seventeen when it ended in 1838. Lan and I had been born in 1838; everything I knew about the war, I knew from history class. It felt peculiar to think that Wash had actually fought in it when he was younger than I was now.

"Anyway, after the war, I had a hankering to see some places no one else ever had," Wash went on. "So I lit out for the Far West. And naturally, I made use of that neat little spell for keeping the flies off."

"What happened?"

"About a week west of the Mammoth, an arrow hawk dove at me. They don't generally have much interest in people, but this one sliced a fair-sized hole through my sleeve and a bit of my arm. Next day there was another one, and two more the day after that. Took me four days to figure out that it was the spell for keeping off flies that was bringing them down on me."

"Why would it do that?" I asked. I'd gotten so interested in Wash's story that I'd forgotten we were only speaking in the way of business.

"I can't say for sure," Wash told us. "But have you ever seen a mob of sparrows drive off a hawk that came too close to where they were all nesting? Those hawks were acting the same way — like I was something they wanted dead or elsewhere in a right hurry."

"You think there's a hawk predator that makes the same noise as your spell for getting rid of flies," Professor Torgeson said.

"Could be," Wash said. "Or it could be something else about that spell that made them angry. All I know is that as soon as I quit using the spell, the arrow hawks lost interest in me."

Professor Torgeson nodded thoughtfully. "Another thing that someone should investigate." She made a frustrated noise. "There is so much that we don't know, and all the research funds the department has can barely stretch to cover five months in the field for one junior professor and an untrained girl. It is very badly arranged."

Neither Wash nor I had any argument with that. For the rest of the day, the professor alternated between questioning Wash about the wildlife he'd encountered during his travels in the West and watching the land around us. I didn't know what she'd really been doing until we got to the wagonrest.

As soon as we had the horses tied up and watered, Wash went to talk to the other travelers who were sharing the wagonrest with us, to see about setting up a schedule for handling the protective spells overnight. Professor Torgeson pulled a pencil and a journal out of the supply pack and started listing all the different plants and birds and animals she'd seen on the day's ride. Then she asked me to mark the ones I'd seen, too, and add any I'd seen that she hadn't. As soon as Wash got back, she asked if he'd be willing to do the same, and he did. When we finished, the list took up two pages, at two columns a page in small, clear printing — everything from grasses and wildflowers to birds and insects and even a white-tailed deer we'd startled out of a little copse of serviceberry bushes.

I'd only added five names at the end of the list, and marked less than half of the things the professor had put down. Wash had seen all but three of the things the professor listed, all of mine, and he still had a dozen more to add. Professor Torgeson stopped him when he started to write them. "I've seen the notes you've sent Professor Jeffries," she said, "and I'd rather have no confusion. Let Miss Rothmer copy the names down for you."

"Whatever you say, Professor," Wash replied, but he didn't grin the way he usually did.

We didn't even start making camp until we finished with the professor's journal, except for watering the horses, so it was getting dark by the time we finished eating. I was worn right out from riding so long, and I went to sleep as soon as we finished clearing up.

I maybe shouldn't have been quite so eager to bed down, because the next morning I was so stiff and sore I could hardly move. But Professor Torgeson wasn't much better off, and she was up at first light, taking notes on which birds started calling first.

We spent that second day at the wagonrest — or, rather, all around it. The professor said that with only two of us doing the survey and only a few months to do it in, I would need to do more than take notes and handle supplies, and I might as well start right off doing it.

So she spent the morning working her way around the north side of the wagonrest, showing me how to list the plants and insects I found, and mark the signs of animals and birds. She wanted a count of different kinds of things, and how many of each kind, and a bit about where each one was — in sun or shade, rocky ground or damp soil, near trees or in the open.

"If you have time, describe or sketch what you see," she told me. "At the least, we'll want to know what stage of growth the plants are at — whether they're just germinating, in early growth, in bud, flowering, or going to seed. Especially if it's something you're not familiar with."

"Wouldn't it be easier just to pick a few for samples?" I asked.

"We won't have room, if we start now," she said. "Besides, we already know about most of these plants; I want the lists here mostly for comparison purposes. So we can see what changes as we get farther west."

I thought about the bare wasteland we'd ridden through last summer, where the grubs and mirror bugs had eaten every growing thing there was. I'd been too busy then to think about exactly where the barren patch started and where it ended, but I was pretty sure the professor would mark it down to the nearest half inch, if she could.

So I spent the afternoon taking notes on a patch of earth near where the professor was working, measuring out a small square of ground and then listing every kind of plant in it and counting how many of them there were. The grasses were hard because they weren't very tall yet, and it was hard to tell one flat, thin blade from another. Acadian thistles and dyeroot were easy. I made sketches of two plants and a butterfly I didn't know the names of. The bugs were the hardest, because they kept moving around and I couldn't be sure whether I'd counted them. I had to put a question mark next to two different beetles, and I gave up on the ants entirely.

In the evening, the professor went over everything I'd done and pointed out things I could do better next time. She even said I'd done very well with my sketches. By the time I curled up in my bedroll that night, I was feeling pretty good about what I'd done that day.

But I was too tired to do any magic practice that night, Aphrikan or Avrupan.

CHAPTER
· 7 ·

NEXT MORNING, WE SET OUT AGAIN, AND AFTER AN EASY DAY'S RIDE we came up on the Puerta del Oeste settlement. Puerta del Oeste was one of the older settlements west of the Mammoth River. The core had been built right after the Secession War, a tiny thing compared to a modern settlement, but in the years since it had been founded, it had grown three big loops off the original log wall, enough to house a passel of new folks from the Eastern states, Acadia, Vinland, and even all the way from Avrupa. Now they had three settlement magicians and a full-time doctor, and the North Plains Territory had just opened a branch of the Homestead Claims and Settlement Office there.

That branch office was the main reason we stopped at the settlement instead of going straight on to the wagonrest. Even though he was acting as our guide, Wash was still a circuit-rider, and he wanted to check on the news that had come in from farther along our route.

The other reason was that Professor Torgeson wanted to recruit an official observer to send information back to the college on a regular schedule. She'd spent the last month looking over all Professor Jeffries's old records, and then she and Professor Jeffries had spent every spare minute for two days holed up in his office, coming up with a list of things they wanted to know and a form for reporting them.

So while Wash went off to the branch office, Professor Torgeson and I headed for the general store. It wasn't too hard to find; it was one of the biggest buildings in the oldest part of the settlement. The professor said that it was the most likely place to find a bunch of different folks all at once, and if none of them was willing to help out, they might still know someone who would be.

At least a dozen people were crammed in between the barrels and boxes that filled Code's General Store, examining tins and tools and fabric while they waited for the proprietor to get around to them. A tall woman in a blue calico dress looked up as we came in and gave a startled exclamation. A minute later, everyone in the store was looking at us.

"Settling out?" a girl asked. "Where?"

"Maury!" the tall woman said. "Mind your manners!"

"But it's what everyone wants to know," the girl said. "Why waste a lot of time asking how they are and how their trip has been so far in order to work up to it?"

"We are from the Northern Plains Riverbank College," Professor Torgeson said. There was a little stir at that, and all the people who'd been pretending not to listen stopped pretending. Most times, when someone from the college was west of the river, it was because one of the settlements was having a problem with the wildlife that the settlement magicians couldn't handle on their own.

"We're doing a survey of the wildlife farther out," I said quickly. "For research."

Everyone relaxed. "I don't suppose you folks brought along any newspapers?" one of the men asked.

Professor Torgeson smiled. "I have three," she said, much to my surprise. "The *New Amsterdam International Weekly*, the *Washington Times*, and the *Long Lake City Tribune*. Also the most recent issue of the *Ladies' Fashion Monthly* from Albion."

There was a hubbub as the professor pulled the papers from her carrypack and distributed them. I found out later that Wash had recommended bringing them. Half of the men bent over the *New Amsterdam International* first of all, shaking their heads over the one-sided battle between the Cathayan Confederacy and the Albion warships and the argument over sending the few survivors back to Albion. The other half went straight to the *Long Lake City Tribune*, looking for news of the national baseball league that somebody had proposed starting up. The ladies all crowded around the *Fashion Monthly* to see what sort of sleeves and necklines they should be having on their Sunday-best dresses. Nobody seemed much interested in what was going on in Washington.

Even the store owner paused to look over the *Tribune* headlines. Then he turned to look at Professor Torgeson. "I assume you ladies didn't stop in just to bring us the news," he said.

"You are right, I confess," Professor Torgeson said. "I'm hoping to persuade someone here to do some work for the college. Or if not, I'm hoping you'll know someone in the settlement who'd be willing."

"What sort of work?"

The professor explained what she wanted, and two men and a woman were interested enough to ask questions. One of the men lost interest once he got it clear that there was no money in it, but the other two didn't seem to mind. In the end, Professor Torgeson decided that having two observers in the same place would be a useful double check, so she gave each of them one of her forms and showed them how to fill it out.

I stood back out of the way while they talked, and just watched. After a bit, I noticed a man in the corner, watching the professor and turning his hat over and over in his hands. He'd come in just after Professor Torgeson started passing out the newspapers, and he looked like he was barely holding himself back from bulling right into the professor's conversation. The longer he waited, the darker his face got. A woman in a poke bonnet next to him put a hand on his arm, but it didn't seem to make much difference. I edged around to the far side of the group. I didn't want to be near anyone who had that much trouble making himself be civil.

Sure enough, the minute the professor finished her talking, he stepped up and cleared his throat. "Excuse me, ma'am," he said, though he didn't sound at all apologetic. "I couldn't help —"

"Professor," Professor Torgeson snapped.

The man looked at her with a bewildered expression. "Beg pardon?"

"*Professor*, not ma'am," she repeated, sounding a bit less cross.

"Professor? You'll be from the college in Mill City, then?" The man sounded like he wasn't sure whether to be pleased or sorry.

"I am."

"I don't suppose — that is, my name's Carpenter, Giles Carpenter. My family and I are trying to get out to Kinderwald settlement, and they tell me we must have a guide or a spell caster to go any farther."

"That you do, unless you're one of them crazy Rationalists," the storekeeper said.

"We've been waiting at this wagonrest for a solid week!" Mr. Carpenter went on. "And I'll tell you straight, ma' — Professor, I'm getting desperate. Could we travel with you? I can pay a little. . . ."

"You will have to discuss that with our guide," Professor Torgeson said. "You are staying at the wagonrest? We will be there ourselves tonight; perhaps he can advise you then."

"The only advice he's like to get is to keep waiting," one of the other men called, and several people laughed. It sounded like a sympathetic sort of laughing to me, not like making fun, but Mr. Carpenter's face darkened.

"Easy for you all to say!" he growled, and for a moment he looked downright dangerous.

"Who's your guide, ladies?" another man called. "If you're heading farther west, you need a good one."

"I believe Mr. Morris is quite competent," Professor Torgeson said in a dry tone.

"That'd be Wash Morris?" the man asked.

Professor Torgeson nodded, and someone in the back gave a low whistle. "Can't get much better than that," the first of the onlookers said, nodding.

"Perhaps we'll see you this evening, Mr. Carpenter," Professor Torgeson said, and motioned me to leave with her. As we left, I could hear the local men razzing Mr. Carpenter like a batch of schoolboys ragging on a new one, and I wondered what he'd done to set their backs up like that.

I didn't think on it much, because we ran across Wash on our way back to the town gates, and the first thing he said was, "You have mail." That was enough to knock everything else out of my head, just like that.

I had a fat letter from Mama, and Professor Torgeson had a thin, official-looking one from the college. She opened hers right off and glanced it over, then smiled and said, "Nothing that can't wait. Miss Rothmer?"

I fingered the envelope. I couldn't think why Mama would write so much, so soon, unless it was a lot of good advice she'd forgotten to give me before I left, and right then, I wasn't too keen on advice. But I couldn't hold everyone else up while I dithered, so I tore the envelope open.

Two smaller envelopes and a sheet of paper fell out, and I felt very foolish. The single page was a note from Mama saying they missed me already but she was sure I was working hard, and that she was sending along the letters from Lan and William that had come just too late for me to get at home.

I thought for a minute, then tucked the letters away in my saddlebag. I couldn't see holding Wash and the professor up, and I figured I'd have time to read them after we got camp made at the wagonrest.

When I finally did get to the letters, I was glad I'd waited. I opened Lan's first. "If you're so determined not to come East for school, why don't you try for one of the ones nearer the border?" was the first thing he said. Then he had a whole list of suggestions, from the Northern Plains Riverbank College where Papa taught to the University of New Orleans at the other end of the Mammoth River. I sighed. I should have known Lan wouldn't give up his notions without arguing.

He didn't say much else about my job with the college, except that he hoped I would have fun and to come back safe. The rest of his letter was about how much fun he was having at Simon Magus. Well, that and complaining about one of his professors, who he said was an idiot who thought he knew four times as much as he really did and what he really did know was wrong. I couldn't follow all of it, because Lan started in on magical theory almost right away, telling me all the arguments he'd have liked to use on his professor.

The last thing he said was that he wouldn't be home for the summer again this year. I wasn't too surprised. He'd only been home about one year in four since he went off to boarding school, and even then, he only stayed for a month or two at most.

This summer, he and three of his friends were working with two of the professors, classifying a batch of new spells the college had imported from the Cathayan Confederacy and trying to develop Avrupan-style spells to do the same things.

That made me frown just a little. Lan had never really been interested in either of the other major schools of magic — the Aphrikan or the Hijero-Cathayan — though he didn't scorn them the way Professor Graham did. But Lan and I had grown up hearing Papa tell his students that the point of getting college schooling was to stretch yourself in new directions, so maybe it wasn't so surprising after all.

I set Lan's letter aside and opened William's. It was a lot shorter, though it covered nearly as much ground as Lan's. William didn't waste a lot of words. First he said congratulations on getting a position with the survey; then he said that he'd be staying in Belletriste for the summer, working for a company there that made railroad cars. He didn't say anything about his father, but I knew William, and I knew that if he was staying in Belletriste, it meant that Professor Graham still hadn't forgiven him.

Apart from that, I could tell that William liked Triskelion University every bit as much as Lan liked Simon Magus. He had a whole list of classes he wanted to take in the fall, and he was planning to study evenings all summer so as to convince the professors that he could handle some of the more advanced material.

I wrote Mama and Lan each a note, saying that nothing much eventful had happened and I was enjoying the work so far. I wrote more particulars to William, because I knew he'd be interested in the way the professor recorded all the little details, from types of plants to daily weather. I left all three letters unsealed. I wasn't sure when we'd stop at a settlement where I could mail them, and in the meantime, I could keep adding things.

About the time I finished up my letters, just when the sun was going down, Mr. Carpenter showed up, looking for Wash. Not that he was hard to find; there were only three groups staying at the wagonrest that night. The wagonrest, like the settlement, had been expanded as the Western settlements grew, by adding two loops to the original log palisade, one on either side of the main circle. Mr. Carpenter's group had made camp in one of the additions; we'd set up in the main circle, along with a family by the name of Bauer who'd come north from St. Louis, heading for some relatives up along the Red River.

Mr. Carpenter spotted Professor Torgeson and me right off. His face went kind of blank when the professor pointed out Wash, talking to the Bauers' guide; then he put back his shoulders like he was giving a recitation in front of a whole school, teachers included, and walked over to join them.

I couldn't hear their talk from where I was sitting, but it didn't take many minutes before the Bauers' guide threw his hands up in the air and walked off in as much of a huff as ever I've seen on anyone west of the Mammoth River. Wash talked with Mr. Carpenter a bit longer, arguing some, it looked like. Eventually Mr. Carpenter stomped off toward his camp and Wash came back to our fire, shaking his head.

"Is there a problem?" Professor Torgeson asked him, glancing after Mr. Carpenter.

"Not for us, Professor," Wash said. "But I don't know what the Settlement Office was thinking, letting that gentleman loose in the West."

"He said he was heading for Kinderwald," the professor replied. "Since the Frontier Management Department has temporarily suspended the building of new settlements, I assume he has family there, or perhaps has purchased an allotment."

"He bought in," Wash said. "And he's in for a shock. For one thing, neither he nor anyone in his family speaks Prussian, and Kinderwald's a pure immigrant settlement — their magician is the only one there who has any English at all. For another . . . well, he seems of the opinion that he can take on the wildlife with one hand tied behind his back, and no need for guides or protection spells."

"He didn't sound so unreasonable when we talked to him this afternoon," the professor said.

Wash shrugged. "Possibly he's not so plainspoken with ladies. From what he said to me, he wants to get where he's going, and he's not much accustomed to waiting. And he didn't take kindly to being told he's best off waiting here. There's more traffic through Puerta del Oeste than there will be farther on."

"Where is Kinderwald?" I asked.

"About a week south of Little Fog," Wash said. "I told him that if he was dead set on it, he could come that far with us, but we couldn't spare two weeks to get him all the way to Kinderwald and then get back to our route. He didn't much like that, either. I gather he intends to pull out in the morning."

"He's a fool if he tries to make it alone," Professor Torgeson said flatly.

Wash shrugged again. "I did my best. Possibly you can talk sense into him."

The professor looked for a minute as if she'd like to try, but then shook her head and went back to her notes. Still, she did stop off at Mr. Carpenter's camp next morning. She came back muttering about pigheaded, stubborn men. Mr. Carpenter's wagon pulled out of the wagonrest about half an hour later, right after the Bauers'. Wash shook his head, and the professor pressed her lips together, but there wasn't much either of them could do except watch him go.

CHAPTER
· 8 ·

WE SPENT THE REST OF THAT DAY COUNTING PLANTS AND ANIMALS
around the wagonrest, the same way we had at the first one.
Professor Torgeson let me do one side while she did the other,
though she came and checked my work around mid-morning
and again a few hours later. She must not have found anything
to complain of, because she just nodded and told me to keep on
the way I was going. Later on, she showed me how to collect
specimens, though she only kept one of the plants she'd collected
herself. She had a special case for them, divided into compart-
ments to hold small vials (for insects and seeds) and press blocks
(for pressing and drying and protecting flowers and leaves).

When we left the Puerta del Oeste wagonrest the next
morning, we made a sharp turn straight west. Wash warned
us that soon we'd be crossing into the area that the grubs
and the mirror bugs had laid to waste the summer before, and
asked if the professor wanted to do any more surveying before
we got there.

Professor Torgeson looked thoughtful for a moment, but
then she said that we had enough to go on with and she was

more concerned with documenting the new growth in the recovering area. I wasn't quite sure what she meant at first. I'd been through some of the area the summer before, when we went to Oak River, and it had looked the way I'd always thought a desert would: barren and dusty and eerily quiet. I couldn't see much recovering happening any time soon.

But two hours later, we were riding past green, green meadows and settlements with fields sprouting. From a distance, it looked almost normal, until you noticed that nearly all of the trees were dead, leafless skeletons. The grubs had eaten away all their roots and killed them. One or two had a single clump of leaves on a high branch, but that was all.

Closer up, you could see that the meadow looked a little too green — there were no long, brown remnants of last year's grass to be seen — and it was barely ankle high. And every hillside and uneven patch of ground had deep, irregular channels cut in them where rain had washed away the dirt. We had to slow down so the horses wouldn't stumble on the uneven footing.

Professor Torgeson made us stop to list the plants and bugs and so on. Wash picketed the horses and stood guard with the rifle while we worked, even though he still had all the protection spells for traveling up.

We ended up spending nearly three hours, and had to stop at the next wagonrest instead of going farther on the way we'd planned. Turned out that the plants that were coming back — bluestem grass, catchfly, fleabane, milkweed — were all natural ones, not magical. Once the professor noticed, we started hunting for the magical plants in deliberate earnest, but we only turned up one stunted flameleaf and a hardy northern sleeping rose in the whole three hours.

"Mr. Morris, is this common, in your experience?" she asked once we were finally back on our horses.

"I can't rightly say, Professor," Wash said. "The grubs that laid waste to this area were a brand-new thing. But now and again I've crossed stretches that were coming back after a wildfire, and as best I recall, the magical plants came back first."

There were a few more magical plants around the wagonrest than there had been along the road — another flameleaf, three clumps of goldengrass, a scattering of demonweed, and a couple of spindly witchvines — and the professor got excited all over again. We didn't leave until nearly mid-morning, and then only because Wash said if we waited much longer, we wouldn't make the next wagonrest by nightfall.

We made pretty good time to begin with, but shortly after noon, Wash pulled his horse to a stop at the crest of a low hill.

"Something wrong?" Professor Torgeson asked.

"Could be," Wash said. He hesitated, then went on, "Would you mind taking over the traveling spells for a few minutes, Professor?"

"Not at all, Mr. Morris," the professor replied. Her eyes narrowed in concentration and she stretched out a hand. After a moment, her arm dipped as if she had caught a thrown ball or a falling plate, and I knew that Wash had handed off the protection spells to her.

As soon as the spell hand-off was done, Wash turned in his saddle to face due south and went still as a stone. His horse shifted once, then stood quietly. I thought he must be doing Aphrikan world-sensing, and without thinking about it much, I took a deep breath and did the same.

It was like stepping out the door on a dead calm day in mid-January when it's so cold it hurts to breathe and it feels like everything is frozen so solid that nothing will ever move again. It was so unexpected that it threw me right back into my own head, which hadn't happened to me when I was world-sensing since my first year in upper school.

Wash was still sitting motionless on his horse. I tried again, slowly, like poking your nose out the door just a little to see how cold it is. I could feel our horses, and Wash and Professor Torgeson, and they all felt normal. But the plants and the ground underfoot felt . . . empty and cold. I poked a little further, trying to sense things that were farther away, but nothing changed. I could barely tell the difference between the top of the hill and the bottom. I wondered what it felt like to Wash.

As I pulled back, Wash shivered all over and took a deep breath.

"What is it?" Professor Torgeson said in a low voice.

"Trouble," Wash replied in a grim tone. He reached for his rifle. "The sort that needs looking into. If I'm not back in an hour —"

"No," the professor interrupted firmly. "Splitting up in the wildlands is asking for trouble. More trouble. Either we head for the nearest settlement for more assistance —"

"That's a good ten miles," Wash said, shaking his head.

"— or we *all* investigate now. If you are confident of handling things alone, the three of us together should manage quite —"

The air at the foot of the hill rippled, and even though I wasn't the one holding the protection spells, I felt them give. A tan-colored streak bounded up the slope toward us. Wash had his rifle to his shoulder, and the professor started muttering a spell. My horse shied and tried to bolt, and so did the packhorse. I heard the first shot while I was trying to get the two of them under control again. At the same time, I felt a spell sweep past me.

Something snarled. I looked up, and the tan streak resolved into a saber cat. It had a large head, with fangs curving down past its lower jaw and chin. It would have been as high as my chest if I'd been standing on the ground instead of up on a horse. From there, its back sloped down to rear legs that were short but powerful enough to send the whole big cat hurtling through the air, even though it was jumping up the hill.

Wash fired again. The bullet caught the charging saber cat in mid-leap, slamming it back and sideways to roll down the hill. As my eyes followed it, I saw something dark moving off to one side. I couldn't seem to get a clear look at it, but I thought it was maybe half the size of the saber cat, and it was moving at least twice as fast.

I raised my hand and, as hard as I knew how, cast the spell we used at the menagerie to push the mammoth back from the walls. It knocked the second creature all the way back to the foot of the hill. A moment later, another spell hit it. It howled in pain, and the air around it rippled. A third shot rang out. The creature jerked and stopped moving.

I was panting, one hand clenched tight around the reins, the other raised in case I needed another spell. Professor Torgeson was still muttering, though neither of the animals looked to be moving any. The only other sounds were the whisper of the wind, the creak of the harness leather as the horses shifted, and the click of the cartridges as Wash reloaded his rifle.

Professor Torgeson finished her spell. A moment later, she relaxed slightly in her saddle. "That's all of them," she said. "At least, that's all that are nearby."

Wash shook his head, but not like he was contradicting her. "How nearby?"

"Half-mile radius," the professor replied. "And yes, I compensated for the sphinx effect."

"Saber cats and Columbian sphinxes travel in prides," Wash said, frowning. "Meaning, more than three."

"Three?" I said before I could stop myself.

The professor pointed past me, to the north. I turned and saw another heap of tan fur partway up the hillside. "Saber cats are clever, cooperative hunters," she said. "When they're stalking, the pride will try to encircle their prey, so that as few as possible will escape."

I'd just barely begun feeling easy, but that made me tense again. "So where are the rest of them?"

"That is a right good question," Wash said. He looked at the professor. "Are you as handy with a rifle as you are with a spell?"

"I can manage, at need."

"Good." He swung down from his horse and handed her the rifle and me the reins. Then he went down the hill to examine the dead saber cats and the sphinx. After a few minutes, he circled the hill farther out, pausing occasionally to study the ground.

"Scouts," he said shortly as he reclaimed his rifle and horse. "The rest of the pride will be back that way." He pointed south. "All three look to be three-quarters starved . . . but they've fed well recently. That'll be why they aren't all traveling together — the pride has killed something large enough to last them a few days." He looked from the professor to me and added, "Maybe a couple of bison, or a mammoth."

I couldn't help frowning a little at that. We hadn't seen any bison or mammoths or even deer since we crossed into the area that the grubs had devastated the year before.

"Starving," Professor Torgeson said thoughtfully. "That explains why they pushed through the protective spells, then."

Wash snorted. "Wildlife comes through the protective spells for all sorts of reasons, and we only know about half of them. If that."

"I take your point, Mr. Morris." The professor hesitated, as if she wanted to say more, then shook her head slightly and waited.

"We need to warn the nearest settlements," Wash said after a moment. "Let's go."

I noticed he didn't say anything more about investigating trouble, but he didn't seem too happy about going on, either. I wondered about that. Wash wasn't the sort to go courting trouble, and searching out a mixed pride of saber cats and Columbian sphinxes looked to me like being more trouble than even a trouble-seeker would ever want.

The horses were still skittish, so we gave the dead cats a wide berth. As we rode away, Professor Torgeson looked over her shoulder and said, "You did well, Eff." Then she went back to concentrating on the travel protection spells.

It made me feel good to hear that, but I didn't feel like I deserved it. I hadn't been much help when the saber cats attacked. Oh, I'd kept my seat and hung on to the packhorse, which at least kept me from causing extra problems, but I hadn't been good for much else, and I didn't like it. I'd grown up on the edge of the West; I ought to have been more use than simply hanging on to a horse and throwing one measly spell.

I stewed over that all the way to the next settlement, a place called Bejmar. They weren't too pleased to see us at first. Like the other settlements that had managed to survive the grubs and mirror bugs, they were hanging on by the skin of their teeth, and they didn't have much of anything to be hospitable with. As soon as the words "saber cat pride" were out of Wash's mouth, though, the man on gate duty hurried off to ring the alarm bell. All the folks who'd been out in the fields dropped what they were doing and came running. By the time we'd finished telling our story to the settlement magician, everyone was inside the walls, and within half an hour of our arrival, the settlement had sent out message riders to the two nearest settlements and started collecting all the people and guns they could spare.

Wash and Professor Torgeson assumed that they'd be going out with the settlers to hunt saber cats. The professor offered to let me stay in Bejmar with our packhorse and supplies, and I even thought about it for a minute or two. Part of me wanted nothing to do with hunting because I was still shaking from the suddenness of the attack and the way I hadn't seen that third cat coming up behind me until after it was shot dead, but another part of me wanted a chance to prove I could do better. There was something else, too — a big, foggy feeling that included the grubs and the dead countryside and the settlements and most of the people we'd met west of the Great Barrier, all in a jumble. I couldn't put a name to it, but it was pushing me to go along and do whatever I could. So I swallowed my worries and told the professor that I thought the hunters needed as many folks as they could get and it wouldn't seem right to stay safe in the settlement.

The settlers were extra careful that none of the livestock got left outside the palisade walls after dark, and the settlers who weren't heading out next morning stood watch all night long. Saber cats have been known to claw their way right over a wall to get at the horses and cows, so everyone was tense.

Next morning, we rode out to take care of the pride: five settlers, Wash, Professor Torgeson, and me. After what we'd seen with only three animals, I wasn't sure that we had enough people, but Professor Torgeson said we'd be meeting up with folks from the other settlements around. A full pride of saber cats and sphinxes was too dangerous to let alone, especially if they were mostly starving, and all the settlements in the area would cooperate to get rid of it.

I had the repeating rifle that Robbie had given me, and most of the settlement folk had something similar, though their weapons all looked well used. The folks from the other settlements caught up with us around mid-morning — five men from Neues Hamburg and three men and a woman from Jorgen. That made seventeen of us. I still wasn't sure it was enough, since we didn't know how many cats there were, but Wash and the settlers seemed to think it was reasonable.

After a quick discussion, they decided on a man named Meyer to be leader of the whole group. He was a bluff blond man with sharp eyes that never smiled even when his mouth did. I didn't care for him, but all the settlers knew him and plainly trusted him to do a good job.

We went on slowly. It took all morning and a bit of the afternoon to go back over the distance that had taken two and a half hours with just Wash and the professor and me. Wash and Professor Torgeson stayed in front, working a variation on the travel protection spells. This time, we didn't want to drive the wildlife off; we wanted them to come out where we could see and shoot them. In order to do that, we had to know when they were coming, and from what direction.

Long about mid-afternoon, we got to the hill where we'd faced the saber cats the day before. As soon as we came in sight of the dead animals, Mr. Meyer signaled everyone to stop. "Mr. Morris says we're getting close," he told us. "We'll leave the horses here. Any volunteers for guard duty?"

After a minute, two of the settlers nodded. They didn't look too happy about staying behind, but someone had to. The horses would panic if they smelled cat, and we'd never get close to them.

'We picketed the horses, and Wash and the professor set up a protection spell around them. Protection spells are usually meant to go out as far as they can, to keep the wildlife as far away as possible, but this time they had to keep it as close in as they could. The men who were staying looked uneasy about it, and I didn't blame them. They wouldn't have much in the way of warning if the saber cats decided to come through the protection spell, the way they had the day before. Nobody made a fuss, though. We all knew that we were hunting for a mixed pride, saber cats and Columbian sphinxes both, and the sphinxes were particularly sensitive to magic. If they noticed any spells, there was no telling what they'd do; they might run off before we could kill them all, or they might charge, the way the three scouts had charged us the day before. So the spell couldn't go much past where the horses were picketed.

As soon as the spell was set around the horses, the rest of us went on, as slow and silent as we could. It hadn't rained overnight, so the tracks were easy to follow, and a good thing, too, because we couldn't use magic to find the pride. Columbian sphinxes aren't just extra sensitive to magic; they also put out magic of their own that hides where they are. It also messes up any magic that their prey might use to tell where they are, and that unfortunately includes most Avrupan detection spells. Even Wash hadn't sensed the cats that had attacked us until they were almost to us.

Mr. Meyer had us fan out in a line, so that if the cats charged, we wouldn't all be likely targets. It was a scary feeling, trying to walk real quiet through the empty, open land. There weren't even any dead trees to hide behind on this part, and the prairie plants were only a little more than ankle high.

Wash and two of the settlement men were a little ahead of us, doing the tracking. The air was warm, just at the point where it's comfortable for sitting in the shade, but not for digging over the garden in the sun. There was no wind, which was good because it wouldn't carry our scent to the cats, but it was also bad because it just made everything seem even hotter and there was no breeze to carry away the bugs. No matter how good you are at sneaking, you can't ever sneak well enough so that mosquitoes won't find you, and no matter how worried and tense you are, or how hard you are trying to pay attention, you just can't help noticing when a cloud of mosquitoes comes for you like you're their first good meal since last fall.

After about ten minutes, one of the trackers pointed off to the left. There was a little cluster of dead trees with some equally dead bushes around and between them. Through the bare twigs, I could just make out a covered wagon, still and silent. My stomach went hollow. As we crept closer, I told myself that the settlers from the wagon must have run across the pride, the same as we had, and left the wagon behind so as to get to a settlement faster. I didn't really believe it, though.

Suddenly, one of the settlers shouted, "On your left!"

Everyone turned to see two saber cats charging up out of nowhere.

CHAPTER
· 9 ·

PEOPLE STARTED FIRING. I WAS IN THE MIDDLE OF THE LINE AND I didn't have a clear shot at either cat. Remembering the day before, I turned, and sure enough, there was another saber cat charging from the right, and two more directly behind us. Without thinking, I raised my rifle and shot, pumped the lever to reload, and fired again. I heard a man scream, and a cat snarl. There were more shots and shouts.

Professor Torgeson cast an area spell, revealing the sphinxes. There were three: smaller than the saber cats, black as night. They had bodies like a lynx, but their heads were set higher above their shoulders, and they had a long, thick mane of black hair. If you didn't pay too much attention to the faces, they really did look a lot like the drawings of the Egyptian Sphinx in my history books.

They were fast, too — even faster than the saber cats. I heard one of the settlers later telling folks back in Bejmar that he'd seen one of the sphinxes actually dodge a bullet. He was exaggerating, I think, but I can't deny they were almighty hard to hit.

I shot twice more, backing up in between shots. All of the saber cats that hadn't fallen were in among us by then, and so were the sphinxes. The animals had each been hit at least once, but they were all mad as blazes and wouldn't go down. It was hard to get a clear shot without maybe hitting someone else. I lowered my rifle and knocked one of the animals back with the spell I'd used before. Someone else shot it.

And then, as quick as it had started, it was over. We'd killed five saber cats and three sphinxes, and three men had been mauled. "Don't let your guard down," Mr. Meyer cautioned as everyone took a breath and started toward the three who'd been injured. "This may not be all of them."

"A full pride is usually seven to ten cats and four to eight sphinxes," Wash said, nodding. "With the ones from yesterday, we've killed seven cats and four sphinxes. We might have gotten lucky and got them all, but best not to take chances."

"I can't believe they got the drop on us," a settler said. "We knew they were there!"

"Quit jawing," his companion advised, "or whatever's left of the pride will catch us with our pants down all over again. 'Scuse me, ladies."

Everyone reloaded, even the ones who were going to look after the injured. All of the injured men were bleeding pretty heavily from bites and claw marks, and one of them had a shattered arm bone where a saber cat had bitten down hard. One of the men from Neues Hamburg had brought a bag of remedies that their doctor had put together for them; he and the woman from Jorgen split up the poultices and bandages and started wrapping up the bites, but there wasn't much they could do about the arm.

After a long argument, Mr. Meyer sent Wash and half the able-bodied through the dead trees to check on the wagon. We drew straws for it; saber cats aside, everyone had a fair notion what they'd find and nobody was any too keen on going to look. I was relieved to get a long straw, which meant I'd stay to help guard the injured.

A few minutes later, we heard another round of shots. A while after that, Wash's group came back, grim-faced. "Two more saber cats, a sphinx, and five cubs," Wash reported. "We got them all."

"They had cubs to protect?" Mr. Meyer said. "No wonder they came at us like that!" He paused for a minute. "What about —"

"The settlers?" Wash shook his head. "No survivors."

"We were lucky," another man said, and spat. "These cats were still half starved. It can't have been more than a day or two since they got the wagon; if they'd had more time to feed on the greenhorn's oxen, they'd have had a lot more of their strength back."

We stayed on guard until the trackers had circled the camp, looking for signs of any more cats. Once they were sure we'd gotten them all, we had to decide what to do next. With three men hurt (two of them badly enough that they couldn't ride), we wouldn't make it to a settlement by nightfall. Half the men wanted to get as far as we could; the rest wanted to stay put and ride out in the morning. They'd all pretty much decided that since the saber cats were dead, they didn't have to follow Mr. Meyer's orders without giving their own opinions first. They had a lot of opinions. Then the three who were most set on having things their own way got to arguing with each other, and even when someone pointed out that the longer they argued, the more likely it was that we'd have to stay put, it only made them argue harder.

In the end, we sent five people to get the horses and the guards we'd left with them, and started hacking down the dead brush for firewood. Wash and Professor Torgeson set up the strongest protection spells they could do at short notice, though as Wash said, it wasn't really necessary.

"A pride of saber cats has been living here for at least three days," he pointed out. "With cubs. Most of the wildlife has sense enough to stay far away from saber cat territory, if they can."

"*Most* of the wildlife?" someone asked.

"Well, I doubt that a steam dragon would be bothered," Wash said, "but it's been seven years since one of them got blown out of the Far West into settlement territory."

That got a nervous laugh from some of the settlers, but I shivered. I remembered that steam dragon. It was the first time I'd ever heard the alarm bell in Mill City ring the wildlife warning. The dragon had flown right over the Great Barrier Spell, and it had taken most of the magicians in town to bring it down.

Once the protection spell was up, Mr. Meyer asked for volunteers to bury the dead and salvage what they could from the wagon. I wasn't too keen on helping with the burying, but I could see that someone should at least try to find out who they'd been and where their people were, so that their family could be notified. I said I'd help with the wagon.

I was sorry almost as soon as I got near. The wagon had had four oxen pulling it, and they and the settlers had been dead in the hot sun for two days. On top of that, the saber cats had been marking the area as theirs. The whole area stank of death and decay and cat urine. I hauled out my handkerchief and tied it over my nose and mouth. It helped, but I still had to breathe shallowly.

Four of the men gathered up the bodies of the settler and his family, while some of the others started in digging the graves. As soon as they said the wagon was cleared out, I climbed up on the driver's seat and started looking around. There was an old sawed-off shotgun lying crosswise right where the driver would have been sitting. Both barrels had been fired. Under the seat, I found a metal box, the sort most settlers used to carry money and family papers. It wasn't locked, and when I opened it I got a shock. The dead settlers were Giles Carpenter, the man we'd met at Puerta del Oeste who'd been in too much hurry to get to his allotment to wait for a travel guide, and his family.

That rattled me more than a little, and I was still shaky from the fight with the saber cats. I'd always known that the settlements were dangerous, and I'd met a few folks who'd been injured by wildlife, but Mr. Carpenter was the first person I'd met who'd actually gotten killed in the West. That I knew of, anyway; about half of my class from the day school had gone out to settlements and I hadn't kept in touch with any of them. *That* thought was even more unsettling. I closed up the box and set it aside, then crawled back into the wagon to see what Mr. Carpenter had brought along with him.

Mr. Carpenter may not have been too smart about traveling with a guide, but he'd done a bang-up job at picking his supplies. There were two more guns packed away, an old smoothbore rifle and a revolver, and plenty of ammunition for all of them. He had a small keg of nails, two barrels of flour and another of sugar, a lot of beef jerky, a large crate of tools for building and mending things, seed for both a field of soybeans and one of Scandian wheat, and a lot of other things. All of it seemed like it would be real useful, even to a well-established settlement like Neues Hamburg, so rather than deciding anything myself, I made a list for Mr. Meyer. I was glad when I finished and got back to the camp, even if it was only a little way from the wagon.

Over dinner that night, the settlers had a solemn talk on what to do with Mr. Carpenter's wagon and supplies. There was too much to just abandon, but nobody wanted to come back a second time. Luckily, one of the men said he could jury-rig a harness for horses from what was left of the straps and the yoke for the oxen. It wouldn't be as good as a proper horse collar, but if they went slowly and some of the men helped push the wagon, it would do. What clinched the argument was that we could put the three injured men in the back. They'd be jolted around — there was no helping that — but there was no way they could ride, and the wagon was better than having to ride double.

As soon as she heard we were taking the wagon, Professor Torgeson asked if there'd be room for one of the dead saber cats. The settlers gave her funny looks. One of them offered to skin one for her right there, if she wanted it that bad, but she said she wanted the whole cat for the college to dissect. Mr. Meyer said that as long as she took care of preserving it herself, and knew what she wanted done with it, he didn't see a problem. So the professor spent the rest of the evening looking at the dead cats to find the one that had been shot up the least. She picked out two, a female saber cat and a male Columbian sphinx, and stayed up through the first watch putting layers of preservation spells on them so they'd get back to the college in good condition.

Just before dark, Mr. Meyer set watches, and the rest of us settled down under the stars to try to sleep. I was restless for a long time, and when I finally did fall asleep, I had the first of the dreams. Even then, I knew it was different. It was sharper and clearer than my other dreams, and I never had any fear that I'd forget the smallest part of it.

I dreamed I was standing in the old well house back in Helvan Shores, where I'd lived until I was five. It was dark and damp and too warm. Someone had left the cover off the well, and a bucket on a rope beside it. I was desperately thirsty, but I was afraid to go near the well to try to draw up any water for myself. Mama had drilled into us all that we weren't to be in the well house without an adult, and if that hadn't been enough, the older childings told all us youngers all sorts of tales about childings who'd fallen in and drowned.

After a while, I crept to the bucket and pulled it back to the wall, where I could look at it without getting too close to the well. There was a little stale water in the bottom, barely a palmful, but I drank it down as fast as I could. It only made me thirstier, but at the same time, I was more afraid than ever.

I decided that it would be best to leave. I peered into the dark well room, but I couldn't see the door. I edged around the wall, peering, and feeling the cool stone with my fingers. After a long time, I tripped over the bucket. I'd gone all the way around, and there was no door. I pressed back against the wall, sure that something would come out of the well and get me. And then I heard rain on the roof.

I woke up feeling terrified and chilled. As soon as I recollected where I was, I went straight to the fire. It had burned to embers, but it still gave off heat enough to warm me a little.

When I was finally warm, I laid myself back down, but it was a long time before I slept again.

───────◆───────

The next morning, we finished burying Mr. Carpenter and his family. Mr. Meyer read a psalm out of the little Bible he carried with him, and Wash said a few words about people brave enough to come across the Great Barrier into the West. He didn't mention people who weren't smart enough to follow good advice when they got it, but that would have been unkind. Then we got to work loading up the professor's dead cats and the three injured men, and started back toward the settlements.

With four horses pulling and five men across the back pushing, we kept the wagon rolling pretty well until we had to part company. We sent the wagon on to Neues Hamburg, because the settlement was old enough and large enough to have its own doctor and two of the injured men were from there. One of the men from Jorgen went with, on account of the other injured man being from Jorgen. Before they left, the settlers from Jorgen and Neues Hamburg both thanked Wash and the professor and me for letting them know about the saber cats. Mr. Meyer even tried to offer a reward, but Wash said helping out like that was a circuit magician's job, even if he was only half on duty, and the professor said that as long as they saw to it that her large samples got back to the university, she'd be more than happy to call it square.

When we got back to Bejmar, we had to go over the whole

business one more time for the settlement magician. "Thank you," he said when we finished. "Both for the warning and the help." He shook his head tiredly. "I'd hoped that with so much forage and cover gone, we'd have a year or two before the big predators came back, but it seems not. Though the smaller wildlife aren't much better."

"Those cats shouldn't have been there at all," one of the men who'd come with us burst out. "They were starving, all of them; since when does a starving animal come to a place where there's no food?"

"They found food, right enough," one of the others muttered, and the first man turned on him.

"There are herds of deer and bison and silverhooves to the west, out past the land the mirror bugs destroyed," he snarled. "Hell, a full pride can bring down a mammoth, and there are plenty of mammoths out past settlement country! Why didn't the blasted cats just stay there?"

No one had an answer.

We stayed in Bejmar just long enough for the professor to find some people to observe the plants and animals for the college, and then we went on our way. The settlement magician and a couple of the other settlers made a halfhearted try at persuading us to stay the night, but Wash and the professor thanked them kindly and said no. We'd already lost nearly two days; if this kept up, we'd be all summer just getting out to the western edge of the settlements, let alone heading north and back around to Mill City.

WHAT WITH THE SABER CATS AND ALL THE STOPPING AND STARTING
to count plants, it took us nearly three weeks to get from Puerta
del Oeste to the Oak River settlement. The professors had
planned for it to be our first long stop because that was where
we'd been staying the summer before when Papa and Professor
Jeffries had been looking into the grubs and mirror bugs, and
because it was the only Rationalist settlement anywhere in the
North Plains Territory.

Since the Rationalists didn't believe in using magic, their
territory hadn't attracted grubs and mirror bugs the way
the other settlements had, and it was easy to tell when we
were getting close. Long before we came in sight of the settlement, we came across bushes and trees that had leafed out. I
hadn't realized what a relief it would be to see a perfectly ordinary tree again, instead of all the bare, black skeletons we'd
been passing. Professor Torgeson got all excited; I think she
would have insisted on stopping to do a survey if it hadn't
been so late in the day, and if we hadn't been so close to
the settlement.

The Oak River settlement looked a lot like the pictures of Old Continent castles from my day school history books, except the castles were made of stone and the settlement was made of wood. The Rationalists had to depend on their walls and watchtowers, because they didn't believe in using magic even for settlement protection, and they'd made quite a job of it. Two log walls surrounded the hilltop, far enough apart that nothing could climb the top of the first wall and then just jump up to the top of the second, and they had manned watchtowers on either side of the settlement.

Oak River didn't have a wagonrest nearby, on purpose. The Rationalists didn't want magic used anywhere on their settlement lands, not even the protection spells that everyone used when they were traveling. Putting up a wagonrest would have encouraged travelers, on top of which they'd have had to keep sending people out to remind anyone who camped there not to use spells. So they'd persuaded the Settlement Office not to build one. Anyone who came by Oak River had to stay in the settlement itself, so the Rationalists could keep a close eye on the magicians in the group.

Papa had sent off a message to my brother-in-law Brant Wilson, to let him and Rennie know we were coming. Sure enough, Brant was waiting inside when the inner gates swung open. He seemed tired and worried, and more than a little fidgety, but he relaxed some when he saw me. "Welcome back, Eff, Mr. Morris," he said. "Glad you made it. We were expecting you last week."

"Nice to see you again, Mr. Wilson," Wash said, touching his hat brim. He dismounted and went on, "We had a little run-in with some saber cats back Bejmar way, and couldn't come on until the main pride had been taken care of. Sorry to be late."

"Saber cats?" Brant frowned. "That close?"

"Mixed pride, saber cats and Columbian sphinxes," Wash said. "We're not sure whether they came in from the west or up from the south. They're gone now, and I doubt there are more to fret over. The ones we killed were starving."

"Toller and the rest of the Settlement Council will want details, I expect," Brant said. "But that can wait." He looked past Wash at me and smiled. "How are you liking rattling around the settlements, Eff?"

"Well enough, so far," I told him. I felt Professor Torgeson come up close behind me, and remembered my company manners. "Professor Torgeson, I'd like you to meet my brother-in-law, Brant Wilson. Brant, this is Professor Torgeson."

"Pleased to meet you, Professor." Brant offered his hand, and she shook it. "You'll be staying with my wife and me." He hesitated, then said, "If you'll all come this way?"

It didn't take me long to figure out what that little hesitation of Brant's meant. The year before, when the whole group of us had come out to visit Rennie and look into the grub problem, most of the settlers in Oak River had just ignored us. Sometimes it was a kind of pointed ignoring, but mostly people pretended we weren't there. This year, the few folks who were out glared, and two women made a point of crossing the street to avoid us.

Wash appeared to take no notice of the reaction we were getting, though I didn't believe for a second that he hadn't seen. Professor Torgeson's eyes got narrower and narrower and her back got stiffer and straighter the farther we walked. I thought it was a good thing we didn't have far to go.

Rennie must have been keeping an eye out for us, because the door of the house swung open before we even got close. She motioned to us all to come on in, and shut the door right quick once we did. We stood there staring uncomfortably at each other for a long minute, and then Albert and Seren Louise came running in and distracted everyone. The baby, Lewis, toddled after them; he was just over a year old, and still trying to get the hang of this walking thing.

I was almost as excited as the childings were. I had other nephews and nieces out East, but these were the only ones I'd seen more than once. Mama had given me presents for each of them — a toy horse for Albert, a rag doll for Seren Louise, and a wooden train engine with a string for baby Lewis to pull along behind him.

I thought the awkwardness with Rennie would go away by the time we got the childings settled down and everyone introduced, but it was no such thing. Oh, Rennie was polite enough, but even the professor, who'd never met her before, could tell that her heart wasn't in it. As soon as the introductions were finished, Rennie gave Brant a dark look and said, "I'll just go and add a bit to the kettle, if you'll excuse me."

Anyone who knew my sister could tell that she meant to turn her back and stalk off. Trouble was, the front room of the little two-room house wasn't large enough for dramatic gestures. It was barely large enough to hold the five of us and the three rambunctious childings.

Brant glanced at the door, then at Rennie's back. He sighed and said, "Albert, have you finished your chores?"

Albert nodded, suddenly too shy to speak.

"Then why don't you and your sister go over to Mrs. Abramson's and —"

"The Abramson girls aren't allowed to play with Albert and Seren Louise anymore," Rennie said without turning.

Brant shut his eyes for just a second. Then he opened them and made a grimace that was maybe supposed to look like a smile. "You three go in the bedroom and play for a minute," he said. "We're going to talk grown-up talk now."

Albert nodded solemnly. He took his sister's hand and ducked between the layers of fly-block netting that separated the front room from the equally small sleeping area. As he did, I frowned. When Papa and Lan and I had stayed with Rennie the summer before, there'd been a spell on the fly-block netting — nothing big or fancy, just a touch of magic to make it work a little better. Now there wasn't one.

There'd been a bunch of other spells like that last summer, little things that Rennie'd done to make life easier and more comfortable, things the Rationalists wouldn't notice. I slipped into the Aphrikan world-sensing, and saw that they were all gone, too. I glanced over at Rennie, but her back was still turned on the rest of us.

"I apologize for the cool welcome, Mr. Morris," Brant said. "Things have gotten a mite tense since you passed through last fall."

I tried to remember back to October, when Wash brought the golden firefoxes to the menagerie, but if he'd said anything about stopping by the Rationalist settlement, he hadn't said it in my hearing.

"Just what is going on here, Mr. Wilson?" Professor Torgeson asked.

Rennie snorted but didn't turn around. Brant raked his hand through his hair. "Like I said, things have been a mite tense. A few of the folks here —"

"A few!" Rennie whirled, still holding the wooden spoon she'd been stirring with. Thick brown drippings ran down the handle and dropped onto the floor, but she didn't seem to notice. "Half the settlement, more than like!"

"Not that many," Brant said with a sigh. I got the feeling from the way he stood that this was an old argument between them. Still, I wished the floor would open up and swallow us. Watching Rennie scold was bad enough; watching her scold while Wash and Professor Torgeson looked on was awful, even if it wasn't me she was scolding at.

"Too many!" Rennie retorted. "And you're just letting it happen. Even when they take it out on your children!"

"Rennie, I've talked till I'm blue in the face," Brant said. "What more do you want? I can't force people to behave —"

"Rationally?" Rennie snapped. She pointed the spoon at Brant. "Next to Toller Lewis, you've more influence than anyone else in this settlement. Use it!"

"If I tried what you're suggesting, it'd split the settlement!" Brant snapped back. "Is that what you want?"

"I want my children to be safe," Rennie said. "And I want them to have choices, and a proper education. And if that means burning your precious settlement to the ground, I —"

Wash cleared his throat very loudly. Rennie broke off and looked at us like she'd only just remembered we were all standing there, then flushed beet red and turned back to her cookpot to hide her face. Brant rubbed the back of his neck, trying and not succeeding very well to look like he wasn't embarrassed.

"Perhaps we should step outside for a few minutes?" Professor Torgeson suggested.

"No!" Brant and Rennie said together.

"Why not?" I asked bluntly. I could see Professor Torgeson was going to keep trying to be polite, in a no-nonsense sort of way, but politeness never worked once Rennie'd gotten up on her high horse.

"Anti-magic sentiment has been growing all winter," Brant said heavily after a moment. "I wouldn't put it past some to try to . . . provoke you into using magic in violation of the settlement rules."

"It's bad enough they know you're here," Rennie put in. "It'd be worse to have you loitering outside our door, making it clear that this is where you're staying."

"If you'd rather we spent the night somewhere else —" Professor Torgeson began.

"There isn't anywhere else!" Rennie said. "And no matter what they say, Eff's family. I've given up a lot, but I'm not giving up that."

I looked at her in surprise as Brant said soothingly, "No one's asking you to."

"You mean, *you* aren't asking me to," Rennie said, but she didn't sound quite as snappish as she had before. "The rest of the settlement's another matter."

Everyone looked at her a little warily, and Rennie sighed. "Oh, sit down, the lot of you. It's too late now; the damage is done."

We looked at each other, then took seats at the little table. Brant glanced once at Rennie's stiff back, then leaned up against the wall with another quiet sigh.

"What happened?" I said when it was clear nobody else was going to ask, or even speak.

Brant didn't pretend to misunderstand. "It started last summer, after your visit. After everyone realized that the whole reason our fields weren't infested with grubs was that the grubs and beetles were drawn away by the magic that all the other settlements practice."

"Like going after bait in a trap," I said, nodding. "Except it wasn't on purpose."

"Yes, well, some of our people feel that we've benefited from magic as a result, even if we didn't do it deliberately," Brant said.

"And they object to that?" Professor Torgeson said. "That's ridiculous! Every adult in this settlement has benefited from magic all their lives long, right up until they crossed the Mammoth River on their way here. Don't they realize that?"

"Some do," Brant replied, "but they still don't like it. We believe that magic is a crutch and people would be stronger and better off if they didn't depend on it. The whole point of this settlement was to show that we don't need magic, not the way people east of the Mammoth do."

"Was it? Even so, you don't sound as if you're sure it's such a good idea any longer," Wash commented mildly.

"I —" Brant glanced at Rennie, then looked down. "I don't know. But it's one thing to refuse to use spells ourselves, and it's another thing entirely to talk of deliberately bringing in a lot of grubs in order to destroy the natural magic in our settlement lands forever."

"What!" the professor, Rennie, and I all burst out at once. Wash just stroked his chin and looked thoughtful.

"I thought you must have heard," Brant said to Rennie. "Charlie came up with the idea last month. I didn't think anyone would take it seriously, but . . ."

"But some of them are," Rennie finished. "I told —" She snapped her mouth shut on the last of the sentence. I was impressed. Marriage must have been good for Rennie, if she'd learned to stop before she finished saying "I told you so."

"That," Professor Torgeson said after a minute, "has to be one of the stupidest ideas I've ever heard, even apart from the fact that it won't work."

"Why?" I asked. "I mean, I can see all sorts of reasons why it's a bad idea, but why won't it work?"

"Because you can't permanently destroy ambient magic," Professor Torgeson said. "Helmholz proved that ten years ago. You can drain an area of magic temporarily, but it always returns to normal within a few years."

"The land does," Wash said. "Draining animals or people . . . that's different."

"Different how?" I asked.

"Animals and people regenerate their magic a lot faster than land. Providing there's anything left to regenerate — drain a living creature too far, and it dies. Hard to recover from that."

"But the mirror bugs didn't drain animals or people," Brant said.

"Not directly," Professor Torgeson said. "Not as far as we know at present."

"Not directly?"

"We actually know very little about the life cycle and abilities of the mirror bugs," Professor Torgeson said. "However, we have considerable evidence that both grubs and beetles could absorb magic from cast spells, and certainly from each other. That is how the trap spell kills them, after all — by using their own ability to drain magic against them. It is not inconceivable that a sufficient number of mirror bugs could drain animals or even people. It's not an experiment I would ever wish to perform."

"I should think not!" Rennie said.

"This is . . . I'm going to have to tell people right away." Brant raked a hand through his hair. "I just hope they believe me."

Rennie made a face, but she just nodded and went to call the children back to wash up for dinner. We had a solemn meal that night, and Brant went off in the morning to talk to his uncle, Toller Lewis, who headed up the Oak River settlement. He returned just before Wash and the professor and I left Oak River, and he didn't look happy. He and Wash had a low-voiced conversation that didn't make Brant look any happier, and then we retrieved our horses from the settlement stable and left. But Wash was real thoughtful all morning.

I couldn't help wondering a bit myself. When I first found out about the Rationalists, I'd thought they lived up to their name. For a while, I'd even wanted to be one. But I could tell from the way Brant and Rennie whisked us out of sight when we arrived, and from some of the talk they'd had, that things had changed in Oak River since I'd been there the previous summer. It just might be that the settlers would be crazy enough to get a lot of mirror bug grubs to clear the magic out of their land, even after what Professor Torgeson said. Heck, they might decide they couldn't believe anything a magician told them, and never mind that Professor Torgeson was a college professor and Wash was a circuit magician with more experience of the Far West than practically anybody! I just hoped that Rennie and Brant would have sense enough to take their childings and get out before things went too far. I had a notion that Rennie would be pleased enough to have a chance to leave, but Brant . . .

I felt a little hollow. Rennie had never been my favorite sister, not by a long shot, and she was in a mess of her own making. Still, she was family. I wanted to help, but all I could think of was to make sure I wrote to her more often. It wasn't much, and it for sure and certain wasn't enough, and I didn't like either of those things one little bit. I didn't have any other choices, though. You can't force folks to have good sense, even if they're family. Maybe especially then.

CHAPTER
· 11 ·

PROFESSOR TORGESON WAS DISAPPOINTED THAT WE DIDN'T GET TO spend more time in Oak River, because she'd hoped to spend several days surveying the plants and animals there. She agreed, though, that we were best off staying out of settlement politics, and we needed to make up a few days, anyway, because of the saber cats. So we made do with riding real slow and watching extra careful until we were off the Rationalist allotment, and then taking a little longer to write it all down when we stopped for lunch.

After we left Oak River, the days fell into a rhythm for a while, like sweeping a floor or hoeing the garden. We alternated days riding to the next wagonrest with days where Professor Torgeson and I worked on the survey while Wash went hunting. If we were close to a settlement, we'd stop and trade papers and gossip, and maybe pick up a few provisions if we were running low.

The settlements we stopped at were all different. If I'd thought about it at all, I'd thought most of them would be smaller versions of Puerta del Oeste, the way Puerta del Oeste was a smaller version of West Landing and West Landing was a smaller version of Mill City. They weren't. Most of them were more like Oak River — a bunch of friends and relatives from the same place, or folks with the same ideas of how to make a go of things, who'd gotten up a settlement group and come West together.

We passed three settlements in a row that were all settled from Scandia. Nobody but their settlement magicians spoke any English at all. Wash said that the only reason all the settlement magicians spoke English was because the Settlement Office made it a requirement, and the only reason they did that was to make sure the settlement magicians could learn any new spells the Settlement Office came up with, without needing a translator. He also said that the Settlement Office couldn't make up their mind whether to assign land so that all the immigrants bunched up in one place or so they were scattered around, so sometimes you got clumps of five or six settlements that were all from one country and sometimes every settlement you came to was different from the last four.

Professor Torgeson did pretty well getting people to collect data for the college, even though she wasn't actually from Scandia. The first settlers on Vinland had come from Scandia, and even though that was a good five or six centuries ago, the language was still close enough to Scandian that she could get across what she wanted. She had less luck at the Polish settlement that came next, but she just shrugged and said the college didn't need an observer at every single settlement we came to.

"This isn't nearly as exciting as I thought it would be," I told the professor one evening when we were setting up camp at a wagonrest.

"Forgotten the saber cats already?" Wash said, raising his eyebrows.

"I'll take boring any day," Professor Torgeson said, nodding.

"I didn't say it was boring!" I protested.

Professor Torgeson just looked at me. "Gathering base data is just as important as making entirely new observations. More important, sometimes; you can't tell whether something's changed if you don't know what it was like to begin with."

As we went farther west, the wagonrests got smaller and the settlements got newer and less finished, until we finally got out where everything was so new they hadn't built up any wagonrests at all yet. We had to camp inside the settlement palisades. The newest settlements didn't have much to spare for travelers, whether that was in the way of space or food or time, so whenever we stopped at one, Wash was real careful about helping out with whatever work was going forward.

Mostly, that meant cutting trees. The grubs had killed most of them by eating away their roots, but the wood was still good for building, as long as someone got to it before the charcoal beetles and the ruby pit borers and all the other things did. Sometimes helping out meant hunting the animals that were coming back along with the plants and ground cover. Usually, they were small critters, like raccoons and foxes and squirrels, but about three miles outside the Greenleaf settlement, we passed a small herd of bison.

When we got to Greenleaf and Wash told the settlers, they reacted like an anthill that had been stirred up with a stick. In less time than it took to tell about it, half the settlers were saddled up with their rifles to hand. Professor Torgeson decided to join them, so I went along, too.

Wash led the group quietly behind some low hills, downwind of the herd. Once he made sure of where the bison were, the hunters crept up to the hilltop and fired down into the animals. All of the bison jerked at the sound of the gunshots, and two of them fell over. In the half second before the whole herd took off running, Wash gave a loud yell. Two of the settlers — ones who'd stayed mounted — did the same.

The bison took one look at the yelling settlers and stampeded away from us. They kicked up quite a dust running away, and I could feel the ground shaking under my feet from the pounding of their hooves. The hunters dropped another one before they got too far away to hit, then most of them remounted and rode after the herd to make sure they kept going. The rest of us went down to start dealing with the dead bison.

One of the settlers rode back to Greenleaf for a wagon to haul the bison skins and meat back to the settlement for smoking and drying and tanning. With everyone helping, we had the hot, dirty job of butchering the animals all done by sunset. The settlers were double happy, first on account of having a lot of meat drop into their laps unexpectedly, and second because they'd gotten to the bison herd and stampeded it off before the bison got into their fields and tore up their crops.

Wash had been over unloading the wagon, but I saw his head whip around when he heard someone say that, and a minute later he was over where we stood, frowning.

"What was that you just said?"

The settler gave Wash a puzzled look. "I said it was a good thing we chased the herd off before they got to the fields. We can't afford to lose any of the crops this year."

"Mmmm." I knew that noise; it was the sound Wash always made when he had a powerfully strong opinion on something, but wasn't going to say it until he was sure he had all the facts. "Where's your Mr. Farrel?"

Sebastian Farrel was the settlement magician for Greenleaf. The settler looked puzzled for a minute, then cupped his hands to make a speaking trumpet and yelled, "Hey, Sebastian! Wash wants a word."

A medium-sized man with thinning blond hair broke away from a clump of people standing near the settlement gate and trudged over to us. He tried to thank Wash again, but Wash cut him off before he could rightly get started.

"How far out do you have your protection spells set?" Wash asked.

Mr. Farrel straightened up a little. "Inner layer goes to the settlement wall; the outer layer runs to the stone markers at the edge of the fields. Why?"

"And have you had trouble with the wildlife getting into your crops? Apart from the grubs the last few years, I mean."

"Not what you'd call trouble out here," the settlement magician said. "The spells aren't a hundred percent effective, but —"

"What have you had that you don't call trouble, then?"

"Some of the natural wildlife has crossed the outer layer of spells a time or two," Mr. Farrel said. "Mainly the larger animals, like the bison, which is why everyone was glad to see them run off. A lone deer or prairie wolf doesn't do much damage before we chase them away, but a whole herd . . ."

"I think you'd best show me your spells close up," Wash said. The two of them went off for half an hour, and when they came back, Wash pretty near had steam coming out his ears. He told the settlers straight out that some of them had been taking shortcuts when it was their turn to help with the spells, and he told Mr. Farrel that it was part of his job as settlement magician to make sure that his helpers did the job right.

Then he told everyone that they needed to take a lot more care about casting spells that might conflict with the settlement protection spells, especially when they were outside the walls, working. He pointed out that they'd been lucky to have just a deer or two get past the outer layer of spells, and not a saber cat or a terror bird. He was perfectly polite about it, but by the time he finished you could just see that half the people there wanted the ground to open up and swallow them right down.

In the end, Wash and Professor Torgeson spent the rest of the evening and most of the next day working with the settlement magician and the settlers, drilling them all on what to do and what not to do. They even had me go over the basic spells, the way they taught them in upper school. I felt awkward and unhappy — it didn't seem right that I would be tutoring a bunch of folks when I'd only just finished my schooling a couple of months back, especially since magic was just about my worst subject. At least Wash didn't try to have me demonstrate anything.

A few of the settlers got grumpy about all the lessons, but Wash just shrugged and said a lot of greenhorn settlers started off thinking they didn't need to be as careful as the Settlement Office and the experienced settlers said, and they were welcome to get themselves killed as long as they didn't take the rest of the settlement with them. That shut up the complainers, and the rest of the settlers were mostly grateful that they hadn't lost their crops or had the protection spells fail at an even worse time.

We stayed at Greenleaf for an extra two days to do a really thorough survey of the plants and wildlife around the settlement (and to make sure the settlers were doing the spells right) and then rode on. We'd gone nearly a hundred and fifty miles west of Mill City when it finally came time to turn north. We stopped that night in an abandoned settlement, one of the seventeen that had failed because of the grubs. The settlers had given up and gone back right before winter set in, when they realized they didn't have enough food to last them, and the settlement was an empty, spooky place.

Wash made the professor and me stay outside the palisade with all the travel protection spells still going strong, while he went in to make sure no dangerous wildlife had taken up residence. A few gray squirrels or daybats wouldn't have been a problem, but a colony of swarming weasels or a black bear could have been trouble.

We were lucky; nothing nasty had moved in, so we put our horses in the stable and made camp. We could have stayed in one of the empty buildings, but nobody suggested it. It was creepy enough camping by the palisade wall with the dim, silent shapes looming behind us.

"I thought the Settlement Office reassigned empty settlements right away," Professor Torgeson said after a while.

"They do, usually," Wash replied. "It keeps the wildlife from homing in. Just now, though, the Settlement Office isn't assigning anyone new to allotments, whether they're brand-new places or ones that someone tried previously."

Professor Torgeson frowned. "That's shortsighted, I think. By next year, something could have moved into these buildings that'll be next to impossible to root out."

Wash shrugged. "When they finally decide on a new lot of folks, I'll come out with the settlement magicians to make sure everything is in order before the first batch of settlers arrives."

"Wash!" I said, slightly shocked by his casual acceptance of such a risk.

"What? I've done it before, more than once. It's part of a circuit magician's job." He leaned back against the palisade wall and smiled at the campfire. "The hard part is making sure all the buildings are fit for living in. Chasing the squirrels and raccoons and daybats out isn't hard, but if quickrot or termites have gotten into the roof beams or walls, the houses can come down without warning."

Professor Torgeson's eyes narrowed. "Has anyone ever done a test to see what conditions promote that sort of rapid deterioration?"

"Not that I know of, Professor," Wash said. "Sounds as if it'd be a right useful thing to do, though."

The professor was looking out into the dark shadows with a speculative expression I'd learned to recognize. I made a bet with myself that we'd be spending an extra day or two here, too, so as to check what wildlife might have sprung up inside the settlement palisade and how it was different from what was outside.

※

That night I had the second dream.

I dreamed of walking down the hall of the house in Mill City where Lan and I had grown up. I climbed out onto the roof of the porch and jumped off, but instead of falling, I flew. First I skimmed over the rooftops of Mill City, watching shifting lights and colors flicker past beneath me; then I rose until I could see the whole patchwork of magic below me. The railroad tracks shone like the obsidian in the science laboratory at the college, slashing through the middle of the rainbow sheen that covered the rest of the city. To the west, I could see the wide silver ribbon of the Mammoth River curling around the city.

I felt the wind whispering through my fingers and tangling my hair. I circled up and away from the glitter of the Great Barrier Spell, hanging like a curtain above and along the center of the Mammoth River as far as I could see. I climbed higher, until I was well above it, and flew west over the settlements that surrounded a patch of lakes and swampland, then farther west over a shining lacework of creeks and rivers that cut through the dark, icy land.

Clouds rolled in around me like thick fog. I tried to fly lower, then almost panicked, thinking I would crash into the ground if I couldn't see it. Just before I started to fall, I dropped out of the clouds and found myself high above Helvan Shores, the town back East where I'd grown up.

The first thing I thought was that Helvan Shores looked different from Mill City. It wasn't just that the shiny black line of the railroad tracks skimmed by the edge of town instead of cutting through the center and coming to a dead stop. The whole town was paler somehow, and less active. The colors moved stiffly, and there were gray areas that didn't shift at all.

I dipped lower, and saw that there was a wall around the outside of the town. It reminded me of the Great Barrier Spell, only it was darker, more solid, and much less shimmery. I flew lower still, and suddenly I started falling.

I flailed my arms around, knowing I had no idea how to stop falling and fly again. The wind whipped my hair and tore at my skirts . . . and I landed with a thump in my bedroll. My eyes jerked open and I found myself staring at the embers of the campfire, cold and panting as if I had been running hard.

I lay there for a while, waiting for my heart to stop pounding, and thought about the dream. I knew it was like the first dream, and yet it wasn't. The first time, I had been terrified the whole time, until I woke up shaking. This time, I hadn't been scared until right at the end when I started falling. I knew they weren't normal dreams. They felt as if they meant something, but try as I might, I couldn't think what. It was a long time before I fell back asleep.

CHAPTER · 12 ·

JUST LIKE I THOUGHT, PROFESSOR TORGESON TALKED WASH INTO letting us spend three days at the abandoned settlement, so we could survey whatever was living inside the settlement walls, as well as what was outside. It didn't take as much time as I'd feared. The settlement had only been two years old, so it had only had the original settlement group to house, and they hadn't wanted to take the time or labor to enclose any more than they absolutely had to. So there wasn't much open ground inside for anything to grow on.

We did find a couple of mud swallow nests and the start of a bluehornet nest up under the eaves of the last house. Professor Torgeson got Wash to bring out a table that the settlers had left behind, and climbed up on it to examine the bluehornets. She spent over an hour standing there still as a stone, watching the hornets fly in and out. When she finally climbed down, she was stiff and frowning.

"Mr. Morris," she said, "would there be any chance of finding another bluehornet nest nearby?"

"I doubt it," Wash said.

"The ones building that nest have to have come from somewhere," the professor persisted.

"We might get lucky and find the old nest within a hundred yards or so," Wash replied. "But bluehornets sometimes fly three or four miles to start a new nest. It'd take a week for us to cover that much ground, even if a lot of the land nearby is cleared. An old nest isn't easy to spot, either. I don't think we have the time."

Professor Torgeson made an annoyed sound. "I was afraid of that. Well, we'll just have to wait, then. Or hope to be lucky. Eff, would you bring me my observation journal and then dig out one of the collection jars?"

I had her journal right there; I'd known she would want it as soon as she came down from the table. I was surprised about the collection jar, though. The jars were specially spelled to preserve whatever was put inside. They were supposed to be for new or unusual bugs we found, and they took up a lot of room, so we hadn't brought very many. The only reason we had them at all was because everyone was still edgy about the mirror bugs. It seemed odd to be using one up on something as ordinary as a bluehornet.

My face must have shown some of what I was thinking, because the professor shook her head. "Explanations later, Miss Rothmer. I need to get my observations down while they're still fresh."

I left to dig through the packs for the collection jar she wanted. I found the little bottle of chloroform, too, though she hadn't asked for it, because I knew she'd need it to kill the bluehornets. It took me a while, but I still had to wait for her to finish writing.

Professor Torgeson smiled and nodded in approval when she saw the chloroform. She put three drops on the little pad of cloth in the bottom of the collection jar, then climbed back onto the table and waited. I thought she was going to catch the next bluehornet that came back to the nest, but I was only half right. She waited for a bluehornet, all right, but when it came, she scooped the whole nest, hornet and all, into the collection jar and sealed it up. Then she handed me the jar and climbed quickly down from the table, and we headed back to camp before the rest of the bluehornets came looking for whatever had vanished their nest.

"Professor," I started as soon as we were well away. "What —"

"Look," the professor said, nodding at the jar.

I held it up. The nest looked a little like a bit of honeycomb made of blackish gray paper instead of beeswax. About half the cells were empty; the others were closed over. The bluehornet was lying at the bottom of the jar with its legs curled up. I frowned. "This isn't — I mean, didn't you want a better specimen? This hornet is missing a leg and one of its wings is crooked."

"That's precisely why I wanted it," Professor Torgeson said. "Every bluehornet I saw this morning had something wrong with it, and they weren't all the same things, either.

Something is wrong with this nest, and I'm hoping to find out what and why. Keep an eye out tomorrow when we're surveying outside the walls."

We kept an eye out the next day, but none of us saw any more bluehornets or found another nest, then or the day after. I expected Professor Torgeson to be cross, but instead she was just thoughtful all through the ride to the next settlement.

Novokoros was a two-year-old settlement that had been started by a group of farmers from the easternmost part of Avrupa who'd been forced off their land by some Old Continent politics. They only had two people in the whole settlement who spoke English, so it was hard to tell whether they were suspicious of strange travelers or just shy of standing around watching a bunch of folks they couldn't have a conversation with.

Once Wash arranged with the settlement magician for us to stay inside the palisade, Professor Torgeson said she had a few questions. The settlement magician frowned. He was a tall, stringy, stern man with an enormous curly beard, and he made it pretty clear that he didn't approve of women being magicians or asking too many questions or riding around the frontier without a wagon and a lot of menfolk for protection.

The professor looked as if she wanted to roll her eyes, but she went ahead and asked very politely where the settlement's mirror bug trap had been. The settlement magician told her, still frowning. The professor thanked him briskly, then turned to Wash and me. A few minutes later, we'd sent our packhorse off to the stable and ridden back out to look at the mirror bug trap.

The mirror bug trap was a spell that Papa and Wash and Professor Jeffries had worked out the previous summer, after I'd figured out how to use the bugs' own magic against them. All the different stages of the mirror bugs' life cycle — the grubs and the striped beetles and the mirror bugs themselves — were attracted to magic. If there was enough of it around, the grubs and beetles absorbed the magic and then popped into mirror bugs like chestnuts popping in a fire. Normally, the mirror bugs' own magic protected them, but I'd found a way to keep their protection from working, so that the grubs and beetles absorbed the mirror bug magic and killed them. Then the grubs and beetles turned into mirror bugs themselves, and the next wave of grubs and beetles would absorb their magic and kill them. The cycle kept on until there was nothing left in range but a few mirror bugs.

The trouble was, the settlements couldn't spare a magician to stand around holding the anti-mirror-bug spell for as long as it took to kill them all, or risk a magician running their magic to exhaustion keeping the spell going, so Papa and the others had come up with a way to use a little of the mirror bug magic to power the spell. Once all the grubs and beetles were gone, the trap spell used the last of its magic to kill the leftover mirror bugs and shut down. It worked a treat; almost all the grubs were gone by the end of summer, and the few that had turned up this spring had been killed off before they could do any more damage, or spread.

I had no idea why Professor Torgeson wanted to see the mirror bug trap. Usually, we did our plant surveying at stops along the ride, or just outside the settlement fields well away from the traps. After all, the whole idea was to find out what plants and animals normally lived between settlements, not what the settlers grew.

Novokoros had two mirror bug traps on opposite sides of the settlement, so as to be sure of drawing all the mirror bugs out of the cleared lands. The settlement magician had told Wash that he'd cast the spell again early in the spring, in case the bugs had laid eggs in the fields before they died the previous summer.

We spotted the trap well before we reached it. It looked like a little windmill with a bag underneath it, fastened to a pole at about eye level. The ground underneath it was bursting with plants. Professor Torgeson made a happy noise when she saw them.

"What is it, Professor?" I asked.

"Later. I want to get this finished by sunset," she replied. "Mr. Morris, would you measure out and mark circles around the pole? One-foot intervals should do. Eff, record the distance from the mirror bug trap along with the usual information. You work from that side; I'll work from this one."

I nodded and got to work. I noticed right off that I was finding a lot of plants I hadn't seen since we got into the area that the grubs had devastated — cloudflower and lady's lace, fire nettle and goldengrass, greater goosegrass and witchvine. It didn't take me much longer to figure out that all of them were magical plants, or that the farther I got from the mirror bug trap, the shorter the plants were and the more natural plants were mixed in.

Five feet from the pole, the number of magical plants fell off sharply and more and more of them looked stunted or malformed. Ten feet away, all I could find were the natural plants of the prairie: bluestem and switchgrass, yarrow and catchfly, milkweed and clover.

We worked until the light started to go, then rode back to the settlement. On the way, I told the professor what I'd noticed. She looked real pleased.

"Just what I was hoping to find," she said. "We'll have to check the settlement perimeter tomorrow, and the other mirror bug trap. And from now on, we'll have to check the traps at every settlement, but I've no doubt they'll confirm it."

"Confirm what?" I said. "That magical plants only grow around mirror bug traps now?"

"That is a symptom," the professor said, nodding. "The grubs and beetles absorbed magic in order to become mirror bugs. When they were killed in great numbers near the trap, they released that magic. So the areas where the grubs grew were temporarily depleted of magic, and few magical plants can grow there, while the area close to the traps has an unnaturally high concentration of magic and therefore a much greater than normal number of magical plants."

Wash pursed his lips, considering. "Interesting idea," he said after a moment. "It'd explain a few things, that's sure."

"It fits our observations so far," the professor said cautiously. "And I suspect that the reduction in the available magic is the reason for the malformed bluehornets we found at the last settlement."

"We haven't seen any of the magical animals, either," I put in. "Well, except for the sphinxes."

"Which were part of a mixed pride," Wash said, looking thoughtful. "With the bison and the deer moving back in, I'd expected to see wallers and silverhooves as well, and maybe some of the critters that hunt them."

"But we haven't."

"Predators will take longer to return than plant eaters," the professor said. "A reduction in the available magic in the soil shouldn't affect the silverhooves or other magical herbivores —"

"Unless they need to eat magical plants," Wash pointed out. "Even if all they need are a few every now and then, they won't come very far back until the plants do."

"It's still only a theory," Professor Torgeson reminded us. "It's a pity we haven't more people available to study the statistical distribution of plant species. This is a once-in-a-lifetime opportunity."

"But next year —" I stopped, remembering what she'd told Brant back in Oak River. "Oh! You mean that by next year, the magic will start coming back."

Professor Torgeson nodded. "And so will the plants. It will take a few years for the balance to get completely back to normal, I expect. We really don't have any data to compare this to. And the distribution of the mirror bug traps — and the magic that's been collected around them — could make a big difference."

We'd nearly reached the settlement gates. I frowned. "Wash," I said slowly, "do you think anyone here grows calsters or hexberries in their kitchen gardens? They're both magical plants, and if the mirror bugs pulled all the magic out of the ground . . ."

"They shouldn't grow much better than the native magical plants are currently growing," Professor Torgeson finished. "Which is to say, hardly at all."

"I'll ask," Wash said. As we rode into the settlement and dismounted, he went on, "Professor, I know you'd like more proof of this idea, but I'm thinking we should let the Settlement Office know as soon as may be. Oats and barley aren't magical crops, but meadow rice and Scandian wheat are, and I've heard talk of settlements trying to make up for the last few years by putting in a second, magical crop once their first one's been harvested."

The professor didn't look too happy about the idea, but she said she'd think on it. Wash went off to talk to the settlement magician, and found out that a lot of the magical plants in the settlement's kitchen gardens hadn't come up at all, and the ones that had were doing poorly. When he told the professor, she got real thoughtful, and next morning she agreed to send a report to the Settlement Office. She even said that as long as we were out as far as we were, we should tell the settlements we passed.

We only spent the one night in Novokoros. The settlers all seemed to have the same feelings about women magicians as the settlement magician had, and Professor Torgeson didn't much like their attitude. Also, she was eager to see if the mirror bug traps at other settlements had the same kind of magical plant growth. We let Wash tell them our idea about the magic, and then we left.

As she'd promised, Professor Torgeson wrote out a short report for the Settlement Office when we stopped for lunch, and we sent it off at the next settlement we passed. She grumbled a little about not having enough proof, though. Wash paid it no heed.

At the next three settlements, we checked the mirror bug traps. They were all the same as the one at Novokoros — lots of magical plants growing around the traps, and none anywhere else. I talked to some to the childings who had the chore of weeding the kitchen gardens, and found that ever since the grubs showed up, they hadn't had any fire nettles or other magical weeds to pull. Also, the hexberries and calsters and other magical plants weren't growing well, or at all.

The more we found out, the happier Professor Torgeson got. She even stopped complaining about passing on rumors, which is what she called Wash telling the settlers about magical crops maybe not growing for a year or two.

We worked our way northward through the rest of June and into July. The hills got lower and more rolling, and we saw larger and larger patches of grub-killed forest. We were moving right along the western edge of the settlement line, so all the places we stopped were new settlements that hadn't earned out their allotments yet. Some were only a year or two old. All of them were struggling to come back after the grub infestation, hoping to finally get a good crop after two years of failure.

The last week in June, we had another run-in with wildlife. This time it was a bear that was hungry enough to push right through the protection spells around our camp to get at our supplies. It took Wash three shots to kill it.

In mid-July, we reached St. Jacques du Fleuve on the Red River, right at the farthest edge of the frontier.

CHAPTER
· 13 ·

St. Jacques du Fleuve was one of the earliest settlements founded so far west. It started as a camp for the Gaulish fur trappers back before the Secession War. The trappers worked all winter, and in the spring they came south along the river to trade their furs for money and supplies. At first, the settlement was a temporary camp that was only set up in the spring and early summer, but after the war when the Frontier Management Department in Washington started trying to get people to move west into the territories, the Homestead Claims and Settlement Office made St. Jacques a year-round settlement.

The palisade at St. Jacques du Fleuve enclosed a lot more space than usual, because every spring the trappers still brought their furs to trade, and they needed space to stay for a few weeks. The north end of the settlement had three long warehouses near the river landings, a couple of rooming houses, and a big empty patch for tents. There was a large corral for the oxen that hauled the fur carts from St. Jacques east to the Mammoth River, two saloons, and a general store with a big cast-iron tub at the back behind a curtain and a sign that said BATH,

5 CENTS; HOT WATER, 15 CENTS and under it the same message in Gaulish. There was also a settlement branch office, so we could collect mail and send off our letters and reports. I had four fat letters from Mama, and a thin one each from Lan and William.

Professor Torgeson and Wash had mail, too. Most of the professor's was from the college; I recognized the seal on the paper. Wash had one letter that he tucked straight into an inside pocket without looking at, and a folded-over note that he opened right there in the front room of the Settlement Office. When he was done reading it, he frowned.

"Professor," he said, "would you object to making a small change in our travel plans?"

"How small, when, and for what reason?" Professor Torgeson asked.

"Three or four days," Wash replied. "If you and Eff wouldn't mind staying in St. Jacques. The Settlement Office wants me to look in at the Promised Land settlement."

Professor Torgeson raised her eyebrows. "What seems to be the problem?"

"The note doesn't say, just that word came from the settlement magician that they'd like a circuit magician to come by as soon as may be." Wash shrugged. "This is still my circuit —"

"And the Northern Plains Riverbank College has an agreement with the Settlement Office," the professor said firmly. "Magicians who teach at the college may be asked to assist with wildlife control or other settlement emergencies."

145

"I don't rightly know that it's an emergency," Wash said.

"It could be, by the time you get there, even if it isn't one now," the professor pointed out. "And that could stretch your 'three or four days' out to a week, if there's anything actually wrong. We can't spare that kind of time, Mr. Morris; you know that as well as I do. How much time would it add if all three of us go off to this settlement together, instead of having you ride out and back?"

Wash thought for a minute. "It's maybe half a day out of our way."

"Half a day plus whatever time it takes to look in," the professor said. "That's much better than three or four. We'll make the detour. Eff and I can work on the plant and animal survey while you're doing whatever needs doing."

"The Settlement Office will be right happy to learn you're agreeable," Wash said easily.

The professor made a skeptical-sounding noise, and Wash laughed. The Settlement Office man who'd given us our mail gave us a funny look, and the professor narrowed her eyes at him. "I don't suppose you know what this is about," she said, waving a hand at Wash's letter.

"No, ma'am," the man replied. "I'm just looking out for things for Mr. Saddler for a few hours. He'll be back late this afternoon, if you're wishing to speak with him."

The professor shook her head, thanked him, and started for the door. As we left the Settlement Office, Wash raised an eyebrow at her. Professor Torgeson smiled slightly.

"Right now, we're looking at going a day or two out of our way," she explained. "But if I come back to talk to this Mr. Saddler, we'll be lucky if we don't have a mountain of paperwork and three more stops to make by the time we get away from him again."

Wash laughed again. "I see you're familiar with the way the Settlement Office works."

"No, but I've dealt with college administrators, and one thing I learned from them long ago: Never give a bureaucrat a chance to hand you more work."

We walked up the street to the more respectable of the rooming houses. I was looking forward to sleeping in a real bed again after so long, and even more to reading my mail.

Mama's letters were mostly family news and fussing about me eating right and behaving like a lady. She said Professor Jeffries sent his regards, and Professor Graham had been ill but was feeling better.

Lan's letter was next. He was still complaining about Professor Warren. They'd rubbed each other wrong from the start, and Lan wasn't too happy about having to work with him all summer on the spell classifications. He was particularly worked up about a Hijero-Cathayan spell for digging out a new lake that he and his friends thought should be like a standard Avrupan excavation spell, but that Professor Warren thought should be in the same class as the Major Spells, like calling a storm or calming the ocean. I still didn't understand half what Lan said, but it was pretty clear he didn't mean me to. He just wanted someone to grumble at who wouldn't argue back.

I saved William's letter for last. He said that building railroad cars was heavy work and he didn't much like it, but it paid well enough, and after that he talked about all the studying he was doing evenings. He especially wanted to take a class that compared all the different types of magic, particularly the three main schools. Since he already knew a good bit of Avrupan magic and had a passing familiarity with Aphrikan, he was studying up on Hijero-Cathayan magic to get ready. He asked how I was liking the Far West and whether I'd seen any interesting critters or had any adventures yet. He didn't ask if I'd heard anything from home.

After I read my mail, I added a bit to each of the letters I'd been writing in the evenings. I'd already told everyone about the saber cats (though when I'd written Mama and Lan, I'd made it sound a bit safer than it really was). I told Lan and William that they were both studying the same kind of magic and they should maybe talk to each other, and I told William what Mama had said about his father.

Then I sat and looked at my letter to Mama for a long time. I'd already said as much about the settlements and the survey as I thought she'd be interested in hearing, but I'd been puzzled as to what to say about Rennie, so I hadn't yet said anything at all.

Mama had been prostrated when Rennie eloped, and they hadn't seen each other since, because Rennie hadn't been back to Mill City. Mama didn't talk much about her, either, not even to worry about her living out in the settlements. They'd written letters, though, ever since little Albert was born. And Mama had quizzed Papa and me and Lan as much as she could manage when we came back from visiting Oak River last summer.

Finally, I started with the children. A year makes for a big change in childings, and I knew Mama would want to hear every detail, even if Rennie had already written her with all of them. When I finished, I thought some more.

Rennie looked tired, but otherwise well, I wrote at last. *I think it wears on her that she hasn't been away from Oak River for six years.* I'd started to write *since she was married,* but I didn't want to remind Mama of any unpleasantness. I certainly didn't want to bring up the anti-magic notions that were growing in the settlement. *Maybe we could invite them to visit in the fall, after they're done with the harvesting? With the boys gone, we have lots of room for them to stay.*

I signed my name and sealed up the letter without reading it over, then gave it to Wash to take to the settlement branch office before I could think better of it. I liked rattling around the big old house since everyone except me, Allie, and Robbie had gone. Sometimes, though, you have to do things for family, even if you'd rather not. I figured I could stand it for a month or so if Rennie came to visit. I just hoped that if it came to it, Mama would be happier for seeing Rennie face-to-face.

I expected to have a restless night, but I slept like a log. The next day, we took our return letters to the settlement branch office to send out, then spent the morning buying supplies. In the afternoon, the professor and I went down to the river to count plants and animals, and the day after, we left.

We followed the Red River north for a while, then cut east through a dead forest. A few of the trees had tufts of green leaves on one or two branches, but most of them had been killed outright by the grubs. "Keep an eye out," Wash said, pointing to several of the trees that were leaning to one side or the other. "If one starts to go down, it'll knock a string of others over."

The professor and I nodded. We got a close-up look at what Wash meant a half hour later, when we had to find a way around a huge tangle of fallen trees. It took us an hour, and we hit two more before we got out of the forested area.

"It's a good thing we're past nesting season for cinderdwellers," the professor said after we passed the second blow-down. "The last thing we need is a wildfire in a dead wood."

"Cinderdwellers don't go for the forests," Wash said. "They're a plains bird."

"Grass fires spread. And this is nothing but a woodpile; all it would take is a spark."

"Too true." Wash nodded. "All we can do is hope for a string of wet summers, the next few years."

"Wet enough for quickrot to get a good hold," the professor agreed. "At least there's been plenty of rain so far this summer."

I stared at them for a minute, then looked at the forest with new eyes. All the dead trees would be drying out more and more as time went by, and there were so many of them. . . . There'd be no stopping a fire, once one got started. Fire protection spells were difficult and draining, so a lot of people didn't bother with trying to find someone to cast them on their homes or even just their roof. Also, the spells only helped keep a fire from starting — they weren't much good against something that was already burning. I wondered what the settlements would do if the forest around them caught fire.

Suddenly, Wash pulled his horse to a stop. His eyes were fixed on the upper branches of a tree about thirty feet in front of us. Near the top was a big untidy mess of old leaves, like an extra-large squirrel's nest. "Razorquarls," he told the professor and me without looking at us. "Back up."

I swallowed hard. Razorquarls were nearly as bad as swarming weasels, and a lot more mobile. Their teeth and claws were bigger and sharper than weasels', and their legs were longer. They had a fold of skin that they could stretch out between their front and back legs to make a kind of wing, so that they could even fly short distances. They looked a little like misshapen black squirrels, and about the only halfway good thing about them was that there weren't ever very many of them. Still, even three or four was too many.

The professor looked up at the tree, nodded once, and then realized Wash wasn't looking at her. "Right," she said in a low voice.

The two of us backed our horses a few steps, then turned them and rode slowly away. I heard Wash start a sort of muttering, half chant and half hum, and I felt the prickle of magic down my arms. "How far?" I said softly to the professor.

"Here," she said, reining in. "Any more and we'll ride out of the travel protection spells. I don't think that would be a good idea just now."

We waited. After about ten minutes, the feel of magic lessened and Wash rode back to join us. He gave us each an approving nod and said, "They'll sleep for two hours, if nothing rouses them. We'll take the long way around."

As we went farther into the forest, the trees started looking less and less dead. It only took me a little while to figure out why. It was just like Oak River — the grubs had been attracted to magic, and the settlement protection spells were the strongest magic around. Wherever there was enough space between settlements, the grubs had been drawn away and hadn't done as much damage.

What with avoiding the razorquarls and all the blowdowns, we hadn't gotten anywhere near the Promised Land settlement by nightfall and we had to camp in the forest. It was the first time on the trip that we'd spent the night outside a wagonrest or settlement, but it didn't feel too different, except that we didn't dare start a cookfire in case a spark got into all the dead wood. We made do with jerky and dried apples, and Wash didn't even grumble about having no coffee. He and the professor set extra-strong spells around our camp, and we took turns watching all night, just in case something nasty came along, anyway. I had the last watch, but all I saw was a white-tailed deer, just before dawn, that bounded away when I moved too suddenly.

We finally reached Promised Land at mid-morning. From the moment we rode out of the forest into the cleared fields, I knew it wasn't the same as the other settlements we'd seen. It felt different, for one thing. I'd gotten used to the cold feeling of the grub-ravaged settlements; it leaked through even when I wasn't doing any world-sensing. But Promised Land felt different — not normal and warm, exactly, but not so bitterly cold as the other places we'd been.

As Wash led us around the fields, I looked for the settlement itself. It took me a minute to find it. Most settlements are on top of a hill, with a high log wall around them and all the houses crowded inside. Promised Land was spread out on flat ground at the far edge of the fields. There was a log wall around part of it, but it only came up about as high as my shoulder. The houses looked short, too, and they weren't made of logs or boards like the ones I was used to seeing. Their walls looked like bushes, all bare and twiggy. People were moving among them, and there were several folk on the far side of the fields with hoes. The whole place was a lot bigger than I was expecting.

"Looks like an interesting place," Professor Torgeson commented with a sidelong look at Wash. "Well established."

I didn't blame the professor for sounding surprised. Except for a few trading towns like St. Jacques du Fleuve, I'd thought all the settlements this far west were only a year old, two at most. The first settlers to come west of the Great Barrier Spell had mostly stuck close to the Mammoth River, so they could get back to safety quick and easy if there was need. The rest of the North Plains Territory had been slowly filling up from there. Nobody wanted to go too far if they didn't have to, on account of so many people not coming back.

"Promised Land was settled shortly after the war," Wash said. "Officially."

"Officially?" I asked.

Wash tipped his hat back and looked out over the fields. "Unofficially, this was one of the latest and last endpoints of the Underground Railroad."

CHAPTER
· 14 ·

Professor Torgeson gave Wash a disapproving look. "You might have mentioned that earlier, Mr. Morris," she said, and then started right in asking questions. Wash spent the rest of the ride answering them.

A few years before the Secession War, the abolitionists who ran the Underground Railroad had started having problems hiding and protecting the slaves they'd helped escape to freedom in the North. Some of the Southern plantation owners started putting tracking spells and control spells on slaves they figured were especially dangerous or likely to run away. A bunch of abolitionists got arrested as a result, and a whole batch of people who thought they'd gotten away ended up being sent back into slavery.

So the Northern abolitionists decided they needed some help. They went to the anti-slavery advocates from New Asante and Tswala and all the rest of the Aphrikan colonies in South Columbia. The South Columbians had been working on stopping the slave trade for years. Some of them wanted to stick to diplomacy and economic methods, but there were plenty of others who were willing to send money and magicians to help out.

The first thing they did was find ways to interfere with the tracking and control spells so that slaves could get away safely. Then they had to figure out where to send them, and someone thought of the Western Territories.

Back then, nobody but a few squatters lived west of the Mammoth River. The magicians in the Frontier Management Department were still working on inventing protection spells to keep the wildlife away from settlers and travelers, and there was still a good bit of safe land east of the river that hadn't been settled yet, so most folks felt that heading West wasn't worth the risk.

But the South Columbian magicians had developed their own ways of dealing with the wildlife, on account of not having a Great Barrier Spell to protect part of their colonies, and everyone agreed that no one would look for runaway slaves in the West. Even if someone followed a slave up to the river, they'd figure that once he crossed, the wildlife would get him for sure, so they'd quit looking.

The abolitionists started sending runaway slaves west to hidden settlements in the unexplored territory. Seven different South Columbian colonies sent money to pay for seed and tools, and magicians to teach the Aphrikan magic they used to protect their own towns. The settlements did pretty well for being new and unprotected; Wash said they had fewer deaths than the first few years' worth of settlements that the Settlement Office approved later on.

When the Western Territories opened up for settlement right after the Secession War, some of the hidden ex-slave settlements applied for official recognition. Others pretended they were ordinary groups of settlers applying for allotments. There was some trouble over it, until the Settlement Office pointed out that all the ex-slave settlements were so far away from the Mammoth River that nobody else wanted to live there, anyway.

Promised Land was one of the last batch of hidden settlements that the abolitionists and ex-slaves had set up. It was founded in the 1820s, just before the Secession War. By then, the abolitionists and the South Columbians really knew what they were doing, so the settlement had done well right from the start. They'd picked a site along one of the creeks that fed the Red River, where there were plenty of trees for building. Just below the town, the creek flattened out into wetlands full of black rice that the settlers could harvest, and they had the trading camp up the river, which became St. Jacques du Fleuve, where they could trade furs for tools and seed with Gaulish trappers who didn't care one way or the other about them being former slaves.

To hear Wash tell it, the settlers were actually pretty relieved when the Secession War broke out, because once it did, they didn't have to fret over the Southern states getting the

Frontier Management Department to send any ex-slaves they caught back to the owners they'd run away from. The settlers were even better pleased when President John Sergeant signed the Abolition Proclamation forbidding slavery anywhere in the United States of Columbia or its territories.

After the war, Promised Land was one of the first of the hidden settlements to get all official with the new Homestead Claims and Settlement Office. They'd been growing at a good clip for the past nineteen years, some from the childings I could see running around and some from new settlers moving up from the Southern states.

By the time Wash finished up all his explaining, we were close in to the settlement, and I could tell that the houses weren't bushes after all. The walls were made of twigs woven together, like the chairs some of the lumbermen made, and the houses were short because they were partly dug into the ground. I wondered what they were like in winter. The settlement was about thirty years old; they had to be warm enough, or people would have changed to a different kind of building.

"Folks here look to be a lot better off than most of the settlements we've been to," I said.

"Promised Land didn't have quite such a bad time of things with the grubs," Wash said. "They only lost about half their regular crop, and they had the black rice to fall back on." Seeing my curious expression, he went on, "Black rice grows in shallow water; any grubs that tried to get at it drowned."

"Only half the crop," Professor Torgeson said thoughtfully. "That's interesting. I wonder why that would be? The woodlands here are as dead as everywhere else."

Wash shrugged, looking uncomfortable. "Promised Land was settled before the magicians in Washington worked out the settlement protection spells, and they weren't official, anyway, so they had to work out other ways to keep safe from the wildlife. What they do must not have been quite so interesting to the grubs as the regular spells."

"Are the other settlements established by the South Columbians in similarly good shape?" the professor asked.

"I'm afraid I don't know, Professor," Wash said. "Most of them are down in the Middle Plains Territory, or even farther south. This is the only one on my circuit."

The professor hmphed. "And probably the only one affected by the grubs, then; I don't think the dratted things got down to the Middle Plains. Still, we'll have to look into it. Do you know what spells these people use in place of the standard settlement protection spells?"

"You'll have to ask them," Wash said.

The professor narrowed her eyes at him. "I'll do that, Mr. Morris."

Right about then, six childings came running toward us, yelling Wash's name. Their ages ranged from six or seven to around sixteen, I thought, and their skin tone from a deep tan to black as widow's weeds. Wash pulled up and called out,

"Lattie, Tam, all of you — stop right there! You know better than to chance spooking a horse."

The childings slowed to a walk, but they kept on coming. "Stop, I said," Wash told them. "Else I'll stable these horses myself, and send you all off to tell Mr. Ajani and Mrs. Turner exactly why I'm slow coming to see them."

All of the childings froze instantly. I was impressed. Either those childings thought Mr. Ajani and Mrs. Turner were fearsome people, or else they really, really liked being the ones who stabled Wash's horse.

Wash dismounted, and the professor and I followed. "Now, then," Wash said, studying the group. "Jefferson, Siri, Martin, why don't you take the horses, and Chrissy can follow to make sure you do a good job." He winked at the littlest childing, who straightened up proudly. "Lattie, if you would go tell Mr. Ajani —"

One of the girls stepped forward, scowling. "Who are they?" she demanded, waving at Professor Torgeson and me. "Why did you bring them? They're Avrupans!"

"No, we're not," I said without thinking.

Lattie stuck her nose up in the air. "I wasn't talking to you. And you are so Avrupan."

"Professor Torgeson is from Vinland," I said. "I'm Columbian, same as you."

The girl looked confused; Wash looked like he was trying to hide a smile. "What are you talking about?" Lattie asked suspiciously.

"You were born here in Promised Land, right?" I said. Lattie nodded warily. "Promised Land is in the North Plains Territory," I went on. "The North Plains Territory is part of the United States of Columbia. I was born out East, in Helvan Shores, but that's still in the United States. So we're both Columbians."

"Now you've got that settled," Wash broke in, "I'm thinking you'd best go let Mr. Ajani and Mrs. Turner know we're here, Lattie."

Lattie gave me one more resentful look, then ran off. "That was an interesting argument," Wash said to me once she was out of hearing.

I smiled, remembering. "Lan and I had that exact same discussion with William, back when we were ten and he was nine. William argued a lot longer, but he's always been stubborn."

A few minutes later, we saw Lattie approaching with a man and a woman. The man's hair was short and snow white, and there was a grayish undertone to his dark skin that made it look like a cloth that's been washed so often that the color's started to fade. His companion looked to be a few years older than Wash. Her hair was still solid black, and she had it gathered up in a ball at the nape of her neck; her skin was about four shades lighter than her hair, more brown than black. They had the sort of look about them that made me want to check that my collar was straight and my hair wasn't windblown.

As they came up to us, a shiver ran all down my spine and a coolness spread across my chest. It felt familiar, but I couldn't place it. At that exact minute, the woman gave me a sharp look.

"Mr. Ajani, Mrs. Turner," Wash said, nodding politely. "It's good to see you again."

"I am always glad to see you, Mr. Morris," the older man replied. "Even when you come to tell me of my most unsatisfactory grandchildren." His voice was deep and precise, and his eyes had a twinkle that told me he didn't mean that the way it sounded.

"Those would be the same grandchildren you spoil unmercifully whenever they're here?" the woman said.

"The very same," Mr. Ajani said, smiling. "I find it most unsatisfactory that they do not spend more time listening to their grandfather."

The woman just rolled her eyes. "Who have you brought to meet us, Wash?" she asked, with a pointed look at Mr. Ajani.

"This is Professor Aldis Torgeson and her assistant, Miss Eff Rothmer," Wash said. "Mr. Ajani, Mrs. Isabel Turner."

"Torgeson?" Mrs. Turner said when we were all done murmuring pleased-to-meet-you. "From Scandia?"

"Vinland," Professor Torgeson said.

Mrs. Turner smiled and nodded, and asked if we'd come inside out of the sun. Mr. Ajani led the way down a few steps into one of the houses. Inside it was as cool as a root cellar, even though it wasn't anywhere near as deep or dark. The windows were a little higher up than I was accustomed to. The floor was made of flat rocks fitted together, with a big rag rug in the center, and a wooden wall split the inside of the house into two parts. The front room, where we came in, was plainly for cooking and eating and talking, just like Rennie's house; I figured the back part would be the sleeping rooms, though we didn't see them.

We sat on wooden benches around a plain table with a white tablecloth over it. Mrs. Turner brought out some cups and a pitcher of cool water, then fussed around with plates and biscuits and fixings, while Mr. Ajani asked the professor very politely why we were out riding circuit with Wash.

The professor explained about the survey of plants and animals west of the Great Barrier Spell, and Mr. Ajani got interested right away. Next thing we knew, the two of them were hip deep in talking and it looked as if we wouldn't ever find out why the settlement had sent a message out asking for Wash.

Mrs. Turner sat down at last and passed a honey jug. She looked at Mr. Ajani and shook her head, but she had a bit of a smile, too. "He never changes," she said to Wash. "Now, as it appears we'll be a time getting to business, maybe you'll tell me more about your student here." And she nodded at me.

I couldn't help staring, though I knew it was rude. And then I recollected Wash saying, "That pendant only moves one way. Teacher to student," and suddenly I knew that Mrs.

Turner had something similar. I'd felt it when I first saw her, and she must have felt mine. It wasn't the first time I'd felt that shiver, either; there was that woman in West Landing, too, only I hadn't known then what it meant. It made sense that there would be more than one, if the pendant was a tool for teaching. I just hadn't thought about it before.

Mrs. Turner's eyes flicked to me just once, then held steady on Wash, but I knew she was aware of every move I made. I froze, the same way the childings had at the mention of her name, though I wasn't sure why. I just knew that I didn't want any more of her attention than I already had, and I had a sight more than she was letting on in public.

"She's more Miss Maryann's student than mine," Wash said calmly.

Both Mrs. Turner's eyebrows rose, but she didn't say anything. She just kept on looking at Wash. Wash smiled. "Five years at the day school in Mill City," he said.

"You think that's more important?"

"I do when it's Miss Maryann."

"She agreed with you?"

"After."

"When it was too late," Mrs. Turner said.

"I didn't say she was best pleased by it." Wash sounded right irritated, though I couldn't have said why.

"I see." Mrs. Turner gave a small sigh. "I do hope you know what you've done."

"After nigh on thirty years, I'd hope so, too," Wash said, looking back at Mrs. Turner just as steady as she'd been looking at him.

By that point, I was getting as irritable as Wash sounded. I'd only just met Mrs. Turner, and I didn't see that she had any call to disapprove of me yet. It wouldn't have been polite to say anything, though, and besides, I was a little nervous of giving her a real reason to dislike me, so I sat up straight and put on my company manners and sipped at my water, pretending they were talking about someone else and I wasn't interested in the least.

There was the sound of a throat clearing. "Isabel," said Mr. Ajani in the same warning tone that I remembered Papa using when Robbie and Lan and Jack were starting to get out of hand.

Mrs. Turner hesitated, then sat back. "All right, if you insist," she said.

"I do," Mr. Ajani said firmly. "We didn't ask for Mr. Morris's presence in order to scold him for decisions that were his to make in the first place."

"I'm right happy to hear that," Wash said. "And I confess to a considerable curiosity as to why you did ask me to drop by."

"Daybat Creek has gone dry," Mr. Ajani said. "All at once, about three weeks back."

Wash set his cup down, frowning. "All at once?"

Mr. Ajani nodded. "And we've had more than enough rain, before and after the creek stopped running. Enough to keep the rice lake from dropping much so far, at least."

"You sent to Adashome?" Wash said, staring out into the air like he was concentrating on something that wasn't there to be seen.

"First thing," Mrs. Turner put in. "The creek is running fine at their end of it."

"So there's more than likely a problem in the Forth Hills," Wash finished. "Giant beavers, maybe; they'd have an easy time of dam building with all this dead wood."

"We'd like to be sure," Mr. Ajani said.

Mrs. Turner frowned. "More than that, we'd like to get the creek flowing again," she said tartly.

"Can't work on that until we know what the problem is," Wash told her. "I'm sorry, Professor Torgeson, but unless you want to ride upstream to the Forth Hills, I'm afraid you and Eff are going to be spending a week in Promised Land."

"Nonsense," Professor Torgeson said before my heart had time to do more than lurch at the thought of staying behind. "It would be foolish to miss a chance to register the plants and animals of an unpeopled woodland. Of course we'll come with you."

I breathed a quiet sigh of relief. I had a notion that I wouldn't have enjoyed spending a week in the same settlement as Mrs. Turner, and now I wouldn't have to.

CHAPTER · 15 ·

MRS. TURNER DIDN'T SEEM TO LIKE THE NOTION OF PROFESSOR Torgeson and me going off to investigate with Wash, but there wasn't much of anything she could do about it. She tried to talk Wash into bringing a whole group of settlement folks with us, in case we needed help with whatever was blocking the creek, but Wash pointed out that Promised Land couldn't spare either the men or the horses for just an "in case."

She did talk him into taking along one extra person — a tall, weedy, cheerful boy about two years younger than me. His full name was George Sergeant Robinson, but everyone called him Champ on account of him winning a shooting contest when he was a childing. He reminded me a lot of my brother Robbie. He brought along a well-worn rifle that his father had used in the Secession War. The first day, he shot a duck for dinner, and didn't waste even one bullet. Wash thanked him, but said that we'd be best off not starting a cooking fire with so many dead trees all around, and after that Champ left the ducks alone.

Quite a few ducks had been nesting along the banks of Daybat Creek. We saw them poking in the muddy creek bed, looking puzzled, or dozing at the edges where the water should have been. Wash made us stay out of the creek bed, though it would have been easier riding. He said that we didn't know what had blocked up the creek, and we didn't know when it would come unblocked, but we for sure knew that we didn't want to be in the creek bed when the water came roaring back.

Between the two settlements of Promised Land and Adashome, the land was forested and hilly. It wasn't easy traveling. Away from Promised Land, most of the trees were grub-killed, and we ran into another blow-down on the second morning and had to go around. Champ thought maybe the blow-down was what had blocked up the creek, but when we finally got past it, the creek bed was still dry and we had to keep going.

It took us nearly three days, but we finally reached the source of the problem. We'd just gotten into the Forth Hills, and riding was hard going. The hills were close together, and the creek had narrowed and cut a deep gash through them. We had our choice of riding up the creek bed or climbing the hill and making our way along the top edge of a thirty-foot slope too steep for horses or people.

Wash was still worried about the creek unblocking itself suddenly, so we climbed. The trees and the bad footing made it hard to stay within sight of the creek. We were just past the top of the second big hill, and Champ was worrying out loud that we'd miss our mark, when Wash pulled up.

"I do believe we've found the problem," he said. "Watch that you don't get too near."

Champ gave a long whistle, while the professor and I just stared. Right in front of us, half the hill looked to have just collapsed into the creek in a huge mess of mud and dead trees. The creek had backed up behind it in the low spot between hills, but it didn't have much place to go. The water was only about halfway to the top of the dam, but it had already made itself a small lake.

"What happened?" Professor Torgeson said after a minute.

"Looks like a landslide," Wash said. "Mr. Ajani said there's been rain recently —"

"A lot of it!" Champ put in.

"— and the grubs ate away all the roots that held the earth in place before." Wash nodded at the dead trees that surrounded us. "Could be a few more spots like this elsewhere."

"Like all the blow-downs," I said, and Wash nodded.

"Well, this looks like a wasted trip," Champ said cheerfully. "It'll take a while for all that to fill up, but by next spring the creek will be back, I'm thinking."

"Maybe," Wash said in the tone that meant you'd possibly missed seeing something important. "I want a closer look."

"So do I," the professor said.

Wash looked around. "Best make camp here, then. We can't get the horses down, and I'm not leaving these two here without protection spells. These woods may not be as dead as they look."

Champ scowled like he was insulted, but I thought about the nest of razorquarls we'd almost stumbled over, and nodded.

It wasn't that simple, of course. Nobody wanted to camp right at the edge of the slope; even if we'd been sure the ground wouldn't collapse again, we couldn't count on all the dangerous wildlife being gone. Even if the magical creatures hadn't come back yet (and we'd already seen signs of the smaller ones), some of the natural ones were just as bad. A hungry family of bears or a pack of timber wolves could trap us against the slope, if they got riled enough to attack.

So we scouted around for a good spot, then spent an hour or thereabouts making it as safe as we could. We had it down to a routine by then — it had been a while since Wash and the professor and I had been able to stay at a wagonrest or settlement every single night, and of course there hadn't been any ready-made protected areas since we left Promised Land. Champ and I unloaded the horses while the professor cast a couple of close-up protection spells to cover the camp for the night.

Meanwhile, Wash took his rifle and walked out into the forest, circling the area a ways out to look for signs of anything dangerous living in the area. The first night we'd had to camp out, he'd found a skunk's den less than ten yards out, which was enough to get us to move the campsite even though a regular skunk isn't exactly a threat to life and limb. I was sure Wash was also doing some longer-range magic, though he didn't say and I didn't ask.

This time, Wash came back in half an hour without spotting anything chancy, so we finished stretching a tarpaulin between two trees to sleep under and went looking for stones to line a firepit. Nobody was completely sure that building a fire would be all right, but all of us were sick to death of cold meals, and Wash said that the woods were still damp enough from all the rain that we could risk a small one, if we were determined on it.

Finding rocks was easy, though I'd never seen any like the ones we hauled back to camp. They were grayish white, of all sorts of sizes and shapes, as if an enormous stone tree had shattered into bits. Some of them had rough textures on one side that looked almost like deliberate patterns. The stone itself was hard, but it broke easily if you dropped it or knocked two pieces together. I commented that the rocks seemed odd, but Champ just laughed.

"A lot of those wash down the creek," he told me. "Just small ones. Miss Blanchard collects them and smashes them up to add to the clay she uses to make pots. She says it makes the clay smooth and shiny, and the pieces come out almost like Cathayan porcelain once they're fired."

"That doesn't make these rocks any less odd," I said.

"Odd appears to be normal in the West," Professor Torgeson said in a dry tone. "We'll take a sample back for the college, though I doubt it'll be anything new to the geologists."

By the time we finished setting up camp, it was late enough that we left heading down to the creek for the next morning. The professor was eager to see what plants were coming up along the creek, and if they were different above and below the dammed-up part, but even she wasn't crazy about the notion of trying to climb back up the slope in the dark.

Next morning, after we'd fed and watered the horses, the four of us made our way down to the dam that was blocking Daybat Creek. It was a tricky business; the whole hillside had sheared away and there were no plants or bushes to grab on to if you slipped. I spent most of the climb down wishing for a rope, or wishing I could have stayed back in camp.

Wash made it to the bottom first. Champ and I were next, almost at the same time. Professor Torgeson was over to the side, about three-quarters down, when we saw her pause and bend over the ground. A minute later, she was scrabbling toward us as fast as ever she could, waving her fist and calling, "Wash! Eff! Look at this!"

I'd never seen her so excited before, not even when we found all the magical plants around the mirror bug traps. She slipped as she reached us, but Wash stepped forward and caught her before she fell into the dam. The professor straightened herself up and caught her breath, then slowly opened her dirty fingers.

Resting in the palm of her hand was one of the grayish white rocks like the ones we'd used to line the firepit — only this one was about two inches long and the exact shape and size of a squirrel's front paw and forearm. If you looked close, you could even see where two of the claws had broken off.

"Huh," Champ said after a moment. "Looks like somebody's been here before us. So?"

"How could that be?" I said. "Nobody'd come all the way out here and bury a broken statue in the middle of a big old hill, especially one that's been around long enough to grow trees all over it. I don't see how anyone *could* do that."

"Maybe it slid down from the top in the landslide."

"That is possible," Professor Torgeson acknowledged. "Though I think it is more likely that it was uncovered when half the hill slid away. If we can find the rest, or even a few more pieces, we may be able to get an historical excavator interested enough to come out and do a proper job."

"Is it magic, then?" Champ asked.

I reached out to the stone with my world sense, the way I'd been taught, and flinched. That bit of rock was even colder and deader and more drained of magic than the land the mirror bugs had been over. I took a deep breath, and realized that Champ and Wash had flinched right along with me.

"No," said Wash. "It's not magic."

The professor looked at him curiously. "We should try to find the rest of the statue," she said. "I hope the pieces are still large enough to identify."

"First things first," Wash said firmly. "Whatever's left of that has been sitting there a good long while; it'll stand sitting a bit longer. I'm more concerned over this dam right at the moment."

Professor Torgeson nodded reluctantly. She pulled out her handkerchief and wrapped the stone paw carefully, then asked to borrow mine so as to give it a bit more padding. Meantime, Wash and Champ inspected the blockage. Wash even climbed out toward the middle, stopping every now and then to have a closer look down the back side. When he came back, he was frowning mightily.

"The dam seems stable enough for the time being," he said. "But it won't last in the long run. Far as I can see, it's a toss-up whether the creek will carve out a new channel through the landslide or whether the whole dam will give way at once. And if the blockage gives way all at once . . ."

"That'd be a problem." Champ looked worried. "Especially if it takes a while before it goes." He stared out over the lake that was building up behind the blockage.

I could understand why he was worried. Even though most of Mill City was high enough above the Mammoth River that it didn't have to worry over flooding, there were still problems every few years, and the barges always had difficulty in the spring. I'd heard that some of the millers and bargemen had proposed building a lock and dam near the falls, to get some control of the water level in the river, but nobody wanted to take the chance on it causing a problem with the Great Barrier Spell.

Daybat Creek was a lot smaller than the Mammoth River, but if it filled up to the top of the dam before it cut loose, the fields and homes along the creek were sure to be flooded, at the very least. If the water was strong enough to carry some of the trees along, there'd be even more damage.

"What can we do about it?" Professor Torgeson asked. "We couldn't dig out a landslide even if we had shovels and the whole of the Promised Land settlement to help."

"We don't need to get rid of the whole thing," Champ said, sounding a little desperate. "Just enough to start a channel through the downfall. The water will take care of the rest. You're one of those college magicians, aren't you? Can't you do something?"

Professor Torgeson sighed. "I'm afraid not. Magic might be some use if we were Cathayan magicians, or a well-trained Avrupan team, or even if one of us was a double-seventh son, but we aren't."

"We don't need to be," Wash said absently. "The real problem is that there's nothing to draw on. The mirror bugs soaked up all the power and moved it elsewhere; it'll be a few years before it comes back this far."

I wasn't sure what Wash had in mind, but I could see he was thinking real hard on something. And if what he needed was magic . . .

"Can you draw on the creek?" I asked.

Wash's head whipped around to look at me. "Draw on the creek? What gave you that notion?"

"They always said that the power for the Great Barrier Spell comes from the Mammoth River itself," I said. "Well, and the Great Lakes and the St. Lawrence on the north side, but that's sort of the same thing. This is just a creek that's backed up into a lake, but it ought to have at least some magic about it."

"That's a true thing," Wash said slowly. He looked down at the dam, then out between the hills. "Professor Torgeson, why don't you three go hunt for the rest of that statue? I'm going to sit here awhile and think."

"But what about —" Champ started, then stopped short when Wash held up a hand to shush him.

"This isn't a thing to do in a tearing hurry, unless there's a powerful need for it," Wash told him. "And it doesn't look much like there's rain coming on, and the landslide is stable for now. I do believe the dam will hold for a few hours while I think."

Champ looked down and scuffed the dirt with the toe of his boot. "Sorry, Wash."

Wash nodded and waved us on. The professor gave him a curious look, but she didn't make any more comments. She just pointed us at the part of the slope where she'd found the stone paw and set us to hunting. She said to gather up anything that looked possible, and we'd sort it out later.

We walked up and down the hill for a while. I wasn't exactly sure what Professor Torgeson wanted; an awful lot of the gray-white stones looked to me like being part of *something*, even if they couldn't all be a squirrel statue. After a few minutes, Champ went down to the landslide and found a branch he could break off. He started digging at the slope with it, while I scrambled up a bit higher.

I'd found a couple of chunks of rock the size of my fist that looked as if they had stone fur on one side when I saw a pointed shape sticking out of the hillside. I leaned forward to grab it. It was stuck pretty firmly in the hard-packed dirt, but eventually I wiggled it free. When I got a good look at it, my jaw dropped.

It was a perfectly formed statue of a barn swallow.

CHAPTER
· 16 ·

THE ROCK FELT AS LIGHT IN MY HAND AS THE ACTUAL BIRD WOULD have been, could I have held it. Carefully, I brushed the last few bits of dirt from the stone feathers. The legs and feet were broken off, but the rest of the bird was perfect. The pointed part that had caught my eye was the tip of the tail feathers poking out of the dirt. The bird's head was tilted, as if it was looking down at something. Two of the wing feathers weren't quite lined up right, just like a real bird that hadn't closed its wings all the way when it landed.

"Professor Torgeson!" I called. "I think you should see this."

"I found it!" Champ yelled at almost the same time. "Look, Professor!"

He was closer to the professor than I was, so by the time I reached them, they were both bent over his find. He held the head of the squirrel. One ear was chipped off; except for that, it was as finely detailed as the paw and the bird. The squirrel's teeth were bared as if it was going to attack something. I wondered what the whole statue would look like if we ever found enough parts to put it together.

The professor was just as excited about my swallow as she was about the squirrel head, but she told us not to dig around on the slope anymore. She said the excavators would want it to be undisturbed, and we should look through the dam instead, since that was already all mixed up.

Inside of an hour, we'd both found a heap of broken statue bits. All of them seemed to be bits of animals, and all of them were perfectly detailed. Most of them were too small to tell what the whole statue had been of, but there were a few that were obvious: a duck's head, a deer hoof, and a whole shrew. Some of them had obviously been magical animals — there isn't anything else that looks quite like a slitherrat — but for the most part we couldn't be sure whether the bits we were looking at had come from statues of natural animals or magical ones.

Finally, the professor told us to stop. "We've already piled up more than we can reasonably carry back to Promised Land, let alone haul along all the way to Mill City," she pointed out. "We'll sort through this and choose the best specimens, and leave the rest for the excavators."

So we sat around the pile of broken statues, hunting for the best bits. Champ and I worked quickly, but the professor went more and more slowly and examined each piece more and more carefully. I could see she was looking for something; she was acting the same way she had when she thought up the business about the mirror bug traps, but hadn't told anyone what she thought because she hadn't checked it yet.

"I wonder why anyone would make so many statues way out here," Champ said after a while.

"I am beginning to wonder whether anyone did," the professor said. "But one way or another, here they are. I expect the excavators will —"

She broke off in mid-sentence and went pale, staring at the rock she held. It was a sizable chunk, nearly as large as my head, which meant we for sure wouldn't be hauling it back with us. On one side there was a patch the size of my hand covered in a pattern of scales. The other sides were all smooth surfaces and sharp edges where the rest of it had broken away.

"Oh, that one," Champ put in. "I knew when I found it that it was too big to take back, but I wanted to show you. See, it looks like the skin on a snake, but it can't have been from a snake statue. The scales are way too big, and so's the rock. I thought maybe you'd know what it was meant for."

"It wasn't a snake," Professor Torgeson said in a strangled voice.

"Professor?" I said cautiously when she didn't say anything more.

"This pattern . . . it's just not possible," she said. She looked up after a minute and shook her head. "This is a perfect rendering of the scales of an ice dragon. Perfect. No one who hasn't actually seen a sample ever gets those waves right, or the overlap. It's a bit off center, and most of the drawings are either too much or too little."

"But ice dragons can't get this far from the tundra," I said. "And why would anyone here carve a statue of an ice dragon, anyway?"

"I don't think anyone did," the professor said more strongly than before.

"How else did they get here?" Champ asked. "For sure nobody would haul a bunch of statues out here and then dump them."

"I don't believe these were carved," the professor told us. "They don't show any tool marks, at least to the naked eye, and they're far more detailed than any sculpture I've ever seen. I wish I'd brought my magnifying glass down with me, but I hadn't thought I'd need it. I'll know more when I've had a chance to look at these in camp. At least, I hope I'll know more."

"If they weren't carved, how were they made?" I asked.

Professor Torgeson pressed her lips together, and I knew right then that she had a notion but she wasn't going to tell it. Sure enough, after a moment all she said was, "I don't know. Yet."

Wash was still having his think at the edge of the landslide, so the three of us began hauling statue samples up the slope to camp. The professor took the big piece with the ice dragon scales on it first thing. She stayed in camp to dig her magnifying glass out of the saddlebags, while Champ and I brought the rest of the bits up a little at a time.

When we finished, Professor Torgeson was still studying the first few pieces we'd brought up, so it was plain she'd be a while. Champ and I went back down to the river to see if Wash had finished thinking yet.

We found him crouched at the near end of the land-slide, almost sitting on his heels. He looked up as we walked toward him and raised an eyebrow. "Where's Professor Torgeson?"

"Camp," Champ said, and frowned. "We aren't childings, you know."

"Could have fooled me," Wash said. "Or have you learned to cast a continuous protection already?"

"It's near mid-day," I said, ignoring his troublemaking. "Are you coming up to eat, or do we have to bring something down?"

Wash unfolded himself. "I'll come up. I need to ask the professor something."

Neither Champ nor I had quite enough nerve to ask Wash what he'd been doing by the creek so long, but we found out as soon as he commenced speaking with Professor Torgeson. He'd been working out what to do about the dam, and he said apologetically that he'd need an afternoon of quiet to set up the spell for the next morning.

Professor Torgeson said she didn't mind staying away from the creek all afternoon, but she was more than a mite perturbed by the notion that he intended to do something about the dammed-up area all on his own.

"What are you thinking of?" she demanded. "It would take at least a five-magician team to remove all that mass, and even if we'd all trained for it, there are only four of us. If you're thinking of burning yourself out by trying it alone —"

"I'm hardly such a fool as that," Wash said. "I have something else in mind."

"You're going to do a working!" Champ cried. "Can I watch? Please?"

"A . . . working?" Professor Torgeson looked startled. Then she gave Wash a narrow-eyed look. "An *Aphrikan* working? I was under the impression you were born in Columbia."

"That I was," Wash said agreeably. "But there are ways to learn Aphrikan magic even here."

"I know just as much of it as I know Avrupan magic," Champ said. He sounded angry, like he thought the professor was questioning his skills.

"Miss Ochiba taught Aphrikan magic to eight or nine of us after school for six years," I put in.

"All right, all right," the professor said. "I just thought . . . Never mind. I, too, would like to watch, if you'll permit it."

"Not this afternoon," Wash said. "It'll be simpler if it's just me. Tomorrow, you can watch if you like. There won't be much for you to see, though." He put just the smallest extra stress on *you*, which made me wonder. Then he said, "Miss Eff, Champ, you can watch, too, as long as you keep yourselves strictly under control," and I knew what he'd meant.

Avrupan spells could do a lot of things, but I didn't know of any that did what Aphrikan world-sensing did. And world-sensing was one of the earliest bits of Aphrikan magic we'd learned from Miss Ochiba. It wasn't exactly a spell. Spells work on things outside you — rocks and tables and weeds and candles. World-sensing is something you do to yourself, inside your own head, so that you can feel more of what's going on around you. Growing up as he had, Champ had to know even more Aphrikan magic than I did, so for sure he knew how to do world-sensing. Professor Torgeson didn't, so she wouldn't be able to tell much of anything about Wash's spell casting.

Suddenly, I felt a little embarrassed. I hadn't really practiced my world-sensing since the hunt for the saber cats. Oh, I'd used it off and on, but I hadn't been working at it the way I should have. At first, I'd just been extra sensitive to the unpleasant, dead feel of the land where the mirror bugs had been, and I'd taken to putting off doing a proper practice session. Lately, it flat-out hurt whenever I tried, so I'd pretty much given it up.

I frowned slightly. Wash and Champ didn't seem to be having problems, and I bet myself that there were plenty of people in Promised Land who did world-sensing every day. I thought back, trying to remember when I'd started having problems. Right after the saber cat hunt, that was when I'd started avoiding my practice. And it had gotten painful after Novokoros . . . no, just before we got to Novokoros, at the failed settlement where Professor Torgeson had taken the blue-hornet specimen.

Right after I'd had the dreams.

I frowned harder. I couldn't see any reason why those two strange dreams should have mucked up my world-sensing, but I was willing to bet they'd done something. I resolved to start doing a proper practice from then on, headache or not.

Professor Torgeson decided that since we couldn't go down the slope to the banks of the creek without bothering Wash, we'd all of us do some plant lists in the woods. With most of the trees dead, the sunlight got all the way down to the ground, and a lot of new bushes and trees had sprouted. Even keeping close to the campsite, so as to take advantage of the temporary protection spells, we found plenty enough things to list.

Next morning, we all went down to the creek to watch Wash work his spell. He sat us down a ways from the end of the dam and told us not to move from there and to be real quiet. Then he walked a few feet out onto the landslide, picking his way over stones and broken branches until he came to a spot that was clear. He sat down cross-legged, facing upstream toward the dammed-up lake, and for a minute nothing seemed to happen at all.

Cautiously, I started in on world-sensing. It was confusing at first, and my head hurt just the way it had been doing since the bluehornet settlement, but I made myself go on. After a minute or two, the headache stopped and everything settled.

To my surprise, the area around Daybat Creek didn't feel anywhere near as icy dead as most places had since we crossed the Mammoth River, just sort of cool with colder patches. The water felt warmest; the coldest part was the dam itself.

Wash reached in his rear pocket and pulled out a jackknife. He opened it up and threw it down into the ground like he was playing mumblety-peg, so that the blade stuck. He dragged it forward along the way the blade was facing, cutting a line in the earth. Then he pulled the knife out and threw again.

Five times, he threw the knife and cut lines in the ground, all in dead silence. I could feel a kind of pressure building up, the way the air feels some days right before a thunderstorm, still and heavy and menacing. Then Wash took the knife and made a cut across the palm of each of his hands. Leaning forward, he slapped both hands down on the pattern he'd made.

I more than half expected something dramatic to happen, but nothing did. The professor stirred and whispered, "What is he doing?"

"Shh!" Champ hissed, and we were still.

I felt a warm spot in the dam. It wasn't very big and it wasn't very warm — just a small patch near the creek bed on the side nearest the water. I focused on that place, trying to sense what was different about it, but at first all I could sense was the warmth.

Then something shifted in my mind, and I knew what was happening. The water that was building up in the lake put pressure on the dam everywhere, but since the dam wasn't really a nice, even shape, the pressure wasn't quite the same all over. The warm bit of the dam was the place where the water was pressing hardest and soaking into the fallen dirt. The warmth of the water was sinking into the dam along with the water itself.

I still couldn't feel Wash's spell casting. I frowned, trying to concentrate harder, and almost lost my focus. Then I realized my mistake. I knew what Avrupan magic felt like, from doing world-sensing in my magic class at the upper school, and I'd been expecting something like that: a cage of magic built up all around the outside of something, to make it change. But Wash's magic was inside the dam somewhere.

As soon as I thought that, I felt it — deep and firm, but also gentle, like Wash's voice. It was all through the dam, but especially in the warmer part, and it felt like it belonged, like it was just another part of the rocks and dirt and trees. I figured that was why I'd had so much difficulty in sensing it in the first place.

I waited, expecting the magic to do something, but it just seemed to sit there. Then I noticed that the warm spot in the dam was growing, and not because Wash was pushing magic into it. It was growing because the water was soaking into it faster, and bringing the warmth of the lake with it. For the life of me, I couldn't see why that should be happening, but it was.

The gentle deepness that was Wash's magic pulled in toward the warm spot in the dam. I still couldn't tell that it was doing much of anything, but the warm spot kept growing and going deeper into the dam.

I don't know how long we all sat there, quiet and near motionless, watching Wash and the lake and the dam. It seemed like only a minute or two. Then the professor's eyes widened and she grabbed my arm and pointed. I lost my focus and the world sense, and I would have been annoyed with her, except that what she was pointing at was water, seeping out from under the landslide on the downstream side.

I grinned and nodded at the professor, then went back to feeling the spell. It took me a minute to get focused again. By that time, the warmth and the water were nearly all the way through the dam, but only in a section about two feet wide. A minute or two later, I could see a rapidly darkening stripe on the front slope of the dam, and shortly after that, water began oozing out of the dirt and running down to join the seepage at the base of the landslide.

Wash hadn't moved a muscle since he'd leaned over and slapped his bloody hands to the ground. I'd have been worried, if I hadn't been able to feel his magic all through the dam. The professor shifted restlessly. Champ glared at her like she was interrupting, and the middle of the dam began to collapse slowly.

It was like watching a dry pea sink through a jar of honey. First the water running down the outside started eating away at the dirt, carving a little channel as it ran. The water ran faster and faster, and then pieces of the softened earth just above the channel started to fall and get swept away. The rut got deeper and wider, and larger chunks began dropping down. Sometimes, everything would pause for a minute when an especially large section fell and blocked up the channel. It took longer and longer for the water to soak through and start washing it away again.

Gradually, the middle of the landslide wore away. When the lake water started spilling over the top, instead of just soaking through, I felt something about Wash's magic shift. I still couldn't tell exactly what he was doing, but the warm, soaked-through part of the landslide settled, like it was hunkering down for a long stay. A minute later, Wash straightened up with a sigh.

CHAPTER · 17 ·

CHAMP AND THE PROFESSOR AND I JUST SAT STARING AT THE CREEK while Wash stretched. The creek was filling rapidly with muddy water, but it didn't look like too much, too fast. The front side of the landslide had a long, sloping channel carved through it about three or four feet wide, starting just below the level of the lake and running down into the newly re-formed creek. The water rushed and swirled around rocks and trees, but it wasn't coming through quite strong enough to sweep them away. It looked like it would be a particularly nasty set of rapids, if you were in a boat.

"What did you do?" Professor Torgeson croaked as Wash came over to us. "That's . . . What did you *do*?"

Wash gave her an extra-wide grin. "It's a mite hard to explain in Avrupan terms," he said. "The best way I can think to put it is that I invited the water that had backed up to soak into the dam and do what it would eventually do, anyway, only faster. Then when I had as much done as I wanted, I asked it to stop."

"Asked it to stop," the professor said faintly. "But —"

"But the creek is still eating away at the landslide," Champ said, pointing. "If it wears through too fast, the rest of the dam will go."

"It won't," Wash said. "Though even if it did, things wouldn't be as bad now as they would be in a few months, when four or five times as much water was backed up."

"How can you be sure?" Champ demanded.

"It was Miss Eff's idea. There's magic in flowing water. Once I got the water flowing through the blockage, I coaxed a little of its magic into the dam. That earth is set to stay put for a while. If I did it right, the water will wear a new channel and empty the lake, but slowly."

"If you did it right?" the professor repeated.

"I'll keep an eye on it for the rest of the day, just in case," Wash promised. "And I'll give it a good looking over tomorrow morning. That's plenty long enough to see the signs, if there's a problem. But I think all Promised Land needs to worry about now is Daybat Creek running a little high and a little muddy for a year or two."

The professor had a lot of questions, but the more Wash tried to answer them, the more questions she seemed to have. Finally, he told her politely that she'd do better to write to one of the professors of Aphrikan magic down at Triskelion University, as they were more accustomed to explaining. Then he took a two-hour nap, and after that he went back down to check on the dam.

I didn't say much through the discussion. It was clear

from the way Champ kept sticking his oar in that he'd seen and understood a lot more of what Wash was doing than I had. It didn't sit right that a boy two years younger than me was so much better at world-sensing, even if he'd probably been learning Aphrikan magic his whole life long. I decided right then to study up, even if doing world-sensing in the grub-ravaged areas was unpleasant.

Wash didn't find any problems with the creek or the dam, that afternoon nor next morning. As soon as he said it was clear, we started packing up the camp. The professor and Champ had a few words over all the statue pieces the professor wanted to bring back with us. Champ said there were too many, and they'd be too heavy for the horses, but the professor said we'd already picked out the best ones and she didn't want to leave any more behind.

Finally, Wash put his foot down. "Champ won't be coming with us any farther than Promised Land," he pointed out. "We'll have one less horse to carry whatever we take. I expect you can fit a few more rocks in the saddlebags if you took out some of those specimens you've been collecting."

"These are specimens," the professor said firmly. "Possibly even more so than you think."

"I thought it was plants and animals you were collecting," Champ said. "Not statues."

Professor Torgeson got a stubborn look on her face for a minute, then sighed. "These are not statues," she said.

"They surely do look like statues to me," Champ said. "Broken ones."

The professor shook her head. "They aren't carved; even under a magnifying glass, there are no tool marks. And look here." She pulled out the magnifying glass and grabbed one of the rocks. "You can see every hair individually. Look at the way they lie — they're not straight and neat when you get this close, even though they look that way without the glass."

We all looked. She was right. They looked like real hairs, too, not just lines scratched into wood or stone like most of the statues I'd seen.

"No artist in the world could create that kind of detail," Professor Torgeson said. "There are no tools that will carve that finely, and no spells, either. And there are hundreds of these here, from all kinds of animals, and every one I've studied has that level of detail. But this is the real key."

She flipped the stone over, so that we could see the broken-off surface. It looked to have cracked off nice and smooth, until she held the magnifying glass over it. Then we could see faint lines. Champ's eyes widened. "That looks like . . ."

"Blood vessels," the professor said, nodding. "On the *inside* of the stone. They go all the way through; I broke off a corner of one to make sure. Bones, too. I'm almost afraid to get these back to the college and find out what they look like under a microscope."

"Nobody could do that," Champ said with conviction.

"But if they aren't statues . . ." I didn't finish the sentence. It was pretty obvious what the professor thought, because we all thought it, too, after seeing blood vessels and bones inside solid rock. I just didn't want to hear her actually say it.

"Just so," the professor said, like she didn't want to say it out loud, either. She hesitated, then went on. "Old Scandia has legends of creatures that would turn to stone if sunlight touched them. That can't be what happened here; we've found too many different species, and too many that aren't magical at all. It could be something similar, though — something about this place, perhaps. That's why I want to bring as many different specimens as we can, so we can find out what they have in common."

Champ yelped. "Something about this place turned all these animals to stone? And you let us camp here?"

"We don't know that for certain," Professor Torgeson said reprovingly. "It's one possible theory, that's all."

"Seems like the obvious explanation to me," Champ muttered. "And I still don't think we should be camping here."

"Whatever did this, it happened long ago," Professor Torgeson said reassuringly. "Centuries, probably. None of the specimens is of recent origin. And we aren't even sure yet that the stones are . . . were animals at all, much less how they got this way. Fossil bones have been found in other places; it's quite possible that these creatures were converted to stone after their deaths, by some natural process we do not yet understand."

I could tell by the way she said it that she didn't really believe what she was saying. I thought about the snarling expression on the stone squirrel's face, and decided I didn't really believe it, either.

"It's a right interesting problem," Wash said after a minute. "But interesting or not, we still don't have room for every bit you've set aside."

The professor rolled her eyes but nodded. "I knew this would happen," she grumbled. "I told Jeffries we needed more than one pack animal. Oh, very well, I'll go through everything one last time. But if Jeffries complains when we get back, I'm sending him to you."

The professor took Wash's words greatly to heart, because she ended up only choosing one satchelful of the best pieces. Champ was pleased that the squirrel's head he'd found was one. So was my barn swallow. She took the piece she said was from an ice dragon, too, but she said she'd leave it at Promised Land. It was too large to haul all the way to Mill City, and the professor didn't think it would be as interesting to anyone else right off, the way the squirrel and the barn swallow would.

Champ and I each took one of the stones ourselves, as mementos. His was another paw, from something considerably larger than a squirrel that Wash couldn't identify. I took a small bird that looked like it had been caught in mid-flight. The head and parts of the wings had broken off, or I think the professor would have taken it instead of my barn swallow.

Getting back to Promised Land didn't seem like as much of a chore as getting out to the dam had been. We dropped Champ off with Mrs. Turner and Mr. Ajani, and told them what we'd found and what Wash had done about it. Mr. Ajani asked some questions about the spell Wash had used, and he gave me an approving look when Wash said I'd been the one to think of using the magic of the creek itself. Mrs. Turner looked skeptical, but she didn't say anything.

Wash told them to keep a close eye on the water level in the creek, and maybe check on the dam again in a few days. Then Professor Torgeson told them about the stones and advised them to be extra careful if they meant to stay long anywhere around the landslide. Even if we hadn't had any difficulties, we still didn't know what had happened there, and it was best not to take chances. Also, the historical excavators would want everything left exactly as it was, or at least as much as possible. Mrs. Turner looked a bit miffed, especially by the comment on the excavators, but Mr. Ajani just said that anyone they sent would certainly take care, and that was that.

We stayed the night in Promised Land and went on the next day. We had to ride longer and harder than we'd planned in order to make up all the time we'd lost, and even then, it quickly became plain that we weren't going to be able to survey the whole circuit the way the college had planned. Professor Torgeson wasn't best pleased, but Wash just shrugged and said he'd have been more surprised if we'd been able to stick to the schedule.

For the rest of the trip, I practiced world-sensing faith-fully every morning. It worked just the way it had when I was watching Wash do the spell at Daybat Creek. When I first started, I'd get a splitting headache, but if I kept at it for a minute, the headache went away, and the only problem was the mildly unpleasant sensation of the grub-devastated land. It got even easier when we finally turned east and left the area that the grubs and mirror bugs had destroyed. Even the headache stopped. And then, three nights before we reached the ferry, I had another dream.

Like the flying dream, it was sharp and clear, and the clarity lingered even after I woke. I dreamed I was stand-ing on the bank of the Mammoth River. It was a clear night, and the stars were bright overhead. I could see Mill City on the far shore, faintly outlined against the sky, but where I stood was only wilderness. West Landing was gone, and so was the shimmer of the Great Barrier Spell that should have hung over the middle of the river. Everything was dark and still.

I felt a breath of wind and saw a light on the opposite bank. As the light moved toward me, I saw that it was a log raft with a waist-high railing around the edge. But the logs weren't logs of wood; each one was a different spell, shaped into a log. The boards that made up the railing were more spells, and likewise every nail that held it all together. The glow of the spells brightened as the raft came closer, until I could hardly stand to look at it.

At last the raft bumped gently against the bank, right where I stood. A gate in the rail swung open, and I stepped on board. The end of the raft where I stood sank lower in the water, then lifted a little. The raft began to move again, back toward the city on the far shore. I felt sad and excited at the same time; sad for what I was leaving and excited by what I was going back to.

Halfway across the river, the raft stopped moving and began to sink. I hit at the railing, trying to break it and release its magic so that the raft would surface and take me safe to shore, but it was too strong. The water crept up to my knees, then my waist. The raft sank completely, and I floundered in the dark until the deep current pulled me down. I woke in a cold sweat, just before I drowned.

I didn't sleep well for the rest of the night, and I wasn't good for much the next day. I was careless enough with the professor's specimen case that she ended up giving me a good scold, and I had to force myself to do my world-sensing practice. I was surprised when it worked the same as always; I'd been expecting more headaches or an upset stomach or something.

Two nights later, on the night before we reached the ferry, I had the dream again. It was exactly the same: the silent river, the glowing spell-raft, the passage halfway across, the raft sinking. I jerked awake in my bedroll, gasping.

Once I'd calmed down a little, I started in on wondering why I'd had the exact same dream twice. I'd heard of folks who believed all sorts of things about regular dreams — that they were messages from people who'd died, or that they were visions of the past, or symbols of the future. If people could believe all that about ordinary, muddled-up dreams, I figured it was possible that the dream I'd been having was more than just a plain old dream. I didn't know how to check on it, though it did occur to me that if I had the same dream again, I ought to make real sure I never climbed out onto that raft.

Wash rousted us out early in the morning so that we could all get cleaned up in West Landing before we crossed back to Mill City. He said he didn't mind turning up a bit shaggy himself, but he wasn't about to face my mother or Professor Jeffries with me looking like a ragamuffin. Professor Torgeson laughed and nodded; next thing I knew, Wash had sent us off to a ladies' hairdresser while he went to the barbershop.

I was more uneasy at crossing back over the Mammoth River than I'd ever been before, but it was an entirely uneventful trip. We didn't even have any problem getting the professor's specimens through the Great Barrier Spell, though I'd expected that the few magical plants and insects we'd collected would be a problem at the least. Wash saw us back to Professor Jeffries at the college, then took himself off to the Settlement Office. I stayed most of the afternoon, helping Professor Torgeson unpack and sort all the specimens she'd brought back.

When I finally got home, Mama had made a welcome-back dinner that couldn't have been fancier if I'd been gone ten years. She'd made Nan and her husband come for it, even though she only found out at the last minute when I was for sure going to be home. She'd have had Jack and Rennie, too, if they'd been anywhere in reach.

It was nice to be fussed over, and nicer still to sleep in a proper bed again. I was surprised by how fast I got used to being home. I fell right back into my old routine, working for Professor Jeffries and Professor Torgeson most of the day and then coming home to do chores. It almost felt as if I hadn't been away, except for the little broken stone bird on my nightstand. And then, a month after we got back, I had the dream again.

This time, when the raft touched the shore at my feet and the little gate swung open, I backed away. For a long moment, the raft just sat there, and then it sank all at once, *boom*. The dark river swooshed in to cover where the raft had been. And then the riverbank collapsed under me, and once again I was sinking in the cold, dark water.

My head went under, but I didn't wake up the way I had before. I opened my eyes and saw the raft, glowing in the depths below me. I knew I couldn't get back to the surface, so I swam down toward the raft instead.

As I drew near, I saw a braided silver rope as big around as my thumb floating toward me. At the far end of the rope, the three strands of the braid separated. One was tied to the raft; the other two strands went off into the dark depths of the river, and I couldn't see where they ended.

Part of me wanted to grab hold of the silver rope, and part of me was afraid of what might happen if I did, and all of me was running out of air and time. I woke up before I died or decided what to do, though at least I wasn't in a panic the way I'd been the last two times.

I still didn't know what to make of the dreams. I couldn't see talking to Mama or Papa about them, and William and Lan were both still out East. Wash was back out in the settlements, checking on some of the ones we hadn't visited.

That left Professor Torgeson, but even after spending over three months with her in the West, I felt a little shy of speaking with her. I didn't have much in the way of other choices, though, so after two days of dithering, I went to her office late in the afternoon when I was done working for Professor Jeffries.

CHAPTER
· 18 ·

PROFESSOR TORGESON'S OFFICE WAS A NARROW LITTLE ROOM IN A back corner of the house that the college had used to hold science classes when it was just starting up, before they got the first two-story classroom building built. Her desk, two chairs, and a bookcase used up every bit of space there was, so she'd found a long wooden table somewhere and stuck it just outside her door to hold all the specimens we'd brought back. When I got to her office, she was standing over the table, fiddling with a skinny, rectangular glass jar and looking harried.

"Eff!" she said in tones of relief when she saw me. "You're just the person I need. I've run out of long-term holding jars, and some of these specimens will begin to deteriorate soon if they're not moved to some semblance of proper storage. Would you mind checking with Dean Farley to find out whether there are any ordinary containers around that will hold a medium-long-term enchantment? Even if they only hold the spells a month or two, it'll save these materials long enough for us to get more jars shipped in from the East."

"Of course, Professor," I said, and went off to see if I could catch the dean. I didn't find him, but I did run into Professor Graham, who said he thought there were some glass containers in the cellar. They turned out to be canning jars with lids too old to be used for canning food, but when I showed them to Professor Torgeson, she said they'd work admirably for temporary specimen storage, as long as nobody banged them around.

"Has Professor Jeffries taught you the spell for preserving samples?" she asked me.

"No, Professor," I said.

"I'll teach you, then. Enchanting all these jars will go much faster with two of us working. You know the general storage spell?"

I nodded hesitantly. "They taught that in second year of upper school." I didn't add that I hadn't ever made it work until I started pushing at my spells with Aphrikan magic. I'd been casting it fine at home as part of my chores since then.

"The sample-preserving spell is based on that one, but it's more advanced — much more specific, and considerably stronger. You shouldn't have any trouble learning it."

"I guess," I said doubtfully.

"It's a bit fiddly, but not actually difficult," she assured me. "Like this." She showed me how to set up the work area, and what the hand motion was, and told me the chant. She was right; it was fiddly. The three white feathers had to be exactly in position, and they had to be laid down first, so that I had to take extra care with every movement I made after that so as not to shift them while I drew the circle around them. The timing of the passes and the chant had to be exact, too — no speeding or slowing the pace. But the motions weren't hard, just a flat-palmed wave three times over the jar and the feathers in the circle, and the chant wasn't a tongue-twister. Mostly, you just had to pay attention and be careful.

"Now you try it," the professor said after she'd enchanted the first jar and walked me through.

I stepped up to the corner of the table. I cleared the work space, then reset everything and drew the circle. Out of habit, I started up my Aphrikan world-sensing and the Hijero-Cathayan concentration exercise that Miss Ochiba had taught me, so I could tweak the magic of the spell directly if it started to go wrong.

I felt a little uncomfortable when I noticed what I was doing. Ever since our first crossing of the Great Barrier Spell back at the start of summer, when Wash had noticed me tweaking the calming spell on my horse, I'd been trying to do all my Avrupan magic properly, without using Aphrikan magic to prop it up if it went wrong. But I hadn't had much call to do Avrupan spells during our time out in the settlements, and since I'd been home, I'd only been working household spells that I knew pretty well already and didn't have much need to prop up. I told myself I was just worried about learning a new spell because I'd been using the Aphrikan and Hijero-Cathayan magic to help learn all through my last year at upper school.

Then I had to put my worrying out of my mind, because I had to pay attention to the actual spell casting. At first, it went fine. I could sense the spell rising up around the little jar, slow and steady, like making a box by balancing jackstraws on each other one at a time.

And then the box started wobbling. Without thinking, I pushed at it, trying to put it back in balance, but that only made the wobble worse. In another second, the whole structure of magic collapsed, leaving three burned feathers and an ordinary, unspelled jar sitting in the middle of the table.

Professor Torgeson didn't seem disturbed. "I did say it was fiddly," she told me. "It took me four tries to get it to stick, the first time. Try again."

She fetched more feathers while I cleaned up the work space, and I tried again. This time, I hadn't even finished the first hand pass before the spell caved in. Professor Torgeson just handed me some more feathers.

By my eighth try, the professor was frowning slightly and I was getting frustrated. I hadn't tried to tweak the spell since my first try, but I was so annoyed by this time that when I saw the magic starting to break down *again*, I couldn't stand it. I made a mental circle around the outside of the box made of magic, like cupping my two hands around it, and held it all in place.

For a few seconds, I thought it would work. The canning jar I was working on started to glow, and Professor Torgeson smiled. Then the spell collapsed inward. There was a bright flash, and when our eyes cleared, the professor and I were staring at a puddle of glass where the canning jar had been. The top of the table was charred black for two inches around the glass, and the feathers were little smears of ash.

"Well," said Professor Torgeson after a minute. "I've never seen *that* happen before."

"I'm sorry, Professor," I said in a low tone. "I just . . . I never have been much good with Avrupan magic. I think you'd better enchant all the jars yourself."

"What?" The professor tore her eyes away from the puddle. "Nonsense! You just overloaded the spell. Though I've never seen quite so much of an overload before." She looked at me with a considering expression. "Your twin brother is some sort of prodigy, isn't he?" She put just the faintest extra emphasis on *twin*.

"Lan's a double-seventh son," I said. "I'm . . . not." William and Wash and Miss Ochiba had spent a long time convincing me that being a thirteenth child didn't make me evil or unchancy, and I mostly believed it myself now, but I was still leery of telling other people. I'd had too much unpleasantness in my life from people who truly did think I was bad luck, and I didn't relish risking more if I didn't have need.

Professor Torgeson didn't let it go, though. "Yes, yes, I can see that you aren't a son," she said. "But what *are* you?"

I sighed. "I'm the older twin, and I'm a seventh daughter," I told her. "Not a double-seventh daughter, though."

"Pity," the professor said absently. "I don't recall ever hearing of a pair of twin double-sevens. I expect they'd be something exceptional, if they ever happened. Still, a pair of twins where one is a seventh and the other a double-seventh is quite remarkable. It might well explain the amount of power you put into that spell."

"I —"

"Frustration no doubt had a fair bit to do with it, too," the professor went on. She tilted her head, studying the table once more. "Why don't you see if you can scare up a pair of work gloves and a cleaning knife? We can't leave this as it is."

I found a pair of work gloves in the kitchen, but I had to go all the way over to the laboratory building for the cleaning knife. When I got back, Professor Torgeson had cleared off the other end of the table and was busy enchanting canning jars. I scraped and pried at the puddle of glass until it came free from the table, then took it out to the waste bin.

Professor Torgeson looked up as I returned. "Ready to try again?" she asked, nodding toward the table. She'd already set up the feathers and the canning jar. All that remained was to cast the spell.

I gaped at her. "You want me to try again? After that?" I waved at the charred spot on the table.

"Of course," Professor Torgeson said as if it was the most obvious thing in the world. "If you don't try again, you'll never learn the spell."

"But —"

"You aren't frustrated now, and attitude has a good deal to do with spell work. Go on, now."

I was so surprised that I did what she said, without using Aphrikan magic or anything. The spell still didn't work, but at least the canning jar didn't melt.

"Again," Professor Torgeson commanded.

"In a minute, please, Professor," I said, staring at the work space. It had been so long since I'd cast an Avrupan spell without using Aphrikan magic to help that I'd almost forgotten what it felt like. Almost, but not quite — and the sample-preserving spell felt different from what I remembered. It needed something, some balance point . . . and then I remembered what it felt like to do the Aphrikan world-sensing. Like building with jackstraws, one at a time, I thought. Only I couldn't build a straw box and keep up the world-sensing at the same time.

Slowly and carefully, I cast the spell again. This time, I didn't use any world-sensing, but I concentrated on the feel of the spell itself. In the back of my mind, I pictured putting jackstraws on top of each other, one by one, very gently so as not to knock anything loose.

I spoke the last word as my hand completed the final pass. For just a second, I thought I'd failed again . . . and then the canning jar glowed, bright but not blinding. The glow faded, and I looked at the professor without even trying to keep from grinning. "I did it!"

"That you did," Professor Torgeson said. "And a good job, too." She plucked the jar out from the feathers and replaced it with another one. "Again."

It took me three tries (it really was a fiddly spell), but I did it. She made me do five more jars before she was satisfied that I could keep it up; then she stacked all the unenchanted jars in the center of the table where we could both reach them, and took herself down to the other end to do some spell casting of her own.

It took the two of us quite a while to finish, and I never did tell the professor about my strange dreams. I was late getting home to dinner. I didn't pay much heed to the scolding Mama and Allie gave me, though I knew I deserved it. I was too busy thinking about the way Professor Torgeson had made me keep trying that spell, even after I melted the canning jar. When I was in upper school, no one ever made me redo my spells once they'd gone badly wrong.

But Professor Torgeson hadn't just made me try again right away, I thought. She'd sent me off to get cleanup tools, and made me clean up first. She'd given me a little time, but not so much that I'd talk myself into a funk over having melted the jar.

The other thing that occurred to me was that I'd been using Aphrikan magic all wrong for near on to a year now. I hadn't really been trying to work my Avrupan spells right — well, I'd been trying to the first time I cast them, but I hadn't been using my Aphrikan world sense to see what I'd done wrong so I could do it the right way on my next try. I'd only ever just watched to see when the magic started going wrong, so I could shove it back into place. And since I never bothered to figure out why things went wrong, I'd make the same mistakes the next time I cast the spell. No wonder I couldn't do Avrupan spells properly!

On the other hand, I'd had a lot of trouble with Avrupan magic before I ever started using Aphrikan magic to force my spells to work. I thought about that all evening, but it wasn't until I was lying in bed, staring at the ceiling in the dark, that I finally figured out why.

I'd never thought of my problems with Avrupan magic as mistakes that I could learn to fix.

First, for years, I'd thought all my troubles were because I was an unlucky thirteenth child. On top of that, I'd been so afraid of what I might do if I went bad that I stopped ever really trying to learn Avrupan magic. Once I found out that I could do spells after all, and stopped really believing that being thirteenth-born was the reason for my problems, I was so used to messing up that I kept right on doing it without thinking. And when I found out that Aphrikan world-sensing could force my spells to work, that's all I'd used it for.

I thought some more. Professor Torgeson had said that the sample-preserving spell was based on the general storage spell, and I'd thought I could make it work the same way I'd been making the general storage spell work. But I'd never really learned how to cast the general storage spell properly, without Aphrikan magic.

I sat up. The house was dark and quiet. I thought about waiting until morning, but I wanted to know if I was right. I slid out of bed, and the wooden pendant Wash had given me thumped against my breastbone.

I snuck down the hall to the linen cupboard and canceled the storage spell. There wasn't much chance of moths getting into the blankets this late in the year, though there was still a month or two before Mama would have to get them out to put on the beds. Holding my breath, I cast the storage spell.

It didn't work the first time, or the second, but on my third try I felt the magic click into place just the way it was supposed to.

I did a little jig in the hallway in my bare feet, and then crept back to my room. Halfway there, I pulled up short. Part of why I'd had such a hard time learning Professor Torgeson's spell was that I hadn't known the everyday spell it was based on. I'd proven that I could learn it after all, but it was just one spell. I hadn't learned any of the basic Avrupan spells, not really, not since Miss Ochiba had left and I'd started upper school. I was going to have to learn all of them all over again.

I trudged the rest of the way to my room. Four years' worth of spells was a lot. On the other hand, I already knew all the theory, and I'd gotten most of them to work by pushing them around with Aphrikan magic, so really, all I had to do was try them a couple of times without Aphrikan magic. Probably.

As I climbed back into bed, I resolved to try. I felt a little tingle from Wash's pendant as I snuggled down to sleep, just a brush across my skin, really. And then I was dreaming again, the same drowning dream I'd had twice before. Once more, I saw the glowing raft come toward me through the night; once more I tried to back away and felt the ground beneath me give as the raft sank; once more I swam through the murky water toward the golden glow. This time, though, I took firm hold of the braided silver rope as soon as I could reach it and started pulling myself toward the raft.

The raft vanished. I paused for a second, then kept pulling myself along. There had to be something at the other end of the rope, whether it was the raft or not. I had nearly reached the spot where the braid had unraveled into three separate strands when everything around me went blindingly white.

Next thing I knew, I was standing in a forest. I took a deep breath. It looked like one of the grub-killed woods we'd seen in the West, all bare trees and silence. I was scared, but nowhere near as scared as I'd been when I'd thought I was drowning.

I still had my hands tight around the silver rope, only it wasn't a rope anymore. I had just one strand of the braid. The other two had disappeared. The strand I held ran off into the forest in front of me. I turned around, but I didn't see it anywhere behind me. When I looked down at my hands, I realized that the strand vanished half a foot behind my fingers. As I moved my hands forward along the strand, the back part disappeared six inches past my grip. I wondered what would happen if I dropped it, but I wasn't about to try it to find out.

I tugged, but nothing happened. Either there was too much cord to pull toward me, or it was fastened to something too far away for me to see. I sighed. I didn't want to stay where I was, and I really, really didn't want to go wandering around this wood without a direction. That only left one choice.

I slid my hands along the silver cord and started walking.

CHAPTER
· 19 ·

I WOKE THE NEXT MORNING TO BIRDSONG AND BRIGHT SUNSHINE. The last I could remember of the dream was walking and walking, with the silver cord slipping through my fingers and disappearing behind me. I didn't remember getting anywhere, though I'd have sworn I'd walked a long way. That was dreams for you, I thought, and put it out of my mind.

That was the last time I had the drowning dream. Since it hadn't ended with me drowning and waking up scared to death, I didn't feel any urgency about talking to Professor Torgeson about it any longer. I might have talked to her, anyway, if one of the daybats at the menagerie hadn't hurt a wing and made things extra busy for the next couple of days. By the time things settled down, classes had started and the professor was busy with her students. After a while, I forgot about it.

I didn't forget about practicing my Avrupan magic, though. At first, I only worked on the householding spells, because I had to do those for chores, anyway, so all I had to do was quit using Aphrikan magic to shore them up. I worked on one spell a day, so that I wouldn't get caught on account of doing my chores slowly and have to explain. By the end of the month, I had all my regular chore spells down cold, and I was starting in on things like the general storage spell that we only had to cast once or twice in a year.

What really surprised me was that getting the spells right was fun. Now that I was actually thinking about what I was doing, I could use my Aphrikan magic to sense where the spells were going wrong, and then figure out how to fix them. Even so, breaking the habit of using Aphrikan magic to force my Avrupan spells to work right was hard. If I didn't pay attention every single time I cast a spell, I forgot and did it the way I'd gotten used to. And every time I did that, it made it harder to remember the next time.

My Aphrikan magic was a lot better, too. I'd never been taught anything except world-sensing and foundation work, and I hadn't noticed much of any change in how I did those since Miss Ochiba left. Oh, they'd gotten a bit easier with practice, but that was all. Even so, I'd kept on with practicing my Aphrikan world-sensing every morning, just as I'd started doing out in the settlements. After that last dream, I started trying to keep my world-sensing up all the time again, except when I was doing Avrupan spells. It was a whole lot easier to do in Mill City than it had been out in the settlements, and a lot more comfortable, too.

That fall, my sense of the world opened up unexpectedly. Up until then, I'd only ever been able to sense my own spells clearly. I could tell when someone else was casting magic, and I could sense really strong spells like the Great Barrier Spell and the working that Wash had done at Daybat Creek, but that was about all. During the trip with Wash and Professor Torgeson, my world-sensing had gotten more sensitive — I could feel everyday things that were farther away, and even things that were out of sight behind trees or rocks — but as soon as I started using my Aphrikan world sense to learn my Avrupan spells properly, I started being able to sense other people's magic.

First I noticed that I could sense some everyday spells without particularly looking for them, the same way I could sense people and animals and chairs. Things like the fly-block spell, or the minder spell that Mrs. Callahan always put on the kettle of beans to make sure they didn't burn. The spells didn't stand out or seem unusual; they were just *there*. After a bit of work, I found that I could sense other folks' magic even when they weren't casting spells. I could feel a lot more normal-strength spells, too, and I could even tell a magical creature from a natural one without looking straight at them and concentrating. And I had less and less trouble keeping my world-sensing going.

The changes seemed important, but Wash was still out in the settlements and no one else in Mill City understood much about Aphrikan magic. I thought about writing to Miss Ochiba, but I hadn't seen her for nearly two years and I felt funny just up and writing out of the blue. So I wrote to William instead.

For once, William wrote back right away. He had a lot of questions, and every time I answered one batch, he sent me a letter with another set. He even asked Miss Ochiba — I still couldn't think of her as Professor Ochiba. All he could tell me was that she'd looked very pleased when he'd talked to her, so I was probably doing something right.

Lan wrote, too, but not as often. He wasn't much interested in how my Aphrikan magic was going, really, though he tried to tell me I'd learn more of it faster if I got more schooling. He skipped right over the parts of my letters where I told him I was having to relearn all my Avrupan spells pretty much from scratch.

In October, the young mammoth in the menagerie got restless again. Professor Jeffries took to having some of his animal husbandry students come by to help with the calming spells, and one of them, Roger Boden, stayed even after November came and the snow fell and the mammoth calmed down.

Mr. Boden was a bit taller than I was, with red-blond hair, blue eyes, and a square, solid build. He was gentle and quiet, good with the animals, and always polite to me. He was also one of Professor Jeffries's favorite students, and he made me very nervous.

After all, I'd gotten my job by doing pretty much what he was doing: hanging about the menagerie and offering to help out and pestering Professor Jeffries with questions. Only there wasn't enough work at the menagerie to hire on another person, so if Professor Jeffries decided he wanted better help, he'd have to replace me. And Mr. Boden was better, by any measure; he was two years older than I was, a lot handier with Avrupan magic, and a lot more knowledgeable about animals, especially wildlife, on account of having finished two years at the Northern Plains Riverbank College already.

One afternoon, late in November, he came over as I was putting away the last of the spell-casting supplies and said, "Excuse me, Miss Rothmer, I was wondering . . ."

"Yes?" I said with a tiny sigh. I'd been looking forward to being done for the day, but Mr. Boden hardly ever spoke to me unless he needed something. "What can I do for you, Mr. Boden?"

"I, ah, was wondering . . . if you are finished for the day . . ." He hesitated. "If I might walk you to your home."

"Oh!" was all I could think to say for a good long minute. "I — yes, I'm nearly done. That is . . . I would like that."

It was a gloomy, raw November day, all gray skies and bare trees. The air had a nip to it that promised more snow soon. We'd had two snowfalls already, early in the month, but neither had been much to speak of and they'd both melted off during the previous week's warm spell. It didn't feel like whatever was coming would be melting again until March.

The chill and the wind didn't make for much conversation. When we came to the front gate, he thanked me gravely for the pleasure of my company and went on his way, leaving me openmouthed in surprise. I went inside and thought very hard for the rest of the evening.

Mr. Boden walked me home again a few nights later. It wasn't long before he was accompanying me two or three nights every week as a settled thing, and I was pretty sure that it wasn't Professor Jeffries or the animals that kept him coming back to the menagerie, or at least, not only them.

It took me a time to get accustomed to the notion that Mr. Boden might be in the way of courting me. What convinced me was Allie's behavior. She was polite enough when he first started dropping in; after all, it was no new thing for us to have students from the college in and out of the house at all hours of the day. By Christmas, though, she was frowning at me and muttering whenever Mr. Boden's name came up in talk. Even Nan noticed, when she came by with her gifts for the family and stayed for dinner.

The three of us — Nan, Allie, and I — were in the kitchen, finishing up the dishes. Even being a married lady with her own house wasn't enough to keep Nan from helping with chores when she was home. Nan asked how things were at the menagerie and winked at me, and Allie started right in muttering, and to my surprise, Nan rounded on her.

"You just stop that right now, Allison Rothmer!" Nan said. "Or do you want to end up like Rennie?"

"Like Rennie?" Allie said, looking startled and offended. She tossed her head. "Ha! I'm not stupid enough to run off with a Rationalist! I can do better than that."

"Maybe, but the way you're acting, you won't even find a gentleman to talk to, much less one willing to run off with you!" Nan said. "If it bothers you so much that Eff has a beau and you don't, go find one for yourself. Fussing at Eff won't help."

Allie stared at her for a second, then burst into tears. Nan rolled her eyes and went to comfort her. I hung back. I wasn't sure Allie would want me reassuring her just then, especially if all her temper was on account of her being jealous of Mr. Boden and me.

Nan seemed to agree with me. She jerked her head toward the door. I nodded and slipped out. Luckily, Mama and Papa had gone into the study to talk, so I could get upstairs without them seeing. A long while later, Allie came up to join me and apologize.

Things were better at home after that, though Allie never did quite explain why she'd acted as she had. I wondered for a while if Allie fancied Mr. Boden for herself. I watched her carefully for a few weeks whenever he was around, and decided she didn't. It was more that she was three years older than me, and all of our older sisters were married. I think she felt like it should be her turn next, not mine.

When I finally figured that out, I felt more than a bit odd. Roger Boden had been walking me home from the menagerie and stopping in to have tea; it was a long way from that to getting married, I thought. It made me a little nervous around him.

It also made me think a lot. I liked Roger just fine, but I wasn't sure that I liked him the way Mama liked Papa or Nan liked her husband, Gordon. I certainly didn't like him enough to run off with, the way Rennie and Brant had, though when I thought about it, I couldn't see him ever asking me to do something like that. The question was, *could* I like him that way, and did I want to? He was an awfully nice man, and Papa and Professor Jeffries both spoke highly of his prospects. I could be happy with him, if I worked at it, and it wasn't like I had a lot of other suitors banging at our door.

But I wasn't sure I wanted to work at being happy with Roger. I didn't want to get married just because most of my sisters had. I'd had a taste of what things were like on the far side of the Great Barrier Spell, and that was what I wanted to do and where I wanted to be. I still didn't know how I could do that, but I was pretty sure that marrying Roger wasn't the way to get there. And I wasn't ready to settle for second best.

Maybe if Nan and Allie hadn't said anything, I wouldn't have noticed what was going on until much later. Maybe by then I'd have fallen in love with Roger and decided he was first best after all; or maybe I'd have felt that I'd led him on and was obligated to marry him. That wasn't the way things worked out, though, and now I had to make a conscious decision. It would have been a lot easier if I could have just let things happen.

So I was downright skittish when, late in January, Mr. Boden asked if he could have a private word with me before our walk home. "Miss Rothmer," he began, "I wanted to tell you . . . that is, I wanted you to be the first to know that I have had some unexpected good fortune."

I relaxed considerably when I heard that. "Good fortune?" I said.

"Yes," he said. "Professor O'Leary was kind enough to recommend me to one of his colleagues at St. Edmund's, in Albion, for advanced study in applied metaphysics and esoteric geomancy, and not only have I been accepted, he's found me a sponsor."

Applied metaphysics and esoteric geomancy sounded plenty advanced to me, but what I said was, "St. Edmund's? In Oxford? That's one of the oldest schools of magic in Avrupa!"

Mr. Boden nodded. "It is a very great honor, and an opportunity I couldn't pass up."

"Well, of course you couldn't!" I said indignantly. "Who would expect you to?"

"I am very glad you feel that way." He hesitated, then went on. "I will be leaving in two weeks, and I'll be gone for a year. May I write you?"

"Um," I said. "I — once in a while, maybe, just as a friend."

I maybe put a little too much emphasis on those last few words, because his face went still. After a minute he nodded slowly. "Yes, that would be best," he said thoughtfully. "A year is a long time; who knows what may happen?"

"Exactly," I said. I didn't mention that I kind of hoped he'd find a nice girl in Albion who'd suit him better than I would.

Roger Boden left Mill City two weeks later, and it was hard not to heave a sigh of relief to see him go. Winter was usually the slow season at the menagerie, what with so many of the animals hibernating, but that year I was busier than a hen with a double set of chicks. Most of the extra business was coming from Professor Torgeson. I'd been helping her out, off and on, ever since we'd gotten back from the settlements. One of the first things she'd done after we'd unpacked all our specimens was to send off a letter to a friend of hers back East, a Mr. Collingsworth, who worked in historical excavation for the Philadelphia Institute of Magic. She'd told him about the stone animals we'd found, and how we'd found them, and she'd even enclosed one as a sample.

In early fall, she'd started getting letters back. First it was a note from Mr. Collingsworth, mentioning that he'd talked her news over with some of his colleagues. Then it was a couple of letters from other folks, asking for further details about the fragment or reporting on their initial study of the sample. They were all hugely excited by the find, and even though none of them was ready to say exactly what they thought it meant, they all agreed that people should know about it right away, so as to get as many more scholars and magicians and scientists in on helping them figure it all out.

In December, Mr. Collingsworth had an announcement published, telling about the stone fragments and how they'd been found. By February, when Mr. Boden left for Albion, Professor Torgeson was getting baskets full of letters every day, mostly from scientists and magicians who had questions or theories, or who wanted one of the stone animals so they could do some investigating of their own. That was when I started spending more time at her office, helping answer the letters. We didn't have enough stones to give one to everyone who wanted one, but the professor sent a few out to particularly well-known scientists and magicians.

The more pieces the professor sent out, the more letters she got back. Most of the scientists were just as excited as Mr. Collingsworth and his friends, but there were also quite a few who said it was all some kind of hoax. Some of them got down-right nasty about it.

I was more than a little surprised by all the fuss. It wasn't as if the stones were any kind of threat to the settlers; they'd been lying there under the hill since long before the settlements went out that far. I was plenty curious about how they'd gotten there and what they meant, but I couldn't see any reason for people to be mean.

The letters kept coming. It got so I was having to spend all afternoon at Professor Torgeson's office answering letters, or she wouldn't have had time to teach. I received one of my own, from Lan, wanting to know all the details of how we'd found the stone animals and why the professor thought they were real animals that had been turned to stone and not fossils or duplications or some other fancy magical thing that I don't recall the name of. Then, early in March, Mr. Parsons from the Settlement Office showed up in person.

Mr. Parsons had replaced Mr. Harrison as the head of the North Plains Territory Homestead Claims and Settlement Office about three months before we'd left on our survey trip. Since the Settlement Office had pushed for the college to start the wildlife survey right away, Professor Torgeson had sent him copies of her official report as soon as she'd finished it, even before classes started in September. She had a few choice things to say about how long it had taken Mr. Parsons to get around to reading it.

Somewhat to my surprise, Mr. Parsons didn't only keep his temper; he actually apologized and said he'd been wrong to take so long to go over the professor's report. Then he asked to examine some of the stone specimens for himself. He and the professor ended up having a long conversation about the stones, and she even let him look at one through a microscope. After he left, she said he seemed fairly sensible, even if all he was interested in was the stone animals we'd brought back.

A few days later, Mr. Parsons came back. He had a map with him, with all the settlements marked. The ones that had failed were in red, and there was a big crosshatched area showing where the mirror bugs had eaten everything away. He and the professor spent most of the afternoon talking about the plants and wildlife we'd found and where we'd found them, and arguing over what it all meant.

I thought Professor Torgeson would be furious by the time he left, but she was actually rather pleased with herself. I figured that meant she'd won the argument, but she said that Mr. Parsons had suggested sending a group back out to Daybat Creek, where we'd found all the stone animals, to collect some more specimens for study. It wouldn't be a proper historical excavation, just collecting pieces that were easy to pick off the ground already, so that we'd have samples to send to all the people who were asking for them. The professor sounded half disapproving and half glad when she said that.

Then she asked whether I'd come along. "I'd be greatly pleased," I said after I got over being stunned at being asked. Then I paused. "Mama will fuss about me going out West again, especially so soon. It may take me a couple of days to talk her around."

Professor Torgeson smiled. "It will be good to have you along."

When I got home after work, I found Mama in the attic with Mrs. Callahan, pulling out bags and trunks. Neither one took any notice of me, so I went looking for Allie.

"Eff!" Allie said when she saw me. "Thank goodness. You'd better start packing; we don't know yet when the train will be leaving."

"Train?" I asked as Mrs. Callahan banged down the attic stairs with a carpet bag on each arm. "Leaving? Allie, what on earth —"

Allie muttered something under her breath. "That dratted boy didn't find you, did he? I knew I should have come to tell you myself. There's been a huge accident out at Lan's college.

Lan and a bunch of other students were badly injured and one of them was killed."

"Lan's — what happened? How bad is he hurt?"

"Bad enough for them to send for Papa and Mama straight off," Allie said grimly. "They're taking you, too, because you're twins. Papa's down at the train station now, making arrangements."

Right then Nan came flying in the door. "Allie! Eff! What's happened? Are Mama and Papa all right?"

"It's not Mama or Papa," Allie said. "It's Lan." She went over the whole thing once more, which gave it a little time to sink in. Nan and I both had a lot of questions, but Allie didn't really know much more than she'd already said. Finally, she went and got the telegraph message, so we could see for ourselves what it said. She was right; there weren't many particulars. All it said was *Accident at Simon Magus. Lan Rothmer hurt bad with seven others, one dead so far. Advise come East now. Ziegler.*

Allie told us that Mama and Papa had talked about waiting a day or two for the mail train to bring a letter with more details, but they'd decided that it would be better to head East right away. Papa said that Mr. Ziegler, the dean at Simon Magus College who'd sent the telegram, was a reliable person and wouldn't have told them to come all that way if he hadn't thought there was reason.

Finally, Nan and Allie went to the parlor to figure out who they'd need to tell and when to write them. Robbie would find out when he got home; there was no sense in sending someone out to look for him, because his classes were done for the day and he was probably somewhere with his friends. They'd wait a day or two before they wrote Rennie and Jack; since both of them were out in the settlements and mail would be slow getting to them, it'd be best to have as many details as possible before writing them. I thought about writing William, but the letter would go East on the same train as we did, so it made more sense to wait in case there was more news. When Allie started in on who they'd need to tell at the college and at church and how soon, I told them to make sure Professor Jeffries and Professor Torgeson got told right off, and to leave Professor Torgeson's note for me to add a line to, because I wanted to say I was sorry I wouldn't be able to go on her specimen-collecting trip after all. Then I went up to pack.

I didn't think about writing to tell Mr. Boden at all.

CHAPTER
· 20 ·

MRS. CALLAHAN HAD LEFT A CARPET BAG BY MY BED. I CRAMMED A few underthings and an extra skirt and blouse into it any which way, then after a moment added my good Sunday dress, just in case. I didn't really know what I'd need. I hadn't been back East since I was thirteen. The last thing I packed was the broken-winged stone bird I'd brought back from Daybat Creek, so I could show it to Lan when he recovered. If he recovered.

I couldn't think. Twice, I found myself standing in front of the wardrobe, holding the door open and staring at my clothes without really seeing them. There was a hard lump in the middle of my chest that wouldn't go away. I didn't even try to tell myself that Lan was sure to be all right. They wouldn't have sent for Mama and Papa so urgently if they thought there was a good likelihood of that.

Dinner was cold meat and bread and cheese that Mrs. Callahan laid out for us to grab as we rushed around finishing things up so that we could leave the next day. I didn't sleep well that night; I don't think any of us did. Mama had dark circles under her eyes when we caught the train in the morning. Papa just looked tired and strained.

It was a long, quiet trip. Mama held tight to Papa's hand for the first few hours; then she held mine. She went back and forth like that for most of the trip. None of us said much. The train still took nearly two full days to get from Mill City to Philadelphia, so it was late in the afternoon when we finally got off at the platform on Broad Street. As we waited for the porter to finish unloading our baggage, a young man came up to Papa.

"Mr. Rothmer?" he said tentatively. He looked relieved when Papa nodded. "I don't know if you remember me, sir. I'm Nicolas Petrakis; we met when you came to New Amsterdam two years ago. Dean Ziegler got your telegram and sent me to watch for you."

"Mr. Petrakis," Papa said. "How is my son?" That told me just how tired and worried Papa was; normally, he'd have made himself introduce Mama and me first, no matter what.

"Lan's still . . ." Mr. Petrakis hesitated. ". . . unconscious. He's in the Philadelphia Hospital, and he has the best doctors in Philadelphia," he added hastily. "I can take you there now, or —"

"Take us there now," Mama said before he could finish.

Mr. Petrakis looked at her and nodded. He and Papa exchanged a few more words, then we loaded our bags onto the carriage he had waiting and drove straight to the hospital. Mr. Petrakis told us where Mr. Ziegler had arranged for us to stay, and took our bags on for us while we went in to see Lan.

We didn't actually get to see him that day. Lan was in a private room in the Surgery and Magical Injuries wing of the hospital, and the doctors all thought he was still in too delicate a condition to have visitors, even us, though they did say we could come back in the morning. Mama was all set to spend the night in the waiting room, but Papa said there was no point in all of us getting more exhausted than we already were. She still wouldn't leave until she got the hospital people to promise to send a message right away if there was any change in Lan's condition. It wasn't until we got to the hotel that we found out any more about how it had all happened.

Mr. Petrakis was waiting for us with two men and a dark-haired, dark-eyed woman about five or six years older than me. "Miriam!" Mama said when she saw them, and hurried forward.

"Frank will be here tomorrow," Miriam said. "He had some trouble finding someone to take over his patients." I realized she must be my oldest brother's wife. I'd never met her; Frank had gotten married while I was still in upper school, and only Mama and Papa had come East for the wedding. Now that he'd finally finished all of his schooling and his apprenticeship, he was a full-fledged medical magician at the New Amsterdam State Hospital, and already pretty important. There weren't all that many folks who took time to learn both medical and magical healing.

Mama gave Miriam a hug, and then we had a round of introductions. The bearded, brown-haired man was Mr. Ziegler, the dean of Simon Magus College, and the stern, thin-lipped man with the dark hair was Professor Martin Lefevre. As soon as we finished being polite, we went off to one of the sitting rooms to talk, and of course the first thing Papa wanted to know was what had happened.

"As far as we can determine, Professor Warren was demonstrating a series of mid-level construction spells for his sophomore class in comparative magic, and something went wrong," Dean Ziegler said. "The injured students are a bit vague as to exactly what, but it is clear that Professor Warren lost control. Mr. Rothmer managed to protect his classmates; I firmly believe that it is due to his quick action that the only serious injuries were to himself and Professor Warren." He gave Papa a solemn look. "Your son is a hero, sir."

Professor Lefevre snorted. "He shouldn't have needed to be. I'll wager anything you please that Warren was messing about with some of that Hijero-Cathayan foolishness he was so fond of."

"Yes, well, we shouldn't speak ill of the dead," Dean Ziegler said. "And after all, one would expect him to pay some attention to Hijero-Cathayan spells in a class on comparative magic."

"A talent such as young Mr. Rothmer's shouldn't have been wasted in that man's classes in the first place," Professor Lefevre went on as if Dean Ziegler hadn't spoken.

"If Mr. Rothmer hadn't been there, this incident would likely have been far worse," Dean Ziegler pointed out. "In any case, I expect that he'll focus on more traditional forms of magic after this experience."

Papa asked for more details about the spell they thought had gone wrong, and the conversation got technical. I stopped listening and started thinking about what Dean Ziegler and Professor Lefevre had said. Lan had written quite a bit about Professor Warren in his letters, and most of it hadn't been complimentary. I wondered what Lan had thought of Professor Lefevre. I couldn't decide whether Lefevre just disliked Professor Warren, or maybe Hijero-Cathayan magic, or whether he was like all the other folks who made a fuss over Lan for being a double-seventh son.

We didn't talk for much longer. Mama and Papa and I were real tired from the train, and Mama wanted to be at the hospital early in the morning. As soon as the three men from the college left, we went up to our room and fell into bed.

Frank arrived sometime in the middle of the night; he and Miriam were waiting for us when we came down to breakfast in the morning. Having a doctor with us helped when we got to the hospital. Even though Frank didn't work there, the doctors were a lot more willing to tell him what they thought, and they even took him in to see Lan. When he came out, he said that Lan was still unconscious, but they expected him to wake up soon and we'd all be able to see him then. Meanwhile, they only let Mama and Papa in for a few minutes.

We spent the rest of the day at the hospital. Lan didn't wake that day, nor the day after. The doctors frowned more and spent even less time talking to us, even Frank. On top of that, the newspapers got hold of the story and went on about Lan being a double-seven and a hero and saving fifty people from a deadly rogue spell, even though Dean Ziegler told us that there were only eleven students and Professor Warren in the classroom at the time and nobody outside had ever been in danger at all.

So Lan had letters and flowers and gifts piling up from people we didn't even know, as well as letters from all the family, even the cousins and second cousins that Mama and Papa hadn't told yet because there wasn't much to tell. Miriam and I were the ones who ended up answering the letters. Miriam took the huge stack from the people we didn't know at all, and I took the giant one from the family. When your father is a seventh son, and most of his brothers and sisters married, there are a lot of aunts and uncles and cousins, and that was on top of Sharl and Peter and Diane and Julie and all the rest of my older sisters and brothers who'd stayed in the East.

I didn't mind writing my brothers and sisters, but I wondered a bit about the rest of the family. Most of them hadn't liked me much when I was little, and I hadn't seen any of them since I was thirteen. The one letter I was sure about was the one to William. I'd written him the day we got to Philadelphia, to tell him what we knew about Lan. He'd written back right away — a short note to Mama and Papa saying how sorry he was to hear it and that he trusted things would work out well and he hoped we'd let him know when they did. There was also a letter to me that was a lot less formal and polite.

I never really believed everything Lan said about Professor Warren, he wrote, *but I guess he was right after all. I don't know why Lan was taking that class, anyway — he doesn't have the temperament for Hijero-Cathayan magic. Write if you need to, but don't feel as if you have to. You have more important things to do right now.*

I wrote him back right away, even though he'd said not to. It was the one letter I really wanted to answer. All the well-wishing from other people was a nice distraction some of the time, but it got real wearing after a while, especially since we still didn't know if Lan would be all right. Writing William was a comfort, because I didn't have to watch what I said or pretend I was sure everything would be fine.

Pretending everything would be fine got harder and harder as the days went by and Lan didn't wake up. The doctors still wouldn't let us see him, except for Frank, and Mama and Papa for just a few minutes a day. Finally, five days after we arrived, Mama cornered Frank.

"I'd appreciate some more information," she told him, in that tone that said he'd better fess up right now, or else.

Frank sighed. "Mother —"

"Your father has been a professor of magic for nearly fifteen years," Mama interrupted. "I've seen my share of student mishaps, though thank the Lord no one has died of them. Still,

I know what is usual and what isn't, and this isn't. You know more than you're saying. Say."

"I — there isn't much to say." Frank looked at Mama, then Papa, then me. "From everything we know — and we've talked to the other students and examined both them and Lan — the critical period was the first seventy-two hours, and —"

"Critical period?" I interrupted. "What does that mean?"

Frank swallowed hard. "It means Lan should have died then, if he was going to. And if he wasn't, he should have started improving."

"But he hasn't," Papa said heavily.

"No." Frank straightened his shoulders. "It's been more than twice as long as we expected, and he isn't improving. None of the treatments we've tried have helped. I don't think he's going to make it, Mama."

I stared at him, thinking that I should feel upset, or cry. I just felt numb and a little dizzy. It should have been a shock, but after so long, it was almost a relief to know, even though it was sad and horrible, too. Papa's jaw tightened, and then his head jerked, just once. Mama's face went a little whiter, and she nodded, too. "Then there's no reason for us not to stay with him, is there?" she said.

"I suppose not," Frank said. "I'll talk to the floor director. They may not want everyone there at once."

"Then they can come and tell us," Mama said. "We'll be with Lan. All of us. Daniel, Miriam, Eff." She raised her chin and swept out of the waiting room, and we followed her. Frank hesitated, then trailed along behind.

That was the first time they'd let Miriam and me in to see Lan. His room was hardly bigger than the box room in the attic at home, and I could see why they didn't want a crowd of people in there. There was just room for the door to open without hitting the end of the narrow bed. The walls were painted gray, and there were plain, heavy curtains at the one window that had been only partly opened, so the light was dim. It smelled of medicine and sweat and the dusty tang of spent magic.

Lan looked very small and white lying on the bed. I could tell just by looking at him that he wasn't sleeping. He had bandages on the left side of his face and his left shoulder and arm; Frank explained in a low voice that he'd been burned when he'd stopped the spell and protected the other students.

I nodded along with everyone else, but I didn't really take in what Frank was saying. I didn't seem to be able to think at all, or do anything except stand and stare. Mama took the one chair squeezed in beside the bed and held Lan's good hand for a while. Nobody spoke much, and when they did, it was in soft voices, as if we were trying not to wake him. I thought that didn't make much sense, since we'd all have been happier than Christmas if Lan had even moved or grumbled a little in his sleep, but I didn't say anything because I didn't want to upset Mama.

After about half an hour, one of the doctors came in and said we couldn't all stay. I could see Mama was ready to argue, so I volunteered to go back and write some more letters if I could trade places with Miriam later. Mama nodded, and Frank said he'd walk me back to the hotel, so that was two less people for a while, and that seemed to be enough for the doctor.

The minute I got out of the hospital, I felt better. I hadn't noticed how odd and light-headed I'd gotten until then. Frank looked worried and solemn. By the time we got to the hotel, I just felt tired. I told Frank I'd answer some letters and then take a nap, and sent him back to Mama.

As soon as he left, I lay down on the bed without even kicking my shoes off and fell straight asleep, and straight into dreaming. I could tell right off that it was another one of *those* dreams, the ones that were too sharp and clear and orderly to be normal dreams. I'd had another few since the last of the drowning dreams back in September — maybe one every couple of months — but I hadn't thought on them much because they weren't frightening. Mostly, they were just dreams of following the silver cord and watching the woods green up.

This one started off that way, with me following the cord through a forest. The light started going, as if the sun was setting somewhere I couldn't see, and a mist came up in the trees. Something tugged on the cord I was holding, and I nearly dropped it. It was pulling me left, instead of straight on, the way I'd been walking. I stopped moving for a minute, and the tug came again. I turned left and started walking again.

The mist got thicker and thicker, until I couldn't see the trees any longer. I tightened my fingers around the cord; if I accidentally let go of it and lost it in the mist, I'd never find it again.

After a long while, the mist cleared and I was standing in the darkened kitchen of our old house in Helvan Shores. I felt unhappy and uncomfortable; I didn't have a whole lot of good memories from there. The silver cord I'd been following was gone. Everything was quiet and empty and very cold.

I shivered and looked around. The big black stove was barely warm to my touch, but when I opened the fire door I saw a few embers still glowing in the heaped-up ashes of yesterday's cookfire. I gave a Rennie-like sniff, wondering who had left the stove in such a state, and set out to mend matters as best I could.

I started by getting the ash bucket and shovel from their place by the back door and clearing out most of the dead ashes. I left just enough around the embers to keep them from burning out. Then I went through the basket of kindling. I found a couple of likely pieces and a wood knife, and splintered off a dozen long, thin strips for tinder. I frowned. I could tell that I was only going to get one chance at this, and the embers were so low that I couldn't be sure that my tinder would catch. I needed something even finer and easier to light.

I thought for a minute, then took the knife to the hem of

my skirt. Once I had a chunk sliced off, I teased the threads apart as best I could in the dark, until they made a light, fluffy ball in my hand. I stuffed the ball in my pocket for the time being, then carefully opened the fire door again. I scraped some of the ashes out, then made a tent of my tinder strips by leaning them against each other over top of the largest and brightest of the still-glowing embers. Then I pulled the thread-ball from my pocket and poked it in between the tinder strips and the ember, and blew gently.

The ember glowed more brightly. The threads smoked, then flared up. They didn't last long, but they lasted long enough to set fire to the tinder. Quickly, I put a larger piece of kindling up against the tinder, and then another as soon as the first piece caught. In a few more minutes, I had a small but steady fire burning. I added a middling log, then another, and adjusted the grate. As the stove began to heat up and the chill left the kitchen, I woke up.

I felt terrible, all achy and stiff, and my chest felt cold. I got up and poured some water into the washbasin to splash my face, then paced a little to get some of the kinks out. Then I sat down to answer letters, the way I'd promised.

I didn't get much written. I'd been asleep longer than I'd thought, and before I'd written out more than three polite replies, Miriam and Frank were knocking at the door to take me back to the hospital to see Lan.

The fresh air felt good, and without thinking too much about it, I relaxed and started world-sensing. Philadelphia was a busy, bustling city, much larger and with more variety than Mill City, and I wished I could have seen more of it under better circumstances. The walk to the hospital was much too short.

When we reached Lan's room, Frank opened the door for me. I hesitated at the threshold. Nothing had really changed since morning except maybe the angle of the shadows. Mama looked up, and I stepped into the room.

Something heated and thumped hard against my chest, like a spark thrown from a fire when a chestnut pops. I yelped in surprise and fell forward.

CHAPTER · 21 ·

Frank caught my arm to steady me. "Watch your step!" he said, and I could tell that he hadn't noticed anything unusual except me tripping over the threshold. I shook my head, partly to clear it and partly because I didn't see how anyone could not notice that something was wrong. The whole room felt sick and smoky green, like something nasty had gotten burned in the fireplace, and suddenly I knew why I'd felt so tired and dizzy when I left the hospital earlier.

I moved closer to the bed, wondering how long I could stand to stay. Papa made room for me. Mama had the only chair, and she was still holding Lan's good hand. I leaned over to stroke my brother's hair. I could feel his magic, sputtering and popping like water dropped on a hot iron pan. It was as crooked as ever any of my Avrupan spells had been, and without thinking I shoved at it a little to get it back in place, the way I'd been shoving at my spell work for the past two years.

Lan made a whimpering noise. Mama jerked and clutched his hand. "Lan?"

He didn't respond. His magic was still crooked and sputtering, though maybe not quite so much as it had been a minute before. I started to shove at it again, but I remembered the canning jar I'd melted back at Professor Torgeson's office, and decided I'd best not try too much of that. I didn't know what to try instead, though. All I knew was that Lan's magic needed straightening out, and right away.

Frank and Papa leaned forward, but neither of them so much as glanced at me. I realized that they hadn't noticed what I'd done, any more than my teachers at the upper school had ever seen that I was using Aphrikan magic alongside my Avrupan spells. They only saw the results.

I brushed my fingers through Lan's hair again, wondering what I could do. It never occurred to me to say anything to Frank or the other doctors. They'd had a week, and Frank had told us they'd tried pretty much everything they could think of. All the Avrupan spells, anyway.

I found myself wishing that Wash was there, even though I'd never once seen him do any healing. In fact, the only really major magic I'd seen him do was when he got Daybat Creek flowing past the landslide. I remembered him trying to explain to Professor Torgeson how he'd done it. *Aphrikan magic works from the inside*, I thought. *But how do you get inside a person?*

The hot spark at the center of my chest got hotter. I reached out with a tiny trickle of magic, the smallest I could manage, and poked at Lan with it like I was trying to get his attention. I felt a reaction in my magic, even though Lan didn't stir a bit on the bed. I poked again and pointed, picturing in my head how everything was supposed to feel, especially where the crooked bits needed to come straight.

Slowly, I felt Lan's magic start to move. I made encouraging noises in my mind, though I didn't think Lan could hear. It went faster and faster, like the water soaking into the dam at Daybat Creek. I held my breath.

And then I felt everything click into place, like setting the very last piece into a puzzle. Lan's magic stopped popping and sputtering, and the hot ember on my chest faded away to nothing. The sick, smoky feeling in the room began to fade, too, like someone had opened a window and let in a breeze.

I looked around. Nobody else had noticed anything, not even Frank. I thought that was more than a little odd, since he was a magical doctor as well as a medical one. Then I thought about saying something about what I'd done, but I decided not to. It didn't seem to have made much difference, and I was pretty sure that Mama and Papa would fuss at me for interfering if they knew.

An hour later, Lan stirred. "Lan?" Mama said.

"He's — I have to get someone," Frank said, and practically ran out of the room. He came back a few minutes later with another doctor, and right away they shooed all of us back to the waiting room. Mama was quite cross about it; if she hadn't been so worried and tired, she'd have given them a piece of her mind.

After a long while, Frank came out, looking hopeful for the first time in days. "Lan's doing a lot better," he said.

"Is he awake?" Mama asked.

"Not yet," Frank said, and he didn't sound like he was hedging or trying to be optimistic. "Probably not for a while. But he's responding to the healing spells and — well, it's too soon to say, still. But he's improving."

"I want to see him!"

"We can come back in the morning, Mama," Frank said, and Papa agreed.

We all went back to the hotel in a much more hopeful frame of mind. As I changed for bed, I thought about the hospital and Lan's magic, wondering all over again whether I ought to tell someone that I'd poked it until it went back into place. I bent over the washbasin and caught sight of myself in the standing mirror.

There was a round, red mark on my chest, about three inches below my collarbone. It looked like a burn. I straightened up, and the little wooden pendant I always wore, the one that Wash had given me almost two years before, dropped into place on top of it.

I stared at it in the mirror for a minute, then slowly lifted the cord over my head. I dangled it in front of me, staring. I almost expected it to look charred, or maybe to suddenly start glowing, but it just hung there, a plain, polished whorl of wood the size of a robin's egg, with a hole at one side for the cord.

Staring at the pendant wasn't going to tell me anything new. It certainly wasn't going to tell me why it had heated up enough to leave a burn on my chest when I walked into Lan's hospital room that second time. I hung it back around my head, knotting the cord shorter so the wood wouldn't rub against the little burn. As soon as I'd finished washing, I turned down the lamp, climbed into bed, and started the Hijero-Cathayan concentration exercise.

It had been a while since I'd practiced, so it took me a lot longer than I wanted to get into the floaty state of mind that told me I was doing the concentration exercise properly. By the time I did, I was half asleep, but I made myself focus on the wooden pendant, and once again, the spells came clear.

The first thing I noticed was that the spells had changed from what I remembered. I was so surprised that I lost my focus and my concentration both, and had to start over, but at least being surprised woke me up a little.

When I got back on track, I studied the change more carefully. It wasn't as big a difference as I'd thought. The magic of the pendant was layered. The older magic curled into a knot in the center, while the rest of the spells wrapped tightly around them. I still couldn't tell exactly what any of the spells were, but it was plain as day that what had changed was the magic in the outermost layer.

Very cautiously, I poked at the changed places. It was like poking a walnut; nothing happened, except that I got a better sense of the changes. They felt familiar — a little like Lan's magic, a little like Mama's . . . and then it hit me. All the changes felt like *my* magic.

Without thinking, I sat up in bed, yanked the pendant off, and threw it across the room. I stared into the darkness, breathing like I'd been running and thinking about everything I'd ever thought I knew about that pendant. After a long time, I fished it out from behind the dresser where it had fallen. I still didn't know what it did, but Wash had given it to me, and I trusted Wash. Trust or not, though, I was tired of not understanding, and so I was determined to study it some more. I didn't put it on; I just held it in my hands while I did the concentration exercise again.

This time, I tried to look at the other layers of magic, the ones that didn't feel like mine. Sure enough, each and every one of them felt different. And the magic in the next layer down from mine felt like Wash's.

I studied the pendant for a good long time. None of the other magic felt like anyone I knew, which wasn't too surprising. Wash said he'd had the pendant since he was three or four, and I wasn't likely to have met anyone who'd worn it before he had. Most of the early spells seemed to be Aphrikan magic of one kind or another; there was hardly any Avrupan magic at all until the last couple of layers, and most of the Avrupan-type magic was in the layers that went with me and Wash. That made sense, too, if the magician who'd originally made the pendant was Aphrikan.

The really interesting thing was all the don't-notice-it spells. They weren't the oldest magic on the pendant; in fact, the oldest layers weren't hidden at all. Then, right before the layers started to have bits of Avrupan-style magic in them, there were suddenly a whole lot of spells for keeping things hidden and unnoticed. I spent a while studying them, trying to figure out how they'd been cast, but I'd never been too good at building spells in reverse, and these weren't like any other kind of magic I'd ever seen or heard tell about.

Finally, I gave up and just sat there with the pendant in my hands, thinking. I laid out in my mind everything I'd learned about it since Wash had given it to me: It was Aphrikan magic, it could draw off a little magic from whoever wore it (and it obviously had), it was passed from teacher to student, it went cold when I was near someone else who wore something like it — I stopped. Something was tickling the back of my brain.

I tried to remember whether the pendant had ever done anything like that at other times. Well, besides heating up when I walked into Lan's hospital room. *Hot and cold*, I thought. *Has it ever heated up or gone cold before?*

And then I had it. Every time I'd woken up from one of those odd dreams, the ones that seemed so clear, I'd been cold. I had connected it with the dreams, not with the pendant, but what if it was more than just the one thing?

It felt right, though I still didn't have any idea why the pendant might be giving me dreams. Maybe I could get Wash to tell me, now that I'd figured out this much on my own. I snorted. He'd probably just smile and nod and look approving without actually saying anything more, and I'd have to study up some more on my own. I made a face. I was surely giving myself a lot of studying to do, for someone who wasn't in school any longer.

I set the pendant on the nightstand and lay back, trying to relax. Even so, it was a long time before I fell asleep. I didn't remember any of my dreams, but I slept better than I ever had in as long as I could remember.

Lan woke up late the next morning, in the middle of all of us visiting. He saw me first and squinted, like he didn't quite believe his eyes. "Eff?"

"Lan!" Mama's lips trembled, like she didn't know whether to smile or cry. I felt tears in my eyes. I'd wanted to believe that he would be all right, ever since I'd poked his magic back where it belonged, but I'd been afraid to believe it until right that minute.

"Mama?" Lan licked his lips. "What are you doing here?" Suddenly, his eyes went wide. "The lake spell! What happened?"

"Lake spell?" Papa said. "I thought you were working on construction scaffolding."

"Later, Daniel," Mama said firmly. "Lan, something went wrong with a spell in one of your classes, and you were badly hurt. We've been very worried, but you'll be fine now."

"What about —" Lan stopped. I could tell he wanted to know something, but was afraid to ask.

"Some of your classmates were injured, but you were the worst of them," Papa said. He smiled. "Dean Ziegler tells me it was your doing that none of the students were more seriously hurt. I am very proud of you."

Lan flinched. "Students," he mumbled. He raised his head, looking scared to death. "And Professor —"

"That's enough talking for now, Lan," Mama interrupted. "You need to rest and recover."

"But —"

"Excuse me," said a polite and utterly unapologetic voice from the doorway. We turned to find yet another doctor standing there. He scolded us for not having fetched someone the very minute Lan woke up, and sent us all back to the waiting room.

We saw Lan again in the afternoon. He didn't say much, and when we left, Mama commented that he seemed tired and it was no wonder after all he'd been through.

I didn't think Lan was tired. I thought he was downcast and worried. I wondered whether they'd told him yet that Professor Warren was dead. The doctors didn't want to say right off, on account of not wanting to give Lan a bad shock when he was only just recovering, but sooner or later, he'd have to know.

Frank went back to New Amsterdam the next morning; he'd been away from his patients longer than he liked already, and with Lan on the mend, he didn't need to stay. Miriam stayed with us for another few days. Mostly, we divided our time between visiting at the hospital and writing letters to everyone telling them that Lan was going to be all right. Papa sent a telegram back to Nan and Allie and Robbie, and Frank said he'd let the family in Helvan Shores know when he passed through on his way to the city, but there was still a heap of other folks to let know.

Since I seemed to do most of the writing, I started a letter to William right off. I wrote Roger Boden, too; it hadn't seemed right to write before, when it would take so long for a letter to get to Albion that by the time he got to worrying everything would be over. I had to put both letters aside a couple of times when Mama thought of someone else who needed to know how Lan was, or to be thanked for inquiring after him. I wrote Roger a straightforward account of everything that had happened, with as much detail as I had about the spell that had gone wrong and the treatments the doctors had used, because I knew he'd be interested in that. William's letter turned into a long ramble about everything that had happened and what I felt about it, including my worries about Lan and the business with the pendant that I didn't feel I could tell anyone else. It was the only letter I didn't mind writing, because it was the only one where I could tell the truth as I saw it.

And the truth was, the more I saw of Lan, the less sure I was that he was "all right," or likely to be so anytime soon. Oh, his burns were healing, and so was the damage inside him that they hadn't told us about right off. The doctors said that with magic as strong as his, he'd be back to normal in no time. Nobody but me seemed to notice the shadows in his eyes, or the way he flinched when anyone talked of the accident (even before they told him about Professor Warren), or that he hardly spoke except when somebody asked him a question.

I tried once to say something about it, but Papa and the doctors said it was a normal reaction to being hurt so badly, and that Lan would be fine once he got his strength back. I thought they were wrong, but it was plain nobody would listen to me, and I wasn't sure what they could do, anyway. So I let it go, and only complained in my letter to William. It ended up being four pages long and needing an extra stamp, and I had to apologize at the end for taking so long to write it when he ought to have been told about Lan straight off, as soon as he woke up.

The doctors let Lan out of the hospital two weeks later. His injuries had mostly healed up, but he was still shaky and weak. Mama and Papa had a long talk one night, and the next day Papa went out and hired a house for a while. Mama and Lan and I moved in, and Papa went back to Mill City and his students.

Slowly, Lan got stronger, but he stayed quiet and gloomy. A week after he got out of the hospital, he came down to breakfast and said, "I'm not going back to Simon Magus, Mama."

"What?" Mama looked up from her tea and eggs with a startled expression.

"I'm not going back to school," Lan repeated in a low voice. "I can't — I just — I'm not."

"It's all right, Lan," Mama said after a minute. "The year is almost over, and after what you've been through, I'm not sure it would be a good idea, anyway. By the fall —"

"I'm not going back ever," Lan interrupted. His right hand was clenching and unclenching at his side; Mama couldn't see it from where she sat, but I was on the same side of the table as Lan, and I could. "Not ever, Mama. I mean it."

Mama looked stricken. "Sit down and have breakfast, you," I told Lan before Mama could come up with something to say.

Lan gave me a look like one of the wild animals in the menagerie about to bolt. I rolled my eyes at him.

"Sit," I said to him. "You don't have to settle everything right this very minute."

"I suppose not." He glanced at Mama, and the wild look left him. He pulled out a chair and sat next to me, bowing his head. He wasn't clenching his fist anymore, but I could see that his hands were shaking before he shoved them under the edge of the tablecloth to hide them.

Mama's eyes narrowed just a hair, and she looked from me to Lan and back. Then she nodded once. I reached for the teapot and poured for Lan, then dumped a big spoonful of eggs in the middle of his plate. He looked up, startled.

"Eat now, talk later," I told him sternly.

"Eff," he started uncertainly, "I —"

"You aren't all the way better yet," I said. "And you're going to need the energy once the knocker starts up."

Lan groaned, but he nodded and picked up his fork. Once word got out that Lan was well, or at least improving, we'd had a steady stream of visitors — first the students who were in the accident with Lan, to thank him for whatever he'd done to save them; then his friends from other classes and from the rooming house where he usually lived; then his professors and a bunch of important folks from all over the city who, as far as I could tell, just wanted to be able to say they'd met a double-seventh son.

Lan was polite enough to everyone, but I could tell that he hated every bit of attention worse than ever I had. He tried to change the subject whenever anyone brought up the accident, and he'd get real quiet if people wouldn't let up on it. Once he even walked out of the room in the middle of a conversation. Mama was not happy, and read him a lecture on manners like he was ten again, instead of almost twenty.

By the end of April, we'd been in Philadelphia over five weeks. Lan was a lot better, except for still being as twitchy as anything. Mama decided that it was time for us to get back to Mill City, and asked Dean Ziegler to get the train tickets for us. The next thing we knew, the college had decided to throw

Lan a farewell dinner. Lan didn't want to go, but Mama gave him another talking-to and he finally agreed.

Two nights before we left for Mill City, the three of us dressed in our Sunday best and went off to Simon Magus College for what we thought was going to be a quiet dinner with the faculty and a few students.

CHAPTER · 22 ·

Simon Magus College had about five times as many students as the Northern Plains Riverbank College where Lan and I grew up, and a whole lot more buildings crammed into a whole lot less space. It was one of the oldest colleges of magic in the United States, and one of the best, too, or at least that's what everyone always said. Dean Ziegler certainly thought it was good; he spent most of the carriage ride from our hired house to the college telling Mama and me about all the awards the school had won, and all the important spells they'd developed since they were founded in 1694. Lan didn't even pretend to be interested, but I don't think Dean Ziegler expected him to be.

When we came to the college and got out of the carriage, Dean Ziegler pointed out important buildings as we walked up to the refectory. Most of them were square, three-story red-brick buildings with white window trim. They looked nice enough, but they were all so similar that even two minutes after Dean Ziegler told us, I couldn't have said which one was the Department of Alchemical Science and which was the Experimental Spell Design Laboratory.

The college refectory, where they were having the dinner, was different. Dean Ziegler said it was because it was the first building they'd put up, and the magicians who'd founded the college wanted it to impress people, so they'd gotten together and used magic to build it faster and better than anything else in Philadelphia at the time. It was two stories tall and made of large granite blocks, with a low peaked roof that stuck out over the front doors. In front, a row of tall pillars held up the stuck-out part of the roof, and a row of narrow windows with pointed tops ran along both sides, like the windows of a church.

When we got inside, it was even more like an old church, because it was all one big room and the windows were stained-glass pictures of important events in the history of magic. The first window showed the Unknown Pharaoh guiding the Nile floods into the Egyptian fields; the second one showed Pythagoras at his desk, writing out the numerical foundations for magic; and so on. The floor — what we could see of it — was stone tiles that made a picture. I couldn't tell what, because most of it was hidden under tables draped in white tablecloths.

The room was full of people, or it seemed that way, even though only about half of the seats at the long tables were filled. Dean Ziegler led us to a platform at the far end, where there was another long table raised up so everyone could see it. Lan and Mama and I were supposed to sit there with most of the faculty, right in the middle with Dean Ziegler and the president of the college.

They put Lan with the president on his right and Mama and Dean Ziegler on the president's right. I was on Lan's left. I was relieved to find Professor Lefevre on my other side; at least I'd met him before. I'd have remembered him from that first day in Philadelphia, when he'd sniffed about poor Professor Warren and Lan needing to be a hero, but he'd also come to the house twice with Dean Ziegler to pay his respects to Mama and Lan.

I sat quietly for a few minutes, watching the crowd, until Professor Lefevre asked how I was and what I thought of the college. I wanted to roll my eyes, but that would have been very impolite, so I only said I was fine and that the college was a lot larger than I was accustomed to. Then he asked what I thought of the refectory.

"It's a pretty building," I said without thinking, "and it certainly holds a lot of people!"

Professor Lefevre snorted. "Under *normal* circumstances, there is more than enough room for students and their guests."

"This isn't normal?"

The professor's mouth twisted. "Three-quarters of Philadelphia society has spent the last week angling for an invitation to this dinner."

"Looks to me as if at least half of them managed to get one," I said before I thought.

Professor Lefevre's lips twitched. "Very nearly," he said. "You disapprove?"

"I'm not used to so many people all at once," I said. "You could fill up two or three whole settlements with just the folks at one table, I think."

The professor gave me a skeptical look.

"Really," I said. "Well, the newer settlements, anyway. The Settlement Office figures on ten families or the equivalent, plus one settlement magician. Those long tables have at least twenty-five people on a side, looks like, so —" I shrugged.

"You're very knowledgeable about the frontier settlements."

"Anyone in Mill City could tell you that much. Everybody knows the settlement rules. But I have a sister and brother who are out in the West, and I spent a lot of the last two summers in the settlements myself. Not *by* myself," I added hastily. "Nobody goes out West alone, except the circuit magicians and maybe a couple of crazy fur trappers."

The professor looked interested, so I told him about Wash and the two trips I'd made, first to the Oak River settlement the summer when the grubs were eating everything, and then with Professor Torgeson and Wash on the wildlife survey. He listened very carefully, and when he started in asking questions about the stone animals we'd found, it was pretty obvious why.

"I've read the published accounts of this . . . discovery," he told me. "It sounds unlikely." I could tell he was trying hard to be polite and not say straight out that it was all a hoax, the way some of the letters to Professor Torgeson did.

I sighed. I'd gotten tired of answering those letters a long while back; it was one of the things I hadn't missed about home since we'd been in Philadelphia. I hadn't figured on getting the same questions out here. "I haven't read what the papers said, but I was there when Professor Torgeson found the first one, the squirrel's paw. What I said is what happened."

"You just stumbled across these . . . statues?" he said, giving me a sharp look. "I thought that area had been thoroughly explored and mapped; it seems unlikely that someone would miss such a . . . unique find."

"The folks at Promised Land said they've been finding bits of the stone in Daybat Creek since they settled there," I told him. "But what washes down the stream is too small to notice anything special about. And the ones we found were mostly in the part where the hill collapsed."

"Ah, yes, that convenient landslide."

I frowned at him. "It wasn't convenient. The settlement at Promised Land would have been flooded for sure, if Wash hadn't cleared the blockage. The professors in the Agriculture and Land Sciences Department said that it probably would have happened sooner or later, anyway, but it happened when it did on account of the grubs eating away all the grass and tree roots that usually held everything together."

"Runoff erosion," Professor Lefevre said thoughtfully.

I nodded. "They had a fair bit of rain in the early summer, so the ground was soaked and the creek was high. And it was a cold, snowy winter before that, and winter ice can cause problems along riverbanks all by itself."

"Very true." The professor looked amused. "That still doesn't explain how a cartload of statues ended up under a hill in the middle of nowhere."

"Nobody knows how many there are," I corrected him. "I'd guess it's a lot more than a cartload, though, especially if there's more than one hill's worth of them. And they're not statues — at least, not the normal sort. Even magicians use chisels and punches and sanding tools to finish off their statues, and there aren't any tool marks, even under a microscope."

"So you, at least, are convinced these are petrified animals?"

"I don't see what else they could be," I said. "They have stone bones and stone veins and stone stomachs and stone everything on the inside. What else would do that?"

Professor Lefevre looked shaken. "Some sort of natural process, then," he said, half to himself. "Like those fossils that Albionese fellow came up with."

"I wouldn't know about that," I said. "And Professor Torgeson won't say what she thinks."

"No?" He gave me another sharp look.

"She hates telling people anything until she has enough information to be really sure it's right," I said. "She didn't want to tell anyone about the problems growing magical plants straight off, either, even though she was sure herself. Wash had to be pretty firm about persuading her that people cared more about getting a good crop that year than about whether she was as right as she wanted to be."

"Magical plants?" said the professor, raising an eyebrow.

So I had to explain about the grubs absorbing magic and the mirror bugs moving it away to where the mirror bug traps were, and how it was going to take a couple of years for everything to even out so that most of the settlements in the grubbed-over area could grow magical crops again.

"Commendable," Professor Lefevre said when I'd finished. "And was there any magical residue where you found those statues? Or whatever they are," he added quickly when I frowned.

"I don't think so," I said. "The grubs had pretty well killed the forest; there were some natural plants coming back, but I didn't see anything magical. Or sense it."

He nodded, pleased. "A natural fossilization process, then."

"Maybe, if it was really fast," I said. The professor gave me a questioning look. "A lot of the stone animals we found looked like they were caught in the middle of moving," I said. "The bird I brought back still has its wings open, like it was landing on a branch. I didn't think natural fossilization could work that fast." I'd learned quite a bit about the subject in the course of answering Professor Torgeson's mail.

"You have one of these statues?" Professor Lefevre sounded slightly disapproving.

"It's not one of the best ones, but I like it," I said. "If you'd like to see it, I have it in my bag back at the house."

"You brought it to Philadelphia? And didn't mention it to anyone?"

"I thought Lan would be interested," I said. "And it's my personal sample. I brought it back my own self, for a memento, not for some laboratory to take to pieces."

"I beg your pardon," Professor Lefevre said stiffly. "I meant no offense."

"I expect not," I said. I gave another little sigh. "You can still look at it if you like, but you'll have to come by the house tomorrow. We're leaving the day after, and Mama and I are going to be packing."

"I shall make time to stop in," Professor Lefevre said. "It's a pity your Professor Torgeson won't send more samples for testing; I'm sure that with the laboratories here we could find out a great deal."

"There aren't any more samples to send yet," I said, feeling annoyed all over again. He gave me a skeptical look, and I glared at him. "We had one packhorse for the three of us, and we'd already collected a fair lot of wildlife samples. And whatever they were once, now they're rocks. There's only so much room in a couple of saddlebags, and only so much weight a packhorse can carry."

"Yet?" the professor said, ignoring all the rest of what I'd said.

"I'm not sure whether I'm supposed to say anything about

it," I said. Then I shook my head. "I suppose it's too late now. Professor Torgeson is planning to take a string of mules out to Daybat Creek to pick up some more samples. Just the loose ones in the part of the hill that collapsed," I added quickly. "She wants to leave as much as she can just how it is, in case they can get some historical excavators interested."

"I won't mention it to anyone," Professor Lefevre promised.

"I can ask Professor Torgeson to send you some of the ones she brings back," I offered.

"I would appreciate it very much, Miss Rothmer."

Right about then, the president of the college stood up and everyone in the refectory quieted down. By then, all the seats were full of people, so it took a minute for the noise to taper off. The president gave a little speech about how welcome everyone was and how we were all there to honor Lan for being a hero. I could feel Lan getting tense and twitchy again, so I reached over under the tablecloth and patted his hand. He gave me a grateful look and settled down.

Dinner was served by a lot of young men wearing vests with the Simon Magus College crest on the left side. Lan whispered that they were mostly freshmen, and they'd probably volunteered because it was the only way they could get in to such a good dinner. After dinner, there were more speeches, and a man came up to give Lan a gold pocket watch from the families of all the students he'd saved from being injured.

When he realized what was going on, Lan went white and grabbed my hand under the table. He held on so hard it hurt all the way through the speech, and almost didn't let go when he had to stand up to take the watch.

"I don't deserve this," he said to the man holding the watch.

The college president smiled. "Let us be the judge of that, my boy," he said.

For a minute, I thought Lan was going to refuse completely, but then he just nodded and took the watch. He held it for a minute, staring at it without speaking. Mama gave him a little frown. He looked at her blankly for a second, then turned back to the college president and the man who'd brought the watch and thanked them politely before he sat down.

I spent the rest of the evening trying to watch Lan without anyone noticing that I was worried about him. Lots of people came up to him to talk once all the speeches were done, including most of the students who'd been hurt and their parents. Lan seemed on edge and unhappy for the whole time. Even Mama noticed. She persuaded the college people that we needed to get home early, since Lan was still recovering.

On the way home, Mama gave Lan a gentle lecture about manners and modesty and not insulting people by refusing their gifts or telling them they were wrong when they spoke highly of you. Lan almost said something to her, but he stopped. Then he just nodded.

When we got to the house, I told Mama I wanted a glass of water from the kitchen. I was hoping to catch Lan by himself and find out what he was brooding about, and sure enough, when I came back a few minutes later, she'd gone up to bed, just as I'd hoped. Unfortunately, Lan seemed to have gone, too. Then I saw the sitting room door ajar, even though it was dark on the other side. I peeked through.

Lan was standing at the front window in the dark. He'd drawn back the curtains, and I could see his silhouette against the yellow glow of the gas lamps all along the street outside. I slipped inside and closed the door.

"Lan?" I said. "What's wrong?"

"They all think I'm a hero," he said, so softly I hardly heard him. "But I'm not."

"Lan —"

"I'm *not*, Eff!" He shuddered. "It was my fault."

"The accident?"

He bowed his head. "I'm the one who made the spell go awry. It's my fault that all those people were hurt and Professor Warren is dead. I tried to tell Dean Ziegler and Papa, but they think I'm just being hard on myself because I couldn't save everyone."

"But you did save some people?" I said uncertainly.

"I suppose," Lan said. "After it all went wrong. But I'm the one who sent it wrong in the first place. And they don't believe me, and they wouldn't listen when I tried to explain, and now it's too late."

I walked over to one of the chintz-covered chairs and sat down. "It's not too late for me to listen," I said. "And I will." I tightened my fingers around the glass I was holding, and waited.

CHAPTER
· 23 ·

Lan stood silhouetted against the window for the longest time. When he finally began to speak, he kept his back toward me, as if he could pretend he was just talking to himself as long as he couldn't actually see anyone else in the room.

"I wrote to you about Professor Warren last summer," he said after a while. "When he had Michael and me working on spell classifications. Do you remember?"

"Yes," I said very softly, once it was clear that he expected me to answer.

"I didn't like him." Lan was quiet again for a long time. "Now I wish I had, even though that would make everything worse, some ways."

I nodded, even though he couldn't see me.

"He taught the class in comparative magic," Lan went on. "You know, Avrupan and Aphrikan and Hijero-Cathayan magic, and how different they are. He says — he said — that Avrupan magic is about analysis and control, Hijero-Cathayan magic is about passion and direction, and Aphrikan magic is about insight and assurance. I never understood what he meant." He paused. "I don't think I ever really tried to understand."

It seemed to me that understanding such a fuzzy description would take a powerful lot of trying, but I stayed quiet.

"Last summer, he had a bunch of us working at classifying some of the new spells the Hijero-Cathayans have been developing. They're really interesting, Eff — the Zhejiang Provincial School of Advanced Magic has done some amazing . . . never mind. The point is, Michael and I wanted to learn some of the spells, but Professor Warren said we didn't have enough control." His shoulders twitched irritably. "So we started working on them by ourselves."

"Lan!" I burst out, horrified. "How could you? Hijero-Cathayan magic is horribly dangerous!"

"It's not that bad," Lan said. He half turned to look at me, and I could see his frown in the dim light from the street lanterns. "They've been doing it for nearly three thousand years, after all. And we didn't have any trouble." He turned back to the window. "Not then," he added so softly that I almost missed it.

After another long pause, Lan went on. "There was one spell in particular, for dredging a lake, that I really wanted to learn. It uses the circulation of the lake water to support the spell, almost the way the Great Barrier Spell uses the flow of the river, and I thought if I could understand it properly . . ."

His voice trailed off, but I knew my brother well enough to know what he was going to say. The Great Barrier Spell was an amazing piece of magic, and nobody really knew how Mr.

Franklin and Mr. Jefferson had gotten it to work. If Lan could explain even one little piece of it, his name would be made. If he could duplicate it, the settlements in the West wouldn't need palisades or even settlement magicians anymore.

A carriage rattled by outside, the only one we'd seen since we'd been sitting there. I wondered how late it was.

Lan sighed. "Professor Warren caught us before we got everything set up to try the spell. He read us a lecture worse than Mama's, and after that, Michael wouldn't help. And you can't cast Hijero-Cathayan spells alone; they all take more than one person."

I nodded again. The way they explained it in day school, Hijero-Cathayan magic takes a team of magicians to work, but it's not like the teams of magicians we use. When Avrupan magicians work together, each of them takes one tiny piece of the spell and does just that one thing. Avrupan team magic takes a lot of control and precision to work, because if everyone's bits and pieces don't fit together exactly right, the whole spell falls apart and nothing happens.

Hijero-Cathayan magicians do the whole spell together, all of them at once, with a master magician or adept guiding the group. That means they have a lot of power — Hijero-Cathayans have spells for damming up rivers and carving roads out of mountains that take just one spell and a few hours to do all that work — but if anyone slips, all that power can burn out the master magician and injure the whole group.

My thoughts stuttered, and all of a sudden I had a sick, awful feeling that I knew where all Lan's rambling was going.

"— took his class, anyway, because I hoped he'd actually teach the spells," Lan was saying. I'd missed some. "But he didn't. He'd show us an Avrupan spell, and then he'd set up for a Hijero-Cathayan spell that did something similar, but he always stopped short of actually casting it. All year long." He banged his fist against the window frame, not hard, just frustrated.

"So last month, when Professor Warren set up for the Hijero-Cathayan lake-dredging spell . . ." Lan paused, and swallowed hard. ". . . when he set up the spell, I went ahead and finished the casting. I thought it would be just for a minute, just to show him it would work, we could handle it. Only . . ."

There was a long silence. "Only it didn't work," I said at last.

Lan gave a harsh laugh. "Oh, it worked; that was the problem. Nobody but me was ready for it to work. I thought I would be the head magician, because I'd finished the casting, but I guess Hijero-Cathayan spells don't work like that. Professor Warren set everything up — he was the teacher, he was the focus. And he couldn't hold us all — he wasn't strong enough. He couldn't . . . he couldn't hold me."

My eyes widened as I realized what Lan was saying. He was the seventh son of a seventh son, with more magic than pretty near any other magician there was. Pouring all that magic into a Hijero-Cathayan spell that no one was expecting in the first place . . . well, I'd wager it'd be a problem for even a really experienced Cathayan adept. For Professor Warren . . .

"I could tell it was all going wrong, but I couldn't do anything about it. Professor Warren was the head of the team. All our magic, from all eleven of us, went straight to him. All of my magic. I couldn't stop it.

"I burned him out," Lan whispered. "Me. My magic. I killed him."

I stayed quiet.

"I almost killed everyone else, too."

"You almost died yourself," I said.

"I should have. I should —"

"No," I said firmly. The word hung in the air almost as if it was a spell, louder and clearer than anything either of us had said.

For a minute, Lan stood like he'd been turned to one of those gray-white stone statues Professor Torgeson had been collecting. Then he turned and, for the first time since we'd started talking, peered into the dark where I was sitting. "But —"

"No," I said again. "I won't say it's not partly your fault, and I won't say you shouldn't feel bad about what you did. But talking about dying makes it worse, not better. It's bad enough that your professor died and people got hurt. More people dying doesn't make up for what happened; it only makes things harder for everyone who's left."

"Everyone who's left?"

"Mama and Papa," I said. "All our brothers and sisters — Robbie and Allie and Nan and Frank and everybody. Your friends here — I don't know their names, but you had more visitors than the hospital would let in, and a heaping pile of get-well notes and letters besides." I frowned at him. "Me."

Lan looked away. "I've let everybody down, haven't I?"

"I don't know," I said. "You messed up, right enough, but it isn't like you meant for anyone to be hurt, let alone —" Lan flinched, so I stopped right there.

"Does it matter that I didn't mean it? People did get hurt, and Professor Warren . . . I don't think I can ever make up for it."

"Lan!" I snapped. "I've been trying to be nice about this, but you're being as thick in the head as the wall the menagerie built to keep the baby mammoth inside! Moping around isn't going to make anyone feel better, not you and not anybody else. If you want to blame someone, you might as well blame me."

Lan's head jerked up. "It's not your fault! How could it be? You weren't even there."

"Exactly," I said. I knew what he was thinking. I'd spent years and years feeling bad about everything that went wrong anywhere around me, because I was sure that it all happened on account of me being a thirteenth child and unlucky, and he thought I was back at it again. But I'd learned a thing or two in the past three years, and one of them was when I ought to figure things were all my fault and when not.

But Lan was just as used to needing to talk me out of blaming myself as I was used to doing the blaming in the first place. I told him that, and then I added, "What you don't see is that for all the times you helped me keep from trouble that hadn't ought to have been mine in the first place, there were just as many times when I helped you duck trouble that really ought to have been yours."

"There were not!"

"Oh?" I shook my head. "What about that time you floated William treetop high when we were ten? All right, you maybe would have let him down easy if I hadn't been there to talk at you, but then again, maybe not. And you were all set to lay into Uncle Earn at least twice when we went out to Diane's wedding, if I hadn't gotten to him first. And —"

"All right!" Lan held up his hands and almost smiled.

"So if I'd come East to school the way you wanted me to, I'd maybe have seen enough to talk you out of making such a mess of things this time, too," I finished.

"You can't blame yourself for that!"

"No more than you should take more blame than you have coming," I told him, ignoring the little voice in the back of my head that said I was, too, to blame. I'd gotten a lot better at ignoring it, but it was still there at times like this. "It's harder for you, because there's no denying that you did something you shouldn't have, and it's only right that you should try to make up for it. But you have to do more than dwell on everything that went wrong."

"If I don't think about it, I might do it again," Lan said. "Not — not a Hijero-Cathayan casting, but something else that'll end up with people hurt and — and —"

"I didn't say not to think about it," I said. "I said not to *only* think. Sitting around doing nothing because you're scared of messing up again isn't going to help anyone."

"I know. I just —" Lan raised his hands, then let them fall helplessly.

Neither of us spoke for a while. Then I said, "I think you should tell Papa what happened."

"I tried!"

"How hard?" Lan was quiet. I nodded. "I think you should try again. Sometime when he isn't so distracted. Then you can figure out who else needs to know and how to tell them."

"I don't want anyone else to know," Lan muttered.

"You told me." I studied the dark shape against the window. "And what about Professor Warren? You're the only one who knows everything that happened; according to Dean Ziegler, all the other students were confused and couldn't explain anything after Professor Warren set up the spell. If you don't say what happened, they'll likely put the blame on him, and that's not right."

"No, it isn't." Lan sighed. "You fight dirty, Eff."

"Think about it, anyway," I said. "You made a bad choice, and some of it can't ever be fixed. But you have a lot more choices coming up. The important thing is to try really hard not to make another one this bad, ever again."

He nodded. We stayed a long time in companionable silence, watching the gaslights and the shadows they cast on the street outside. Finally, Lan pushed away from the window and walked over to where I was sitting. He didn't speak; he just put a hand on my shoulder and gave a gentle squeeze, then went on out of the room.

Lan was still quiet and unhappy at breakfast, but not quite as much as he had been. Not that I had a lot of time to watch him. It was our last day in Philadelphia, so everyone we'd met came to call and wish us a good journey, and a bunch of new folks dropped in because it was their last chance to meet up with us.

Professor Lefevre came early in the day, and I showed him the stone bird with the broken-off wings. He'd brought a magnifying lens, and he studied it carefully the same way Professor Torgeson had when we first found the statues. I could see he was surprised, and right away he started muttering about his laboratory and testing. I took my bird back before he could get too excited, and promised him again that I'd make sure we sent him a good sample as soon as the collectors got home.

Next day, we boarded the train for the two-day trip back to Mill City. It rained most of the way. Mama occupied herself with tatting a lace trim for a baby bonnet to send off to the next grandchild, and Lan and I sat and read.

As soon as we were home, I went back to work for Professor Jeffries and Professor Torgeson. I was surprised to see Professor Torgeson that first day. I'd expected her to be off collecting more stone animals, but she said that between finishing up teaching her classes and making arrangements for all the mules and a guide, she'd be lucky to leave town before July. Then she asked if I still wanted to come along.

I hesitated. Lan was still brooding, and I didn't want to leave him on his own. Of course, with Mama and Papa and Allie and Robbie, he wouldn't exactly have been alone much. Professor Torgeson very kindly gave me some time to think on it, and that night over supper, I brought it up.

The next thing I knew, Papa took the notion to send *both* me and Lan along with the professor. He'd noticed the way Lan was dragging around the house, and he decided that a trip to the West would be just the thing to take his mind off his troubles. That's what Papa said, anyway; I had a strong suspicion that he and Lan had finally sat down for that talk I'd suggested, and Papa wanted Lan off doing something useful when he broke it to the rest of the family.

What with the sample-collecting trip being mostly a college project, it wasn't too hard for Papa to arrange for Lan to go on it. For the next couple of weeks, Lan came over to the office house with me. Between the two of us, we got caught up on all the mail the professor had gotten, and we even made a list of all the people who'd asked for samples of the stone animals after we ran out.

Working with the professor seemed to cheer Lan up some, but he wasn't the same as he had been. Robbie commented on it once when Lan wasn't around, and Allie lit into him good and proper. She said that almost dying from a bad spell was enough to sober up anyone, and Lan was a lot more grown up now, and that was a very good thing.

Robbie shook his head, but he didn't try to argue with her. I was pretty sure he suspected more than he let on, though. He'd spent more time with Lan when we were growing up than Allie had, and knew him better than any of our other brothers. I half expected him to badger me for information, but he didn't. He only came close to admitting that he was worried once, when he and I were talking about the sample collecting.

"You'll be safe out there?" he asked me.

"I expect I will," I said. "It's plenty dangerous, but we did all right last summer."

"Fine for you," Robbie said. "But I don't know about Lan, after all that's happened." He paused, then looked me straight in the eye. "You take care of him."

"Of course I will," I said. "He's my twin."

"Right, then."

And that was all he ever said about it in my hearing.

Once the semester was over, it didn't take as long as Professor Torgeson had predicted to get the sample-collecting trip put together. The Homestead Claims and Settlement Office had been working on it all along, and by the second week in June, two days after Lan and I turned twenty, we made the crossing to West Landing.

There were so many of us that we pretty near filled the ferry all by ourselves. There was Lan and me and Professor Torgeson, plus two of Professor Torgeson's students who were to help with the specimen gathering. All of us had horses, plus two pack animals, and the college had arranged for two mule-teers and eight mules to meet us on the far side of the river.

Our guide was a tall, whip-thin man with raggedy blond hair and three scars down the side of his right cheek where something had clawed for his eye and barely missed. His name was Lawrence Jinns, and I never met a grumpier, more close-mouthed man. He knew his job, though. Mules and all, we got on the road out of West Landing less than two hours after the ferry docked.

The trip out to Daybat Creek took us a bit under two weeks this time, even with the mules. Instead of swinging south around the lakes and marshes straight west of Mill City, we went north and then angled west and north through Water Prairie, Mammoth Hill, Wyndholm, and Hoffman's Ford to Adashome. From Adashome, we followed Daybat Creek downstream through the hills to where the landslide had dammed it up.

The third day out from West Landing, we ran across a bison herd, and later on we saw a couple of prairie wolves following it. Luckily, the wolves were interested in the bison calves, not us, and they didn't give us any trouble. Mr. Jinns shot a porcupine one day and made soup at the wagonrest later. It was pretty good soup, too. Other than that, we didn't see much wildlife except for a few birds.

Once we passed Mammoth Hill, the land was still coming back from the grub-killing. Where there was open prairie, the only sign left was a lack of magical plants, but the natural plants like bluestem grass and coneflowers and catchfly had grown back so tall and thick that if you didn't look close, you wouldn't know anything had happened. Wherever there'd been woods, though, the bare, dead trunks still stood black against the sky. Even in the dead woods, though, there was new growth — young birches and aspens poking up knee-high like they were in a hurry to replace what was gone, and weeds and bushes that had only needed light to sprout up.

Lan wasn't talkative on the trip out, but he didn't seem as gloomy as he'd been. I thought it helped that he was out of doors and away from people he knew. Mr. Jinns and the students didn't know anything about what had happened in Philadelphia, and Professor Torgeson knew there'd been an accident, but she didn't much care about details.

When we finally started down Daybat Creek, it didn't take long before we began seeing bits of gray-white stone scattered along the banks. Professor Torgeson was pleased and excited, but she wouldn't let us collect any of them. "We'll leave them for the historical excavators," she said. I couldn't help wondering just how many acres of hills she expected them to dig up, but I knew better than to say such a thing straight out.

The place where we'd found the landslide blocking the creek turned out to be about a day and a half west of Adashome. It would have been less, but the hills were covered with grub-killed trees, and we had to make a wide swing around one where the dead trunks had all fallen down in a tangle.

After nearly a year of the creek washing it away, plus all the snowmelt from the winter, the landslide looked more like narrow rapids than a dam that had cut off the creek for a while. Most of the dirt in the middle of the creek had been washed away, though you could still see the steep, bare slope of the hill that had sheared away and a weedy heap of dirt covering the bank of the creek by the bottom of the slope.

We made camp at the top of the hill, in the same place we'd been before. Professor Torgeson asked Lan if he'd help set up the protection spells around the camp, but he declined. The professor tried to persuade him, on account of him being a double-seven and therefore able to do stronger spells and cover more ground for all the people and mules we had with us. Lan went white and absolutely refused. The professor gave him a sharp look, and went off with Mr. Jinns to work the spells. Lan just sat with his head down for a while.

Once we'd finished setting up camp, we all headed down to the creek to collect bits of stone. Digging through the collapsed part of the hill was a lot easier with proper shovels and buckets. The professor had brought along a couple of gadgets like big wire sieves to separate out the rocks from the dirt. We cleared off a patch of ground next to the creek, then Lan shoveled dirt into the sieve and I shook it and cleared out the rocks. There were a lot more rocks than just the stone animal pieces we were looking for.

Professor Torgeson sent one of her students to walk along the creek shallows, looking for bits of stone that might have washed downstream as the water cleared away the dam. The other man she set to washing off the stones we collected, and then carrying them up to camp in a bucket after she'd sorted out the best ones.

We got about half a packful of fragments from that first day's work, so the professor figured we'd be at it for at least a week. By the end of the first full day, I was wishing I'd stayed in Mill City. It was hard, hot, heavy work, no matter what job you were doing. Even wading along the creek was only fun for about five minutes; after that, your back ached from bending over and your eyes got sore from squinting to see through the sunlight on the water and your feet hurt from banging against all the rocks that weren't stone animal pieces.

So I was plenty glad when, a few hours after noon of our third day at Daybat Creek, I heard Professor Torgeson say, "Mr. Morris! What brings you out this way?"

I turned to see Wash riding toward us along the bank of the creek. "Wash!" I cried.

"Afternoon, Professor, Miss Eff, Mr. Rothmer." Wash touched the brim of his hat. "All's been well?"

"We've had no difficulties I know of," the professor said, frowning slightly. "Why?"

"I was hoping you'd say that," Wash replied. He looked us over, and his eyes narrowed. "You have a guide?"

The professor nodded toward the top of the hill. "Mr. Jinns. He's up at camp."

"Ah." Wash sat back in his saddle, considering. "I'll have a word with him in a bit, then." He dismounted, staying well clear of the area we'd been working on.

"What's wrong?" the professor asked.

"Maybe nothing," Wash said. "Or maybe more trouble than is normal, even out here. I was down Lindasfarm way last week, when I got an urgent message from the magician at the Big Bear Lake settlement a bit north of here. Seems they had an Acadian fur trapper come through in early spring complaining about something running off the animals, breaking up his traps, and ruining his catch."

"Isn't that what trappers always say?" Lan asked.

"In the general way of things, yes," Wash said, grinning. Then he sobered. "This one, though, was considerably more exercised about it than most. He claimed some of his catch had been turned to stone."

Professor Torgeson's eyes went wide. "Turned to stone?"

"That's what he said, at least once he'd drunk enough," Wash said. "They didn't pay him much mind until one of their hunting parties came back hauling a stone fawn. Said they'd found the doe with it, but they couldn't carry both

283

of them. That's when the settlement magician sent me the message."

"But — you're saying these are newly petrified animals?"

"I'm not saying either way just yet," Wash replied. "I haven't seen them for myself. But I've known Bert Macleod for a good ten years, and he's a good magician and a reliable man. He used to ride circuit closer in toward the Mammoth River, before he decided to settle in one place and let trouble come to him instead of running around looking for it. If he's worried, I'd say he has reason.

"I'd heard you were out here digging up some more rocks," Wash went on, "and since it was nearly on my way, I figured I'd stop by and let you know."

"And check that nothing strange was happening here," I said before I thought.

Wash nodded. "It seemed like a reasonable thing to do, being as how this is the only other spot we know of where anyone's found stone animals."

"Yes, but these are not recent," Professor Torgeson said. "Besides, someone would surely have found something before now, if animals were still being petrified."

"That depends," Wash said. "Nobody's gotten much farther west than Wintering Island in the Grand Bow River. There's plenty of strange things out there that we don't know about yet."

"Nobody knew about the mirror bugs until about three years ago," Lan put in.

"Big Bear is a new settlement, relatively speaking," Wash said. "It's only three years old. Doing well, but then, they're a timbering town, and north of the grub-kill. They're as far west as anyone's settled up at that end of the circuit, so if there's anything coming east that we haven't seen before, they'd be one of the first to spot it."

"Still, you'd think some of those fur trappers would have noticed something," Professor Torgeson said.

Wash shrugged. "Maybe some of them did. There's always a fair few that don't come back from the bush every year."

There was a moment of silence as we all considered that. "Well," Professor Torgeson said after a minute, "I'll have to think about this. Will you be riding on right away, or can you stop for a bit?"

"It's late enough in the day that I'll be better spending the night here, if you're willing. Safer, too — the big animals haven't moved back into the woods, and the small ones aren't likely to attack a large group. Especially with four of us to renew the protection spells," he added, looking at Lan.

Lan's eyebrows drew together. "Three," he said.

Wash's eyebrows rose, but all he said was, "Three, then."

"You're more than welcome," Professor Torgeson said.

"Thank you kindly," Wash replied. He tipped his hat again and then rode off to camp. The rest of us got back to work picking rocks until dinner. Thanks to the professor's wire screens, we'd found a lot more good specimens than we'd expected, though we still didn't have any that were completely whole. Everything seemed to be missing the thin, fragile bits — legs or feet or tails or ears. The closest we came to a whole animal was a loon with its feet tucked up. The head had broken off, but we found it, too, so there were just a couple of missing chips around where the break was.

Wash's news made for quite a conversation over dinner. Lan was particularly excited. "It proves that the petrification is some kind of spell," he said.

"It doesn't prove anything of the sort," Mr. Torre, one of the students, said. "Until somebody actually sees it happen, we can't know for sure. And I think it's some kind of natural process."

"Fast enough to petrify a live animal all at once?" Lan said scornfully. "That's ridiculous. The only natural petrification we know of is fossilization, and fossils take thousands of years to form."

"Obviously they're not fossils," Mr. Barnet, the other student, said. He'd just graduated, and he and Lan didn't get on. I thought it was because he felt that being two years older and finished with college made him the next most important person in the group after Professor Torgeson. Lan thought he was just an idiot. "But they can't have been the result of a spell; they haven't any magical residue at all."

"Neither does anything else around here," Lan shot back. "The grubs and the mirror bugs ate it all."

"That's an interesting theory," Professor Torgeson said. "I'd assumed that the lack of magic was a feature of the stones themselves, but it might very well have happened later."

"Professor!" Mr. Torre said reproachfully, like he'd expected her to side with them because she was their professor. She just looked at him, and he drooped a little. Then he straightened up. "But most of the stones we're finding were buried in the hill," he said. "I could believe that the mirror bugs absorbed the magic from all the ones near the surface, just like they did with everything else, but could they have pulled magic from that far underground?"

"Something did," I said.

Everyone looked at me. I sighed. "It's just common sense. Everything that's alive, and a lot of things that aren't, has magic. Natural animals only have a tiny bit that doesn't do them a lick of good, but they still have it. Even rocks and dirt have magic, most places — Professor Torgeson said last summer that the magical plants can't grow here because the grubs absorbed it all and it'll be a while coming back."

"Yes, yes," said Mr. Barnet. "What does that have to do with the petrification problem?"

"If all these stone animals used to be live critters, they had magic in them when they were alive," I said. "It has to have gone somewhere."

"Very true," Professor Torgeson said. "Which is why you and I are going on with Mr. Morris tomorrow morning, Miss Rothmer." She looked at Lan. "Since you are something of a volunteer, you may come or stay as you see fit. The rest of you will stay here with Mr. Jinns and continue with the sample collecting. You know how by this time."

In spite of the professor's no-nonsense tone, that caused a bit of uproar. Both of the students thought they should be the ones to go with Wash and the professor, if anyone was going, and Lan and I should stay to collect samples. The professor told them that they'd been hired to collect samples, not to do scientific investigations. She said that I was along as her assistant, and she wouldn't do without me, and Lan wasn't employed by the college or the Settlement Office at all and could do whatever he liked.

"We could all go," Mr. Torre suggested.

"Well, now, I'm sorry to disabuse you of that notion," Wash said, "but a group travels a sight slower than one man alone, and the larger the group, the slower it goes. The professor here talked me into taking her and these two, but that's my limit. It was an urgent message, after all."

"And I'm not sitting around babysitting a bunch of mules, waiting for all of you to get back," Mr. Jinns growled. He glared at the two students and added, "Not that the two-legged mules are likely to be any better, to my way of thinking."

Once the students were finally convinced that they'd have to stay, they wanted to know how long we'd be gone.

"It's about two, two and a half days' ride if we nip right along," Wash said. "Call it five days for travel, and one or two when we get there to find out what's actually happened."

"A week, then," Mr. Barnet said. "What if we finish filling all the packs before then?"

Mr. Jinns snorted up his coffee. I got the feeling he didn't think much of their chances of being done in a week, but he didn't actually say anything.

"If you finish before we return, you will of course take the samples back to Mill City," the professor said. "We'll probably catch up with you on the way; you'll travel more slowly with the mules to see to."

I could tell that the students still wanted to argue, but I knew it wouldn't do them any good. Professor Torgeson was in charge and it was clear that neither Wash nor Mr. Jinns would back them up. I poked Lan and nodded at the dishes, and the two of us collected them and took them down to the creek to wash up. We stayed a mite longer than was strictly necessary for dish washing, so that by the time we hauled everything back to camp, the argument was over and done with.

And the next morning, barely after dawn, Lan and Professor Torgeson and I rode out with Wash, just as the professor had said in the first place.

CHAPTER
· 25 ·

Traveling with Wash when he was in a hurry was a lot different from the way we'd traveled the previous summer. We didn't take a pack animal, and we alternated trotting and walking so as to go as fast as possible without foundering the horses. When Lan asked about speed-traveling spells, Wash said that he'd only ever used one once, west of the Mammoth, and he'd only do it again if someone was likely to die if they didn't get somewhere on time. Mostly, if there was a real emergency but nobody dying, he'd gallop and walk, then trade his tired horse for a fresh one at the next settlement. We couldn't do that because settlements only had to provide mounts for circuit magicians, and anyway this wasn't an emergency yet.

Wash's estimate for time was dead-on. We got to the Big Bear Lake settlement near sunset of our second day traveling, mainly because it was high summer and the sun rose early and set late, and we rode pretty nearly every minute it was up.

The settlement folks were surprised to see us; they'd only expected Wash. They found room for all of us, though, in the newcomers' longhouse. That was a big, plain building three times as long as it was wide, meant for new settlers to stay in until they got their own houses built. Most settlements built one first thing, and then after they earned out their allotments they turned it into a general store or town hall. Professor Torgeson said the settlers got the idea from the Scandians and Vinlanders, who'd been building longhouses since medieval times.

It was too late in the day to do much in the way of talking, especially with three of the four of us well and truly tuckered out from the fast ride. Wash was the only one who didn't seem bothered by it. The rest of us turned in as soon as we could and slept as late as they let us, which wasn't much later than we'd been getting up at the camp.

Right after breakfast, Wash collected the rest of us and took us to see Mr. Macleod. He was a sturdy gentleman with short graying hair, dressed in an old blue work shirt and bright red suspenders. He lived and worked from a log house right inside the palisade gates. He'd divided the inside in half with a burlap curtain; the front part was where he met with people and did official business, and with five of us there it was pretty cramped. Practically before he had a chance to say anything, the professor asked whether we could talk to the trapper who'd first come in with the news, and she was a mite put out to learn he'd moved on long ago.

"Trappers have itchy feet, ma'am," Mr. Macleod said. "About the only time you see them in one place for more than a week or two at a time is at the annual St. Jacques assembly or if they've been snowed in. Old Greasy Pierre came through back in late March; there's no way he'd still be here now."

"Just like the summer men," Professor Torgeson said, nodding. "I'd hoped for better, but I can't say I'm surprised."

"Summer men?" Mr. Macleod said.

"Vinlanders who cross to the mainland to hunt every summer," the professor replied. "We lose a few every year who insist on staying just a few more days and get caught by an early winter storm. Once that happens, they rarely make it back before the ice dragons come down from the north."

Mr. Macleod nodded. "Same thing, really. Pierre took it particularly hard on account of these last few years being so good. He got accustomed to taking enough animals to get his summer supplies without so much work, so when things went back to normal, he was right put out."

"The last few years have been good ones?"

"For trappers," Wash agreed. "All up the Red River and down to the Middle Plains Territory. Maybe farther."

"Likely it was all the animals forced out by the grubs," Mr. Macleod said. "Leastwise, that's what everyone says."

"Forced out by the grubs?" Lan said. "But they just ate plants!"

"And when the rabbits and deer and bison and giant beavers and rainbow squirrels have no plants to eat, they leave, and the saber cats and foxes and jewel minks and dire wolves follow," Mr. Macleod said.

"Why would this year have been a bad one, then?" I asked. "The grub-killed land is coming back, but it's not the same, and it won't be for a long time. There might be enough for the rabbits and ground squirrels to eat, but for sure not the giant beavers and deer."

"Who knows?" Mr. Macleod said. "All I can say is that every trapper who came in from the Far West this year had a scanty catch."

"Now, there's an odd thing," Wash said, rubbing his beard. "I hadn't rightly thought on it before, but most all the trappers who work south of the Grand Bow River brought in as many furs as they could carry. There were a lot more new critters among them, too."

"More new animals?" Professor Torgeson said.

"There are a lot of things in the Far West that we don't have names for," Wash said.

"Every so often, the boys bring in something strange," Mr. Macleod agreed. "There's a fox with a gray patch on its forehead that they're partial to, when they can catch one, and a thing that looks a bit like a fat squirrel that's had its tail bobbed. Come to think on it, there's been more of those furs these past few years than there used to be. But then, the boys have been working farther west."

"Have they?" Wash said in a thoughtful tone. "The way the trappers I talked to were complaining, I got the notion they haven't ever gone much past their usual runs."

"How far west would that be?" Professor Torgeson asked.

"Most of the trappers on the North Plains work between here and . . . well, draw a north-south line through Wintering Island on the Grand Bow, and that's about as far west as they've ever gone," Mr. Macleod said. "I don't know about the Gauls and Acadians. They call themselves *coureurs de bois*, and they're right out of their heads, if you ask me, the chances they take."

"They aren't accustomed to having a safe place nearby," the professor pointed out. "Acadian settlement isn't more than halfway along the Great Lakes yet."

"If the trappers had their way, they'd stay there," Mr. Macleod grunted. "They were right pleased when the Settlement Office held up on allowing any new settlements last year."

"All this building has been eating up their hunting ground," Wash said, nodding.

"Speaking of hunting," Professor Torgeson said in a pointed tone. "I believe Mr. Morris indicated that one of your hunting parties brought in something interesting."

"Yes, well, just let me get it and you can see for yourselves." Mr. Macleod disappeared behind the curtain for a minute. He came out carrying a stone fawn.

From the look of it, the fawn wasn't more than a week old. Its legs were folded up under it, but its head was up and its eyes were wide, as if it had just seen or smelled something and was wondering what to do. The stone it was made of had a faint pinkish cast to it, but aside from that it looked just like all the other gray-white stone fragments we'd been collecting for days.

"Yonnie Karlsen and three of his friends were hunting off to the west when they came across it," Mr. Macleod said as we looked it over. "He said there was a doe, too, caught standing. The others wanted to get out of there right quick, but Yonnie made them rig a sling to carry this little one back with them. Said he didn't want folks calling it another tall tale."

"How far west?" Wash asked.

"T'other side of the Red River," Mr. Macleod said. "They were about a week out, which is why they needed the sling. This statue isn't very heavy, but it's awkward to haul around for very long."

The professor had pulled out her magnifying glass to study the fawn more closely. "Except for that pink tinge, it's just like the others," she said. "Well, the pink, and that it's not broken."

"It was a fair bit pinker when they brought it in," Mr. Macleod offered. "It's faded out quite a bit over the last two weeks."

"So they brought it in two weeks ago," the professor said. "And they found it a week before that."

"Early June," Mr. Macleod confirmed.

"I'm not liking the look of this," Wash said.

"What? No, no, it's amazing!" Professor Torgeson said. "We'll have to get it back to Mill City somehow without breaking it. I don't suppose you still have that sling, Mr. Macleod?"

"I don't think that's what Wash meant," I said.

Wash nodded. "Studying up on that statue is your job, Professor. Mine is keeping the settlements safe."

"I sent word as soon as I saw it," Mr. Macleod said. "Up here, white-tailed deer birth in mid to late May, most years. This fawn looks to be a week old or thereabouts, so it must have been petrified in late May or early June."

"So three or four weeks ago, whatever does the petrifying was a week's travel from this settlement," Lan said. "It seems to me that if it was coming this way, you'd know by now."

"Maybe," Wash said. "Or maybe it just travels a whole lot slower than Mr. Karlsen's hunting party."

"If we're lucky, it won't be able to cross the Red River," Mr. Macleod said. He frowned. "I purely do hate depending on luck."

"You're assuming that this fawn was petrified this year," Professor Torgeson said reprovingly. "We have no evidence that that is the case. You're also assuming that whatever it is can move, which is likewise unproven."

"Professor, ma'am, that's true enough," Mr. Macleod said, "but out here, it's better safe than sorry, because generally speaking, too much of the time sorry means you're dead."

"I would like to speak with your hunting party, if any of them are available," Professor Torgeson said.

Mr. Macleod allowed as how the Anderson brothers had gone right back out to look for game, heading north this time instead of straight west, but he thought Mr. Karlsen was still about. He went off to fetch him while the professor returned to studying the statue.

"It feels wrong," I said after a while.

Wash nodded, but Lan and Professor Torgeson gave me questioning looks. "It just feels wrong," I repeated. "There's no magic in it, not even a little bit, and there ought to be."

"Just like the ones back at Daybat Creek," Lan said, nodding.

"No," I said. "Those are old, and they're used to being the way they are. This one is . . . fresh. New. And it's wrong."

"How can you tell?" the professor asked.

"This is some of that Aphrikan magic you learned from Miss Ochiba, isn't it?" Lan said at almost the same time.

I glanced at Wash, but he didn't give me a hint what to say, one way or the other. So I nodded. "The ones at Daybat Creek just feel like old rocks. Kind of peculiar rocks, but just rocks. Whatever they used to be, they've forgotten. This one hasn't."

Professor Torgeson's eyes narrowed. "And what does all that mean? Rocks don't think!"

"I'm sorry, I can't explain it any better than that," I said.

"Aphrikan magic never has been easy to explain," Wash said.

"Insight and assurance," Lan muttered. Professor Torgeson gave him a questioning look, and he said, "It's what my professor in comparative magic used to say — Aphrikan magic is about insight and assurance. I never did figure out what he meant."

The door banged open, and Mr. Macleod came in. With him was a middling-tall man of about thirty with a long face and hair the color of fresh-cut oak planks, whom he introduced as Mr. Karlsen. "Nah, just call me Yonnie," the man said. He spoke with a thick Scandian accent. "Bert says you're wanting to hear about my hunting trip?"

"That we are," Professor Torgeson said, and launched into a whole series of questions about where they'd found the stone fawn, whether they'd seen anything unusual, whether they'd been there before, and a whole host of other things.

Mr. Karlsen answered patiently, for the most part. He and his friends had been in that area before, though he couldn't swear to the exact spot. He hadn't noticed anything odd; no strange plants or odd smells. It wasn't an area for sinkholes, just plain old prairie running endlessly on toward the west.

"You could maybe be asking the Andersons if they noticed anything more than I did," he said at last. "They'll be back by tomorrow."

"They might be back tomorrow," Mr. Macleod said. "They might not. Hunting's not so easy to say."

"They'll be back by tomorrow, or I'll be going out to look for them," Mr. Karlsen said firmly. "Nils promised."

Mr. Macleod looked skeptical, but early that afternoon there was a shout from the lookout and a few minutes later a boy came running in to tell us that the hunting party was back, moving fast, and they'd brought someone with. We'd taken the fawn outside so as to be out of Mr. Macleod's way (and to have better light and more space to work in), and the professor had spent most of the time taking measurements and studying the fawn through her magnifying glass, while I wrote down measurements for her in a little notebook. Lan had gotten bored and wandered off to talk with some of the settlers, and Wash and Mr. Macleod were holed up in Mr. Macleod's front room, but they came out as soon as they heard.

So we were all standing around just inside the palisade gates when the Anderson brothers came through. I thought at first that the boy had been wrong, because I only saw the two men, but then I realized that the second horse carried two men riding double. The one in front sagged forward in the saddle, and only the other man's hold on him kept him from falling right off.

The first man through the gate fairly leaped down from his horse and ran to help the other two, yelling for Mr. Macleod. He got Wash and Mr. Macleod both, and the three of them eased the unconscious rider down to the ground. As he came off the horse, I heard the first rider say, "Beware for the leg! It will not bend."

I started forward to see if I could help, but Wash turned and shook his head at us, then he and Mr. Macleod and the first rider clustered around the man they'd brought back.

"For God's sake, get the gate shut!" the second rider shouted, and the boys who were on gate duty jerked out of their fascination and shoved the gates shut. The rider sidled his horse away from Wash and the others, then dismounted.

By this time, half the settlement had gathered. "Nils, what happened?" one of the settlers asked as the second rider handed the two horses over to one of the gatekeepers.

"I don't know," the man said. "Olaf — we should never have gone."

"Gone where?"

The man shook his head and twisted to stare at the little clump of people crouched around the man on the ground.

"Is that Greasy Pierre?" someone said. "What's he doing back here?"

Right about then, Mr. Macleod stood up and came over. "Eric, Thomas, we need your help carrying him inside. My place. Yonnie, you stay with Nils. Anfred, we're going to need two bottles of that whiskey you brought back from Mill City; I'll see you're paid for it later."

"Bert, you can reverse it, can't you?" Nils Anderson said. "We brought him back as fast as we could — there's still time, isn't there?"

"Maybe time to save his life," Mr. Macleod said. "But I'm afraid we're going to have to take his leg off to do it."

"No!" a young woman cried. She pushed through from the back of the crowd and Mr. Macleod caught her just before she tried to run for the man on the ground. "No, you can't!"

"We have to, Martha," Mr. Macleod said gently. "It's turned to stone."

CHAPTER
· 26 ·

THE YOUNG WOMAN BURST INTO TEARS AS A BUZZ OF CONVERSATION
and questions broke out. I found out later that she was Martha
Anderson, Olaf's wife, so she had plenty of reason for tears. A
couple of the women came and huddled around her, but
nobody else moved. Mr. Macleod frowned, and then he started
snapping at people to do as he'd said, and didn't they have
more sense when a man's life was at stake, and a few other
choice words. That got people going, right enough, though
there was still plenty of jawing about what kind of spell accident he could have had.

I stayed long enough to see them carry the man into Mr.
Macleod's house, then I went back to the longhouse. I'd heard
tales of all the amputations in the Secession War, when the
doctors had only been able to save half their patients, and neither Wash nor Mr. Macleod was a doctor. Even if I didn't
know the man, I didn't want to be anywhere near when they
started working on him.

Lan stayed just inside the gates with most of the settlers.
Mr. Karlsen took Nils Anderson back to his house, away from

the operation. I heard later that he got Nils roaring drunk so as to take his mind off what was happening to his brother. Olaf Anderson was the man who was losing his leg; the third rider was Pierre Le Grise, the Acadian fur trapper that Mr. Macleod called Greasy Pierre.

Just before dark, Professor Torgeson came in to say that they'd gotten the leg off and Olaf was still alive. If he hadn't died by morning, they could stop worrying about the shock of it killing him and start worrying about infection and gangrene. They had hopes that it wouldn't come to that; that's what they'd wanted the whiskey for. Everyone knew that if you poured whiskey over a bad cut, it wasn't so likely to take an infection. Nobody knew if it'd help something this bad, but at least they would try.

We still didn't know what had happened. Except for Nils Anderson, everyone who knew anything was holed up in Mr. Macleod's house, and Nils was passed out at Mr. Karlsen's. When Wash and the others finally came out, they were too exhausted to say much except that they needed folks to sit with Olaf and Olaf's wife in case he needed more caring for in the night than she could handle. Lan offered straight off, but so did everyone else in the settlement, and they thought familiar faces would be the best if he woke. So Lan slept in the men's half of the longhouse after all.

It wasn't until the next morning that we found out what had happened. Olaf was still alive and looked to be staying that way for a while, so Mr. Macleod left Martha to sit with him and gathered everyone else into the longhouse. "I know all of you want to find out what happened to the Andersons," he told us. "This is the best way I could think of for everyone to get the whole story as soon as possible."

"And without it getting twisted when it gets passed along," Wash added sternly.

Several people shifted uncomfortably.

"Nils, you first," Mr. Macleod said.

Nils Anderson stood up from his place next to Mr. Karlsen. He seemed a little hesitant at first, but once he got going he didn't seem to want to stop. He and his brother had started off looking to hunt deer or bison — they didn't much care whether they got one of the natural varieties or a magical one, as long as they could eat it. They'd run across Pierre at one of the fords where the trappers and hunters were accustomed to water their horses, and the three of them had gone on together. They figured that whatever they shot, the Andersons could take the meat and Pierre could take the skin.

They hadn't expected the trip to take very long, but about all the game they could find were rabbits and squirrels and such like. Everything larger seemed to have gone missing. Then they came across a stone bear with its paws full of early bison-berries, and they decided that if something was turning things to stone and had scared off all the game, they ought to be scared off, too.

The three of them cut back toward Big Bear Lake. Back by the ford, they found some strange tracks. "Not more than two hours old, and the strangest thing I've ever seen," Nils said. "The prints were flat and stretched out, like a hand pressed down on a tabletop, and all four toes were thin and triangular, almost like fingers."

"I have never before seen such a thing," Greasy Pierre put in, nodding. "Not even in the Far Northwest, where I am one of the few who are bold and daring enough to lay traplines in winter."

Several folks snorted at this, and then someone in the back called, "How big were the prints?"

"So," Pierre said, measuring what looked like four or five inches between his two hands. "It would be the weight of a young horse, I think."

The three men had dismounted, and Pierre and Nils went to examine the tracks, while Olaf took the packhorses a little way downstream to water them and adjust their loads. Pierre had his rifle handy, but the other two were relying on the travel protection spells to at least give them warning of anything nasty coming their way.

Wash frowned when Nils said that, and Greasy Pierre sniffed and looked superior.

"It was my turn to hold the travel protection spells," Nils said. "They were fine, I swear — no sign of anything for half a mile out. And then the horses spooked. Olaf grabbed the lead line for the pack animals, but his riding horse took off for the far side of the ford — ripped the branch right off the bush Olaf had him tethered to."

"He should have used a larger branch," Greasy Pierre commented, but not very loudly.

"I went to try to calm the other horses," Nils went on. "And then . . . it felt like something hit me on the back of the head. I went out like a blown candle. When I woke up, Olaf . . ."

He choked up and stopped speaking. Mr. Macleod told him to sit down and let Pierre take over, since the trapper was the only one who'd seen all the rest. Pierre stood up with considerable relish; I could see he liked being the center of attention. He didn't tell a straightforward story, the way Mr. Anderson had; he kept gussying it up with comments about his other adventures and how brave he was. The heart of it wasn't hard to come at, though.

When the horses spooked, Greasy Pierre jumped for cover and raised his rifle. He saw the three packhorses dancing around Olaf, and Olaf's horse bolting. Then he heard a noise like an owl hooting, only he said the hoot went on a lot longer than an owl's would have. He saw Nils collapse, just as the travel protection spells came down, all at once. An instant later, Olaf let out a yell and fell over backward into the creek, and all three of the packhorses turned gray-white and froze motionless. It wasn't until Pierre had a chance to look at them later on that he realized they'd all turned to stone.

Pierre let off four rifle shots as fast as ever he could, aiming for the brush along the bank where he thought the hooting might be coming from. The hooting stopped abruptly, and he heard rustling heading away from the ford. He didn't figure he'd hit anything, only maybe scared it off, but that was good enough for the time being. He peeked out from behind the tree and fired again a couple of times, just to make sure, then went to the creek to fish Olaf out.

Olaf was pale as a new sheet, and when Pierre got a good look at him, he didn't blame the man one bit. His left leg had turned to stone from just above the knee on down. Pierre hauled him out of the water and left him by a tree with the rifle while he went to see what had happened to Nils. He was a mite surprised to find Nils still alive but unconscious.

"It was a state most dire!" Greasy Pierre said dramatically. "For alone, I could not hope to return two injured men to safety, and the creature might return at any moment! What could I do? I approached the stone horses to see what I could learn!"

What he was after was the medical kit in the Andersons' pack, and whatever else he could salvage. Turned out he could salvage as much as they could carry. The packhorses had turned to stone, but their packs and gear hadn't. Pierre grabbed another rifle and all of the ammunition, and the medical kit, but he didn't figure on taking much more than that. It was more important to get out of there — and bring the news of what had happened back to Big Bear Lake — than to try to haul their supplies back to the settlement.

By the time Pierre finished digging through the packs, Olaf had passed out and Nils had woken up. Nils was too drained to cast even a fire-lighting spell, and he had a headache powerful enough to make his eyes cross, but he could ride. Pierre got him up on one of the two remaining horses, and between them, they loaded Olaf in front of him, and then they left. They didn't even take time to recast the travel protection spells, though Pierre had sense enough to do a strong speed-traveling spell once they were away from the ford. They'd covered what was normally a day's ride from the ford to the settlement in less than an hour, hoping that Mr. Macleod would know what to do for Olaf.

There was a long silence when Mr. Le Grise finished his tale. Then someone in the back said in a shaky voice, "Turned to stone? His leg just . . . really?"

"I can attest to that," Mr. Macleod said. "Or if you'd like to look for yourself, we have it under a preserving spell, so that the magicians in Mill City can take a closer look at it."

"You don't need a preserving spell for stone," a hard-faced man in front objected.

"You do if it used to be somebody's leg and it's still flesh for about half an inch around the bone down the center," Mr. Macleod said grimly. "At least, it is as far as we could tell."

Several people in the audience turned green, and Mr. Anderson made a strangled noise. Mr. Macleod shook himself and said, "Yonnie, why don't you take Nils back to my place and let Martha come on here? You can sit with Olaf. Pierre can tell us anything else we need to know."

"What else do we need to know?" someone muttered as Mr. Karlsen and Mr. Anderson left.

"How to stop the thing, whatever it is," someone else said.

"Why did it get all three of the packhorses, but only Olaf's leg?" the hard-faced man demanded.

Pierre shrugged. "He was standing behind the horses; perhaps they blocked the spell, so that it only struck his leg. Or perhaps it is because he fell into the water, and that is what saved him. I was not watching closely to see exactly what turned to stone when, you understand."

"You said it took down your travel protection spells?" a woman in a blue calico dress asked.

"But yes," Pierre replied. "Without a warning or any signal. It was most sudden and mysterious."

"I'd call a bunch of spooked horses something of a signal," Mr. Macleod said dryly.

"Might be," Wash put in. "Though it'd help to know exactly why they spooked. And not all of them did spook, right at first, if what Mr. Le Grise says is true."

"Of course it is true!" Pierre said indignantly. "I do not lie!"

"It's just a turn of phrase, Pierre," Mr. Macleod said. "Nothing to get peeved about, especially since we've more important matters to hand."

"We don't know enough about this critter," an older man grumbled.

"You are welcome to go back to the ford and investigate further," Greasy Pierre said politely. "You cannot miss it; there are three stone packhorses in the middle of the path."

"Barely a day's ride away," a woman whispered. "What if it comes here?"

"There's no reason to think it will," the hard-faced man snapped. "We've been here for three years now. We'd have seen some sign of it before, if it was common. Or the trappers would have."

"Perhaps," Professor Torgeson said reluctantly. "However, there have been indications that some animals that usually live in the unexplored West have been moving eastward over the past four or five years. Possibly longer than that; we don't have observations from much earlier."

"Indications?" the hard-faced man said, narrowing his eyes. "What kind of indications?"

"Over the past five years, the Settlement Office reports have noted more frequent sightings of unique and unknown animals within settlement territory or within sight of settlements," the professor said with more assurance. "The number of unusual creatures brought in by trappers such as Mr. Le Grise has also increased by a small but significant amount along the entire length of the Mammoth River during that time."

"The Settlement Office has adjusted the protection spells twice in the last five years," Mr. Macleod commented. "Both times on account of needing to keep out new critters."

"Why haven't we heard of this?" a woman cried angrily.

"Because it's my job to handle the settlement spells, not yours," Mr. Macleod shot back.

Professor Torgeson cleared her throat. "Be that as it may, it seems at least possible that this incident may, like the mirror bugs, be a case of a previously unknown creature moving in from the wilds of the West."

"Why? Why would it come here?"

"I have no idea," Professor Torgeson said in her best classroom lecture voice. "There are a great many possibilities, but we do not have enough information to speculate about which of them might be true. There may have been a fire in the Far West that's driven animals eastward, or some other act of nature. We know little about the country between here and the Grand Bow River, and nothing at all about the unexplored land west of that."

I thought of the pride of saber cats we'd killed that shouldn't have been anything like so far east. I could surely understand why they'd come east, if some creature that turned things to stone was moving in from the Far West. But what would drive a critter east if it could turn things to stone?

"Why isn't important at the moment," said a man who'd been quiet up till then. "Why is for later on, when we can stop worrying over what's happening and start worrying over how to keep it from happening again. The real question right now is, what can we do about it if this thing that turns people to stone shows up here?"

"I still say it's unlikely," the hard-faced man repeated. "Why would it come farther east after Nils and Pierre here gave it such a scare?"

"Why not?" the quiet man said. "Better to be ready for trouble that doesn't come than have trouble arrive when we're not ready."

"There's another possibility to consider," Wash said, "and that's that these critters are more drawn than driven."

Half the settlers looked at him with blank expressions.

"The most recent batch of critters that we know came from the Far West were the mirror bugs," Wash said. "We still don't know all the hows and whys, but we do know they were attracted to strong magic. Could be that there's other critters that are like that."

"That's speculation," the professor said sharply. "There's no evidence for it in this case whatsoever."

Some of the settlers looked relieved, but then the woman in the blue calico said, "There's no proof against it, either. And it's like Christoffer said — better to be ready than not."

The talk ran on like that for quite a while. Mr. Macleod let it go without saying much, except when someone's temper looked to be running a mite high. About all that happened in the end was that the settlers decided to call the stone-making critter a "medusa" after the old Greek stories about the lady with snakes for hair who turned folks into stone with a look. Nobody knew what the critter looked like, though we were pretty sure it wasn't a lady of any kind, but putting a name to it made folks feel a bit better.

Eventually, the meeting broke up so people could get back to their everyday tasks, though most everyone who'd planned to head outside the settlement palisade decided it'd be a better day to stay home and fix up something they'd been putting off. Professor Torgeson went off to Mr. Macleod's place to look at the stone leg and double-check the preservation spells Mr. Macleod and Wash had put on it. She asked if I wanted to join her, but I turned her down.

Mr. Macleod and Wash set up a roster of folks to reinforce the settlement protection spells, which gave everyone something constructive to do and perked a lot of them right up. I noticed Lan didn't volunteer to help, which he normally would have, so when the settlers filed out of the longhouse at last, I took him aside to ask about it.

"The last time I tried helping with settlement spells, it almost got me and everyone else killed," he said.

"The last — oh! At the Little Fog settlement two years back," I said. "But if you hadn't helped, we wouldn't have worked out how to stop the mirror bugs."

"And if you hadn't been at Oak River for me to call on, or if you and Wash and William had been a little later getting there, the whole settlement would be dead, and me and Papa along with," Lan retorted. "You can say 'what if' as much as you like; it was still a harebrained thing to do." He hesitated. "Besides, I think Wash could be right."

"About what?"

"About that medusa thing being like the mirror bugs. Drawn to strong magic," he explained. "The way it took down the travel protection spells . . . well, it sounds awfully similar. If it is —" He shivered.

"If it is, the medusa will be following along after Mr. Anderson and Mr. Le Grise," I said slowly.

"Speed travel takes a lot of power," Lan said, nodding. "And it leaves a trail for at least a day. Even if the medusa can't move very fast, it's had plenty of time to get pointed in this direction."

"And once it gets close enough, it'll sense the settlement spells," I finished. "I can see why you wouldn't be keen on pumping a lot of extra power into them just now."

"Of course, the settlement spells may keep it off, the way they're supposed to," Lan said. He didn't sound any more convinced than I felt.

"At least there's only one medusa," I said after a minute.

"Probably," Lan added.

I nodded very slowly. We were both in a very sober frame of mind when we left the longhouse to see what help we could be.

CHAPTER
· 27 ·

THE WHOLE SETTLEMENT HAD A TENSE AND SOLEMN AIR FOR THE
rest of the morning. People gathered in little knots, talking.
You could feel the fear growing as everything sank in. Settlers
were accustomed to the dangers of the wildlife, but a creature
that turned three horses to stone all at once was more than
anyone had signed up for.

What worried people the most was the way the travel protection spells had come down. Mr. Macleod was acting like the
settlement spells would stay up, especially since he knew to
expect a problem, but most folks could see that he was just trying to reassure people.

The trouble was, nobody had any good idea what else to
do. People came up with notions, of course, but they had
no more back of them than hoping. One of the settlers took to
carrying a hand mirror with him, because the Greek lady with
the snake hair had finally been killed by a man who only ever
looked at her in a mirror. As soon as word got out, more than
half the settlers went looking for mirrors of their own. One
man smashed his big looking glass and offered people the

pieces. Lots of folks ended up with cuts from handling the broken glass, and slashes in their clothes, but they still carried them around, even though nobody knew for sure whether they'd help.

Pretty soon, a few folks started talking of heading back to Mill City "for a few weeks." Mostly, it was the families with childings doing the talking, but I was still surprised to hear it. Big Bear Lake was three years into its five-year commitment — anyone who left now would be giving up their share for the Settlement Office to reassign.

Around mid-afternoon, Lan and I were sitting on the ground outside the longhouse when we saw Wash and Professor Torgeson come out of Mr. Macleod's house. They made a bee-line for Mr. Macleod and started talking a mile a minute. Lan's eyes narrowed. "You stay here, Eff," he said. "I'm going to talk to them."

He stood up and I stood up with him. He turned and glared at me. "Eff —"

"I know that look, Lan Rothmer," I interrupted, "and I'm coming with you, and that's that."

Lan made a face. "I suppose I can't stop you," he grumbled, and set off for Wash and the others.

As we came up on them, the first thing we heard was Mr. Macleod saying, "— not. I can't let you take a chance like that. Besides, we need you here, to protect the settlement."

"No, you don't," Wash said. "The settlement protection spells are as strong as may be, and you've plenty of people to trade off holding them up so that they'll stay that way. The next thing to do is to get rid of this medusa critter before it causes more trouble. Waiting here for it to show up doesn't seem like the best plan to me. And taking chances is a circuit magician's job."

"It's not a professor's job!" Mr. Macleod said.

"Mr. Macleod," Professor Torgeson said, "I am a Vinlander born and raised, and I've spent my time in the wildlands of a summer. Furthermore, my job is to find out more about the petrified animals we've been uncovering, and this is a golden opportunity to do so. And finally, it is not within your right to detain me should I wish to leave this settlement. Which, I must tell you, I am feeling more inclined to do the longer you talk."

Wash hid a smile behind his hand and pretended to cough. Mr. Macleod sighed. "Professor, ma'am, I don't — what do you two want?" he said as he saw Lan and me.

"You're going to go out hunting the thing that turned the packhorses to stone, aren't you?" Lan asked Wash.

Wash nodded, at the same time as Mr. Macleod said, "No, they're not!"

"Well, I want to come with," Lan said.

I snapped my teeth closed over an objection so fast that I bit my tongue. Telling Lan not to do things only made him stubborner about doing them.

Professor Torgeson frowned. "Mr. Rothmer, while you are not one of my students, you are in some sense my responsibility.

This is not a lark, and I will not allow you to accompany us without a very good reason."

"I have a very good reason," Lan said steadily. "Two, actually. First of all, there's a good chance this creature absorbs magic, the way the mirror bug beetles did, and I'm the only person here who's had experience holding protection spells against that kind of drain."

"Then you should stay here!" Mr. Macleod said.

"When was that?" Professor Torgeson said at the same time.

"Two years ago, at the Little Fog settlement, when my sister figured out how to beat the mirror bugs," Lan said. "You may have heard about that part. I was inside the settlement, holding the protection spells against all the grubs and mirror bugs, while Eff figured out how to turn their magic back on them."

Mr. Macleod's eyes narrowed. "You held the settlement protection spells? All of them? How?"

"I held all of them," Lan replied. "As to how — that's the other reason I should go along on this hunting trip. I'm the seventh son of a seventh son."

"All true," Wash said. "I was with Miss Eff at the time." He rubbed his beard in a thoughtful fashion. "It hadn't occurred to me, Mr. Rothmer, but you have a point. You could be a right handy man to have along."

"Sounds to me as if the one you want to take is his sister," Mr. Macleod growled.

"Both of us, or neither," I said, nodding.

"What? No, Eff, you can't —"

"I already said, Lan — both of us, or neither. I let you go off to Little Fog without me last time, and look what happened! Not again." Which wasn't exactly fair; I hadn't particularly wanted to go with him last time, because it was supposed to be just a boring day of fiddling with the broken settlement protection spells at Little Fog and getting them to work properly again. The effect on the grubs and the mirror bugs was something nobody had expected, and it had been a very good thing that I was outside where I could do something about it, once I went chasing after Lan. But I certainly wasn't going to point any of that out now.

I especially wasn't going to point it out when I knew I wasn't being completely truthful about why I wanted to go with Wash and the others. Oh, I wanted to keep an eye on Lan, right enough, but if the only thing I'd wanted to do was watch out for him, I'd have put my energy into making him stay behind. What I really wanted was to go along, too. I wasn't sure why. I didn't have anything to prove to myself, the way I had with the saber cat hunt the previous summer, and I knew this would be even more dangerous. We wouldn't have anything like as many people; the settlement couldn't spare them, and Wash wouldn't wait for messengers to recruit folks from nearby settlements. We didn't even know what we were hunting, much less how long it would take to find.

Even so, I wanted to go. I looked hopefully at Wash and Professor Torgeson.

"That seems reasonable," Professor Torgeson said briskly. "Who else, Mr. Morris? We don't want too many people, or we'll move too slowly."

"Pierre, if he'll come," Wash said. "And if Mr. Macleod can spare us a marksman who's willing to come, I think that will do."

"Wash, you —" Mr. Macleod shook his head. "All right, I can't stop you. I suppose the only questions left are, what do you need and how soon do you leave?"

"Tomorrow morning, for leaving," Wash said. "I don't much fancy spending the night outside walls when there's wild-life about that laughs at the travel protections. As to what we need, I was hoping you'd have some suggestions."

The two of them walked off, deep in discussion. Professor Torgeson looked at Lan. "Mr. Rothmer —"

"Yes, I'm sure I want to do this," Lan broke in. "Just . . . I'm sure, all right?"

"I was going to ask about your experience with the mirror bugs," the professor said mildly. "Mr. Anderson indicated that whatever interfered with his spells was similar to an abrupt blow, but the accounts I've heard of the mirror bugs sounded more like a slow draining."

"Oh," Lan said. "I — well, the mirror bugs were small. One at a time, or spread out the way they normally were, they didn't absorb enough magic for anyone to notice." He went on describing what had happened at the Little Fog settlement, with the professor asking pointed questions every so often, and I could see some of the stiffness fade out of his shoulders.

He didn't expect it to be so easy to get included in the hunt for the medusa creature, I thought. I couldn't figure out why, though, much less why he'd been so keen to go in the first place. He was up to something, and I was pretty sure I wouldn't like it once I figured out what it was.

The news that there was a hunting party being sent out got most of the settlement folks calmed down. There was still some quiet talk of leaving, but it had more the sound of planning for the worst than panic. Some of them even laughed a little at Greasy Pierre's posturing when he agreed to help hunt for the creature.

I didn't sleep too well that night. Growing up in Mill City, and later on working with the professors and coming out to survey the plants around the settlements, had given me a powerful respect for the wildlife of the West, and there was a sight of difference between running afoul of a cloud of mirror bugs or even coming across a pride of saber cats, and going out looking for trouble. But I couldn't let Lan go alone.

We left early the next morning. There were six of us: Wash, Professor Torgeson, Greasy Pierre, a settlement man named Sven Grimsrud, Lan, and me. It had been over a day and a half since the Anderson brothers and Pierre had their run-in with the medusa creature at the ford, and we didn't know how close it might be if it had followed them, so Wash and Pierre and Mr. Grimsrud had their rifles ready.

After some arguing, we'd settled it that we would ride a lot farther apart than folks usually did when they traveled out in settlement country. The idea was to make sure the medusa thing couldn't catch us all at once, the way it had with the Andersons' packhorses.

We had two sets of travel protection spells going, one that was mostly to detect anything alive that stretched out as far as Professor Torgeson could stretch it, and one that doubled up the standard traveling spell with one to keep off magic that was as close in and as strong as Lan could make it. I was paying extra-close attention to my Aphrikan world-sensing, and I was pretty sure Wash was, too.

Greasy Pierre had the job of backtracking the route he and the Andersons had taken. It wasn't hard; even I could sense the residue of the speed-travel spell he'd used to get them all safely back to the settlement. Wash rode next in line, then the professor, Lan, and me, with Mr. Grimsrud bringing up the rear.

We rode for about three hours, then stopped for a break. You'd think that just riding along keeping a sharp lookout wouldn't be much harder than the normal kind of riding through settlement country, but it was. I was glad to dismount for a minute or two.

Two hours later, Professor Torgeson signaled for a stop and motioned everyone to come close enough to hear. "There's a . . . blank area over that way," she said, pointing at a slight angle to the direction we'd been traveling. "No animals, hardly any birds."

"This is suspicious," Pierre said solemnly.

"Is it moving?" Mr. Grimsrud asked.

Professor Torgeson looked irritated. "There are animals everywhere else, and they are moving. Up that way, there is none."

"How large is the quiet area?" Wash asked.

"About ten degrees at the far edge of the spell," the professor replied. "We're about a mile and a half away, as best I can estimate. It doesn't exactly have sharp edges."

"We'll head in that direction," Wash said. "Let us know when we're close, or if anything changes, Professor."

We rode a lot more cautiously after that. Wash took us north and around, hoping to come up behind the critter, if that was what it was that had caused what the professor's spell had detected. I was a bit annoyed because even with my Aphrikan world-sensing, all I could tell was that the animals nearby were more nervous than usual. It wasn't until we were nearly right up to the quiet area that I felt anything different.

Right about then, Wash stopped and signaled everyone to dismount. He and Pierre had a quick talk in low voices, and then Wash took the lead. The forest was dead quiet, except when a breeze rustled the trees. It was even spookier than the grub-killed forests farther south; those at least had birds and mice and ground squirrels coming back. Everyone tried to make as little noise as possible. Even the horses moved carefully.

Suddenly, Pierre let off a low whistle. Even though I knew it was a signal to Wash, the unexpected noise made me jump. He and Wash examined the ground, and Pierre pointed. We started off again, angling more toward the north. When we got up to where Wash and Pierre had been, I looked down and saw a paw print — four long, thin, triangular toes stretched out from a squared-off pad. I moved my horse around so it didn't step on it.

A short while later, we found the first petrified animal — a rabbit, caught in mid-leap. Wash had us spread out even farther, for safety. And the farther apart we got, the more nervous I felt.

We didn't know how the petrification magic worked, really. Mr. Macleod had said that Mr. Anderson's leg had still been part flesh on the inside, and I couldn't help wondering whether the horses and the animals that turned to stone had been, too. The ones we'd found at Daybat Creek had been stone through and through, but they were old. Maybe the magic had changed. Or maybe it didn't work all at once; maybe it turned things to stone slowly, from the outside in. I wondered what that would be like. Would it hurt? Would you feel the stone creeping slowly inward, knowing what was happening, or did the magic just kill things and then turn them to stone? It hadn't killed Mr. Anderson, quite. I shuddered, and decided not to think about it anymore.

We followed the tracks for a long way, until Pierre signaled again. "Not far now," he said.

Wash nodded. "I think —" He broke off, raising his head like a deer scenting a saber cat on the wind. I felt it, too — a ripple right at the edge of my world-sensing, from the direction we'd come. Wash muttered something I figured it was just as well I hadn't heard clearly. "It's cut back toward the track we made coming in. At this rate, we'll circle each other for hours."

Mr. Grimsrud gave Wash a puzzled look, but he didn't ask how Wash could know such a thing.

"It likes horses," Lan said. "We could use ours for bait."

Pierre and Mr. Grimsrud looked at him as if he was clean out of his wits, but Wash thought on it for a minute, then nodded. "It's worth a try. If we lose them, we're still close enough to walk back to the settlement. Professor, you can drop your detecting spell for now and grab a gun. Miss Eff —" He paused, scanning the woods. "You have your rifle? Good. Take yourself back there behind those boulders, and keep an eye out. Don't make a sound, and if you think something's coming, shoot first and ask questions later." He pointed out positions for everyone else, then turned to Lan. "Mr. Rothmer —"

"Lan."

"— Lan, as soon as we have the horses tied and are in position, drop the travel spells and get back to the boulders with your sister."

"Drop the travel spells?" Mr. Grimsrud said doubtfully.

"So the critter can find us," Wash said. "And so it doesn't get a big boost to its magic by draining Lan here the way it did your Mr. Anderson." He'd already fastened his horse good and tight to a tree. "Hurry up, before it gets out of range."

Mr. Grimsrud still looked doubtful, but he went ahead and did what Wash had told him. I went back to the little heap of boulders and crouched down behind it. I was surprised that Lan hadn't objected to Wash's directions. He'd never much liked being left out of whatever was happening. I was even more surprised when I felt the travel spells drop and he didn't join me back of the boulders.

There was a long, tense silence. I could still feel the strange ripple out at the edge of my world-sensing, but it didn't seem to be getting nearer. Lan made no move to find cover; he just stood there next to the horses. And then I felt a bright blaze of magic all around me, and the ripple paused and began to move straight toward us. I whipped around to glare at Lan, and as soon as I saw the reckless grin on his face, I knew exactly what he was doing.

Lan was using *himself* as bait.

CHAPTER
· 28 ·

Right away, without even thinking about it, I stood up and ran over to Lan. He looked startled; he looked even more startled when I smacked his cheek as hard as I could. It knocked him sprawling backward. "Eff! Cut it out!" he whispered.

"You stop that this instant!" I hissed at him. "That thing will be here in a minute."

"Good," Lan said, getting up. "Don't whack me again; I don't want to be distracted."

"Lan, stop it!" I grabbed his arm and tried to drag him back to the boulders, but he was taller and stronger than I was, and I didn't get him very far. I could feel the ripple getting closer, and then I felt something, some magic, come at us. At Lan.

I twitched it aside, the way I'd been twitching and tweaking my Avrupan spells for nigh on two years. It was more difficult to do than I'd expected; whatever it was, it was homing in on Lan like a pigeon headed back to its nest. I just barely knocked it off course enough to send it whizzing past Lan's left ear.

"What —"

"Turn it off, Lan!" I felt another bolt of magic come toward us. I shoved this one harder, but when I did, it tried to latch on to my magic like a leech. It didn't quite succeed. I think it was confused by the waves of magic coming off of Lan and by the fact that I was using Aphrikan magic. Even so, it sucked out enough of my magic to make me dizzy before I pushed it away.

"Eff!"

I blinked up at Lan's worried face. I realized that he'd caught me as I started to fall, and pulled both of us back behind the boulders. But he was still shining his magic out just as hard as ever he could. "Stop it," I croaked, and finally he did.

"Eff, what —"

"Later," I said. "Quiet now." And for a wonder, he was.

I pushed myself upright. My head hurt like anything, and getting my Aphrikan world-sensing working again just made it hurt worse. At least I'd hung on to my rifle. Then the horses started rearing and pulling against their tethers. A moment later, I heard a hooting noise, just like Pierre had described.

Two of the horses went gray and froze. An instant later, something large flew through the tree branches and landed just on the other side of the horses from me and Lan. I got an impression of gray-brown scales and lots of sharp teeth as the thing whipped its head side to side. I couldn't get a shot with all the horses plunging and pulling at their tethers, but somebody fired. I thought they'd missed, because the thing didn't react, but then there were three more shots in quick succession, and none of them hurt the thing, either.

The creature slid forward, just past the horses, and I finally got a good look at it. It was an enormous gray-brown lizard. Its front legs were short, but even standing low to the ground, its head would have come as high as my chest if I'd been fool enough to stand beside it. In back, its legs were longer and more muscular, like a frog's back legs. They looked strong enough to kick a dire wolf halfway across the Mammoth River, and I didn't wonder that it could jump so high and far as it had. It had a large head with a mouth like a bird's beak with teeth, long enough that they could take off a man's arm to the elbow in one bite, if it had a mind to.

I pulled the trigger, but my shot had no more effect on the thing than anyone else's. Well, it had one — the medusa lizard hissed and turned its head toward Lan and me. As I pumped the lever to reload my rifle, I saw a bump in the center of the lizard's forehead, covered by a patch of white scales. As I watched, the scales pulled back, like a third eyelid, revealing a glossy black knob underneath. It opened its mouth, and I got a real good look at all of its sharp teeth.

Lan's eyes narrowed, and he let his magic loose again. I grabbed at his arm, but before I could say anything, I felt him give a *push*. An enormous wave of magic went past me. The creature gave a high-pitched shriek and reared back on its hind legs, shaking its head. Four rifles cracked, and bloody holes appeared on its underbelly. It fell over and lay still.

I glanced over at Lan. He was staring at the medusa lizard, his lips twisted. "It couldn't handle me any better than Professor Warren did," he said, so low that I was pretty sure I wasn't supposed to hear.

After a minute, Wash appeared from behind a tree. He kept his rifle at the ready as he walked to the lizard and examined it. Then he lowered his gun and called, "It's dead."

We came out from behind the boulders. Lan staggered and leaned against the nearest one, looking tired and drained but satisfied. The others appeared from behind trees. Professor Torgeson went to join Wash beside the medusa lizard. Pierre and Mr. Grimsrud went for the remaining horses, to try to calm them. And then I felt another ripple, *behind* me. *Close* behind.

I shoved Lan down and crouched beside him. One glance was enough to tell me he wouldn't be any help; he'd used up everything he had on the first critter. Everyone but Lan and me was on the far side of the horses. I swallowed hard and poked my head out from behind the boulders, sighting along the rifle barrel and hoping I would get a clear shot at the thing before it hurt me or Lan. And with all my heart, I wished that it wouldn't see me before I saw it.

Wash's wooden pendant went ice-cold against my chest, and I felt all the don't-notice-it spells unwrap from around it and expand just a little. Just enough to cover me and Lan, as well as the pendant. A second later, I felt the magic leeching, looking for us, but it slid away without finding either of us.

I saw a flash of movement between the trees and everything slowed. My world-sensing spread out around me, clearer and stronger than ever before. I could sense the ants hurrying up and down the bark of the trees in front of me, and the beetles burrowing in the ground below. Farther out, behind a screen of leaves, I felt the second medusa lizard pull the scales back from the knob on its forehead and open its mouth to send its petrifying magic straight at Lan and me. More important, I could sense exactly where the lizard was, even if I couldn't see it, and I knew the track my bullet would take when I fired. I moved my rifle barrel a hairsbreadth to the left and squeezed the trigger.

The bullet hit square on the black knob in the lizard's forehead. It didn't even have time to shriek before it fell over and died.

The world speeded up back to normal, and I felt the not-noticing spells pull back and wrap tight around the pendant once more.

"Got it," I said, but I pumped the lever to reload, just in case.

This time, nobody lowered their rifles until Professor Torgeson had cast every detection spell she could think of, and at least one that she made up right there on the spot, to make sure there were no more medusa lizards around. Wash stood beside her with his eyes narrowed, and I knew he was pushing his Aphrikan world sense as hard as it would go, checking for the same thing. They both nodded at about the same time, and everyone relaxed at last.

Wash came over to Lan and me. He was frowning and his eyes were still narrowed. "Which of you was playing games with this thing?"

"I — what — how did you —" Lan finally just stopped and stared.

I sighed. "He knows the same way I knew. Aphrikan world-sensing. You should have stopped when I told you to."

"We needed better bait," Lan said unrepentantly. "And it worked, didn't it?"

"After a fashion," Wash said. "You'll be the one that over-loaded the first one, too, I expect. We'll talk later, Mr. Rothmer."

"I — yes, sir."

Wash gave him a small smile and added, "It was a dread-ful chance to take, and I wouldn't recommend doing anything like it ever again. But I do believe we'd have had a lot more trouble with that first one if you hadn't done as you did."

"Thank you," Lan said.

"Mr. Rothmer, if you have any abilities left after your attempted heroics, I could use your help with a preservation spell," Professor Torgeson called. "We have to get this back to the college for study."

"It's fifteen feet long!" Lan objected, but he headed toward her.

Wash cocked an eyebrow at me. I was pretty sure what he wanted to ask. I put one hand to my chest, over the spot where the pendant lay hidden against my skin. "It was what I needed to know," I said.

"Ah," was all he said, but he looked pleased.

With only four horses left and the medusa lizard to haul back, we had to walk back to Big Bear Lake. None of the horses would have the medusa lizard anywhere near them, preservation spell or not. We finally had to rig up a sort of sled for one of them to drag along behind, and tie the dead medusa lizard to that. Between that and walking, it was well past dark when we finally got to the settlement.

The settlers wanted to make much of us for killing the medusa lizards, but Wash wasn't having it. He went into plenty of detail about the fight, and made an especial point of how fortunate we'd been that the first critter reared back and gave us a shot at his underbelly, and that the second one had gone down to a lucky shot. He didn't mention Lan lighting himself up like a beacon for bait, or me using Aphrikan world-sensing to help aim, for which I was grateful. He also suggested that the settlers use an express rifle, or at least something a bit more heavy-duty than our repeaters, if they had occasion to hunt medusa lizards in the future.

"In the future?" one of the settlers said. "You mean there are more of those things out there?"

Professor Torgeson snorted. "You think there were only two of them in the whole wide world? Of course there are more!"

"Though hopefully the rest of them are still out in the Far West, where these two came from," Wash put in.

———◆———

We stayed on at Big Bear Lake for nearly a week, because Wash wanted to head out with Pierre to see for sure and certain that there weren't any more medusa lizards around. They found a few petrified animals, but only ever tracks from the pair we'd shot, which went a fair way to reassuring the settlers. By the time we left, Olaf Anderson was on his way to mending, though he and his wife hadn't gotten so far as to decide whether they'd stay on in the settlement.

On our way back to Mill City, Wash and Lan had a couple of long conversations. I didn't ask what they said, and Lan didn't tell me, but I could see that Lan was feeling a lot better.

I spent a lot of time on the ride talking with Professor Torgeson. She was particularly interested in the way I'd felt the first lizard's magic leeching, and in the way I'd twitched it aside. She and Wash had been so busy concentrating on killing the lizard that they hadn't had time to pay attention to its magic, and that was going to be important if they were going to figure out a way to add it to the settlement spells.

As soon as we got back, Professor Torgeson disappeared into her lab, along with Professor Jeffries and the carcass of the medusa lizard. That left Wash and Lan and me to explain things to the Settlement Office and everyone else. The newspapers got hold of it, and it was a right circus. A week later, the professors put out a short, dry, extra-scientific summary of what they'd found out so far from examining the dead medusa lizard, and that set the whole thing off again. It would have been even worse if the professors had told them everything.

"The trouble is, the thing was gravid," Professor Torgeson told Lan and Papa and me. She'd asked us and Professor Jeffries to dinner in order to talk about their findings — Papa, because he would be working on the changes to the settlement spells with them, and Lan and me because we'd been there and they thought we ought to know. They'd have asked Wash, too, but he was back out riding circuit already.

"It's a good thing we got it when we did, then," Lan said soberly.

Professor Jeffries nodded. "It was carrying nearly fifty eggs, ready to lay ... and the preservation spell worked well enough and fast enough that I believe we could hatch at least some of them, under the right conditions."

"Why would you want to?" I asked.

"It's a totally new species," Professor Jeffries said with a little frown. "Think of how much we could learn from live specimens!"

"Think of the trouble it would cause if someone irresponsible got hold of one of those eggs and hatched out a creature that can absorb more magic than the mirror bugs," Papa said.

"And do it faster than the bugs, and on this side of the Great Barrier Spell. Not to mention turning people and animals to stone."

"Exactly," Professor Torgeson said. "That's why we're keeping it a secret, for the time being." She gave Lan and me a pointed look, and we nodded.

Professor Jeffries looked thoughtful. "Yes, but we've been intending to open a study center west of the Mammoth River for some time. Getting live specimens through the Barrier Spell to this side is always a problem, and they generally don't do as well here. This would be the perfect opportunity."

"Perhaps," Papa said. He looked at Professor Torgeson. "How much have you been able to determine from the carcass?"

"Not nearly as much as I'd like," the professor replied. "It's clearly not native to the area where we found it."

"Thank goodness," Papa murmured.

Professor Torgeson nodded and went on, "Its flesh has a magical affinity for certain kinds of rock, most of which aren't present on the Western Plains. I've a request in for a geologist to assist in making more specific determinations. It appears to absorb magic via a special organ near the brain. Even dead, it is difficult to detect with magic — it resists what it cannot absorb."

"You were extremely lucky," Papa said to Lan and me. He looked back at Professor Torgeson, frowning. "How on earth are we to incorporate something like this in the settlement protection spells?"

"I have a few ideas," Professor Jeffries said. "But we're going to have to talk the college into that study center. We must have a place where we can research these things, and test our spells before we try to adjust anything in the field."

"What we really need is a research expedition," Professor Torgeson said. "Everyone who's gone out for the past thirty years except for McNeil has been exploring, not researching, and even so we still don't have proper maps for the territories past Wintering Island. And I suspect our scaly visitor came from well beyond there."

"What makes you think that, Professor?" Lan asked.

"The rock affinities I mentioned before," Professor Torgeson replied. "But I need that geologist to confirm it for certain."

———◆———

Professor Torgeson got her geologist, and pretty near everything else she asked for. The settlements had been in an uproar since the news came out about the medusa lizard, and the Settlement Office was disposed to be cooperative. All of a sudden, Professor Torgeson didn't have to try so hard to get them interested in hiring historical excavators to go out to Daybat Creek, and they brought in nearly a whole trainload of scientists and magicians to help study the dead lizard and all the petrified animals we'd brought back.

I spent more time working for Professor Torgeson than I did at the menagerie. The professor was too busy with the medusa lizard to worry about all the questions coming in, so I handled as many of them as I could. I sent off samples of the petrified animals we'd brought back from Daybat Creek to everyone who'd asked for them (though I made sure I sent Professor Lefevre his first), along with the summary of what the professors had figured out about the medusa lizard. The most interesting part, though, was looking up information for her when she had questions about settlement country. It kept me busy through the rest of July.

Early in August, Lan came and found me down at the creek. It was a Sunday afternoon and so hot that even the mosquitoes were drowsing instead of biting people. I'd gone down to the wide spot where there was a bit of a breeze and I could hike up my skirts and dangle my bare feet in the cool water as if I were a childing. He sat down beside me and pulled off his boots, and we sat in silence for a while.

"I'm not going back to Simon Magus this fall," he said abruptly.

I just nodded. "Have you told Papa?"

"This morning." Lan looked down and kicked at the water. "He isn't too happy, but he's not making a fuss. I think he understands that I need more time."

"You're not going to just mope around the house, are you?"

Lan shook his head. "I'm going out to the settlements for the rest of the summer," he said.

"Circuit-riding?" I asked.

"Not by myself," Lan said. "Sort of as an assistant."

"Circuits finish up in October. What are you doing after that?"

"I think I might do some work for the Settlement Office. They have all these reports full of information that I don't think anyone has ever looked at properly."

"Anyone could do that kind of job."

"Not anyone," Lan objected. "It takes someone who can organize and think and —"

I poked him. "I meant, it doesn't take a magician."

"I know," Lan said quietly. "That's why I want to do it. I want to try not being a magician for a while."

"Then why are you going to ride circuit? That does take a magician, and a pretty good one, too."

Lan sighed and splashed the water again. "I want both. I want to do something real with all this magic I have, but . . ."

"So you're trying it both ways," I finished for him. "Working with your magic, and without it." It seemed a strange way to think of it to me, but I'd never thought I wanted to do great magic, the way Lan always had.

Lan nodded. "For a year."

I smiled and flopped back in the grass that covered the bank. "It'll be good to have you home, even if it's just for a year. Maybe you can get Wash to drop by more often."

"Maybe." He gave me a sidelong look. "Are you going to keep working for Professor Torgeson?"

"Probably," I said. "At least as long as she has things for me to do. After that, I'll go back to the menagerie for a while."

"For a while?"

"I want to go back out to the settlements," I said. "Not as a settler. Riding circuit would be nice, but I don't think I have the magic for it. Something else."

"You'll have to invent it, whatever it is," Lan said after thinking for a moment.

I smiled again, pleased that he was listening to what I wanted for a change. "Maybe I can work for the new settlements, surveying the plants and animals they have on their allotment to see if any of them are valuable."

"Or maybe the professor will get her research expedition going and take you along."

"That would be nice."

Lan flopped back on the grass to join me, and we stared at the sky and splashed our feet in the creek water. "It looks like we're both on our way," Lan said after a minute.

"On our way where?"

"Wherever we're going." He swept his hand out in a grand gesture that took in the creek and Mill City and all the land beyond in either direction. "Even if we don't know yet exactly where that is."

I thought about that for a minute. "Starting is good. You can't get anywhere at all if you never start."

Beside me, I felt Lan nod. "Now all we have to do is keep going."

"Keep going?" I smiled without taking my eyes from the endless blue sky. "I can do that."